Thank You!
Dann Collis

BURNIN' DAYLIGHT!

A novel set in the period of the Great American Civil War

Dann Wallis

authorHOUSE™

1663 LIBERTY DRIVE, SUITE 200
BLOOMINGTON, INDIANA 47403
(800) 839-8640
WWW.AUTHORHOUSE.COM

First published by AuthorHouse 09/26/05

ISBN: 1-4208-7661-9 (sc)

Library of Congress Control Number: 2005907371

Printed in the United States of America
Bloomington, Indiana

This book is printed on acid-free paper.

It is for my only grandchildren, Chelsea Savannah Campbell and Nicholas McDaniel Hawthorne that this book is really written; in the hope that they also will get swept up in the exciting history of this wonderful country, and swell with pride to be a child of this the greatest nation on earth!

"This country, with its institutions belongs to the people who inhabit it. Whenever they shall grow weary of the existing government, they can exercise their constitutional right of amending it, or their revolutionary right to dismember or overthrow it."

First Inaugural Address…..Abraham Lincoln, 4-March-1861

"If I could save the Union without freeing any slaves, I would do it---and if I do it by freeing some and leaving others alone, I would also do that."

President Abraham Lincoln….. 22-August-1862

"It is well that war is so terrible; else we should grow too fond of it."

General Robert Edward Lee

"War is for the participants a test of character; it makes bad men worse and good men better."

Joshua Lawrence Chamberlain, Congressional Metal of Honor for action at Gettysburg, 2-July-1863.

Acknowledgements....

I am blessed to have had so many people in my life and in my history that have not only encouraged me to write this book, but provided the continuing inspiration to do so. Without that collective inspiration and support this story would still just be floating around in my head, keeping me awake at night.

They are:

John Wallis (1843 – 1877), my great-grandfather and a Private in Company E, of the 19th Iowa Volunteers, Union Army. It was my reading of his war-time experiences during the Civil War and then falling heir to his 1862 Springfield rifle and other surviving pieces of his uniform that initially launched my curiosity about the history of the great American Civil War.

Colonel Robert Fleet (1921 – 2001), United States Army, Retired after three wars and 30 years of service to his country. His intense passion for the history of the Civil War proved infectious to those of us fortunate enough to have been in his classrooms. He had forgotten more of the history of the Civil War than most of us would ever learn.

Harry D. Wallis (1909 – 2004), my father. Before his death he read the initial draft of the first eight chapters and he offered, "It would make a damn good movie and Tom Selleck should play the lead!" It was not possible for me to stop writing after such a review.

Deanna Batson Cheves and Nancy Turner, very good friends who volunteered to served as my "Test Readers". It was their long hours that produced many, many suggestions; their attention to the detail, the accuracy, and the continuity of the story-line that finally turned my ramblings into a story that I am now not embarrassed to show to others.

All of the members of the **"Civil War Roundtable"** group of Okaloosa-Walton College. Not only have they continually encouraged me to finish this book when I became certain I never would, but their research and classroom reports added numerous interesting historical facts to the narrative.

My thanks to each of you and may God Bless you, as my knowing each of you has blessed me!

H. Dann Wallis

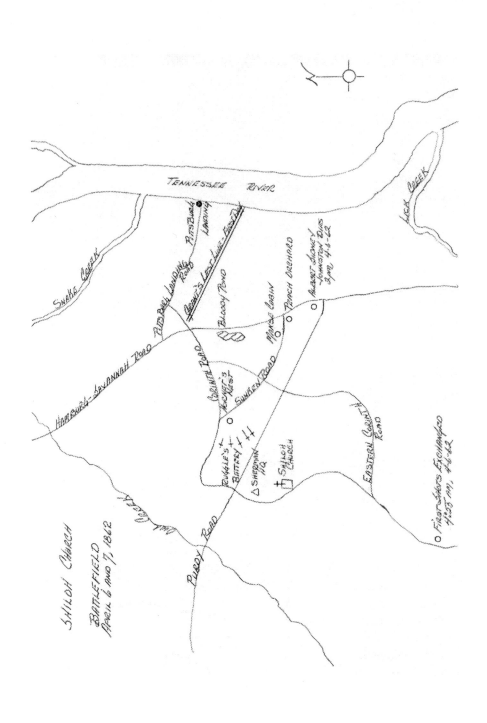

Tennessee River

Lick Creek

Snake Creek

Pittsburg Landing

Grant's Last Line April 6

Hamburg-Savannah Road

Pittsburg Landing Road

Bloody Pond

Eastern Corinth Road

Peach Orchard

Bragg's Advance Johnston's Divs April 6 & 7

Hamburg-Purdy Road

River Road

Sunken Road

Hornet's Nest

Ruggle's Battery

Sherman HQ

Shiloh Church

Eastern Corinth Road

Final Union Encampment 4:25 pm April 6

Purdy Road

Owl Creek

SHILOH CHURCH
BATTLEFIELD
April 6 and 7, 1862

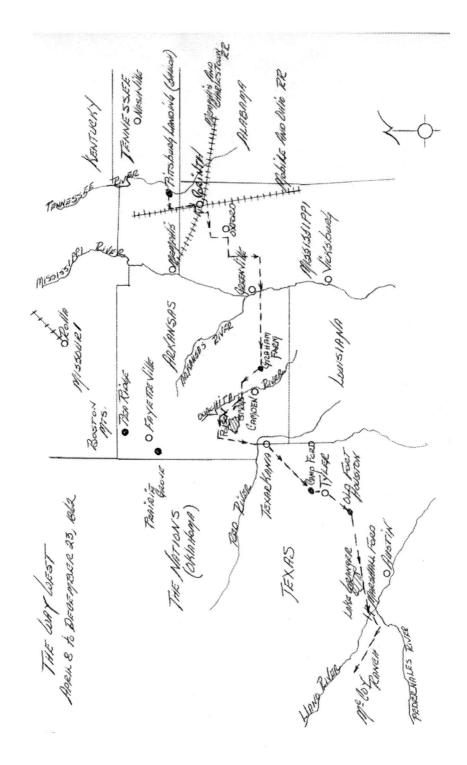

THE WAR WEST
April 8 to December 23, 1864

PROLOGUE

The People

Ulysses S. Grant

During the month of July of the unusually hot summer of 1861, a slight build man, perhaps five foot seven inches tall by 155 pounds, with dark probing eyes and a shaggy, untrimmed beard sat alone brooding over the map board in his lap. Close at hand, as usual, sat an uncorked bottle and a small glass both only partially filled with amber liquid. The man was seen to study his map, make a few marks on it, reach without looking to the glass beside him and take a sip, and then puff until his pipe bowl was glowing again. He much preferred cigars but his financial situation kept them a luxury he could not abide.

The place was the small Union army headquarters in Ironton, Missouri, and the man was Ulysses Simpson Grant. Until two months earlier that year he had been a clerk, working for his two younger brothers in the family's leather goods business in the small Illinois town of Galena. He was now a newly appointed Brigadier General in the Federal army, commanding the District of Ironton,

Western Department. While he waited for an army to be gathered for him to lead, he was finalizing a strategy for the western campaign that he would eventually execute to strike deep into the heart of the Confederate States of America.

The General's given name was actually Hiram Ulysses Grant, but the confusion in his registration at West Point had him enter The Academy under his Mother's maiden name. Thus, he was enrolled as Ulysses Simpson Grant, and the name the army gave him would remain with him throughout the balance of his life.

His developing plan was to combine efforts with the river navy and move his army south along the great river waterways; the Tennessee, the Cumberland and the Mississippi, to carry the war deep into the heartland of the western Confederacy. The rivers were the highways that would transport his army and their supplies to victory and then he would make the rivers safe to commerce for the Union. The final key to that free commerce was unlocking the Confederate grip on the lower Mississippi River for the 130 miles from Port Hudson, LA, to Vicksburg, MI. The stronghold at Vicksburg was the ultimate key to that lock. When it fell to the Union, Grant knew the war in the west would have been won and the Confederacy split, east from west. .

His tactic would be to apply constant and unrelenting pressure to the Confederate armies in his path. He would wear them away with the superior numbers and the superior armament of the Union. Unlike his Union counterparts in the eastern campaign, he would take to the attack and stay on the attack, never letting the pressure off. Lastly, he would apply what he had seen demonstrated by General Winfield Scott in the Mexican campaign, do not be tied to your base of supply but cause your army to live off of the land as it moves. The Grant plan for the conduct of the war in the west was actually one part of the plan originally developed by the now General-in-Chief of the army Winfield Scott, called *Anaconda*, after the large South American snake. *Anaconda* contained three elements to strangle the Confederacy: create an army to operate against the Capital of Richmond; a naval blockade to isolate the South from the aid and markets of Europe; and gaining control of the inland rivers and splitting the CSA into two or more parts. But supplies would come slowly to the western commanders; Grant's 48th Ohio was finally equipped with rifles only two weeks prior to their being committed in the battle for Shiloh Church. They had trained using small tree limbs and broom handles.

Grant knew his new opposite commander well. He was a fifty-eight year old former brigadier general in the Federal army, Albert Sidney Johnston, now a full general and commander of the Confederate Department No. 2, including all, or portions of seven states of the new Confederate nation. As such, Johnston was the over-all Confederate Commander in the West, but with the impossible task of implementing the orders given him by Confederate States President, Jefferson Davis to, "yield no territory of the Confederacy". That would require that Johnston secure a 600 mile defensive line from the Cumberland Gap to the Mississippi River. Johnston had just relieved a West Point classmate of President Davis, Major General Leonidas Polk. Prior to Polk's appointment by Davis, with no previous military experience, Polk had been a bishop of the Episcopal Church attempting to start a college at Sewanee, Tennessee.

Johnston graduated from West Point in 1826, eighth in his class but shortly resigned from the army to care for his terminally ill wife. He and Grant had served together in California before Grant's resignation from the army. Prior to that duty, Johnston had served with distinction in the 1857 campaign against the Mormons in Utah and was brevetted a brigadier general for that action. He commanded forces in the Texas revolution of 1836, and commanded the 1st Texas Rifles in action during the Mexican War. On July 16, 1838, forces under the command of Albert Sidney Johnston engaged Chief Bowles of the Cherokee Nation and associated tribes in a decisive battle by which the organized tribes were forever driven from East Texas. Grant had said of Johnston, "I expect him to be the most formidable man that the Confederacy will produce." Johnston was universally considered to be the finest military leader of either the North or the South. Confederate States President, Davis wrote, "I hoped and expected that I had others who would prove generals, but in Sidney Johnston I knew I had one."

Jefferson Finis Davis was likewise a West Point graduate, class of 1828. He was active in combat in the various Indian wars against the Pawnees, Comanches and the Black-hawk war of 1831. Davis resigned from the army in 1835 to marry the daughter of his commander, Zachary Taylor and became a planter in Warren County, Kentucky. He was elected to congress from Mississippi in 1845, then served with distinction in the Mexican War and was wounded at Buena Vista. Appointed to the U.S. Senate in 1847, he became a strong supporter of the Missouri Compromise of 1850 as a way to retain the peace in the western U.S. Senator Davis did not take any active part in planning or hastening secession, but followed his home state when, on January 9, 1861, Mississippi elected to succeed. One month later, he was appointed President of the Confederate States of America.

The Davis strategy, now imposed upon Johnston, would dictate the building of strong points with which to anchor defensive lines and then hold firm against attack, "never surrendering an acre of southern soil". Grant would counter with a strategy of probing for weakness, or flanking Johnston, and then siege his armies into surrender. The keystone to Grant's offensive was to combine soldiers and gun boats in the "river war". But Grant's biggest worry remained, would the people of the North and the Federal administration possess the will to fully prosecute and win the war in the face of the heavy losses that would certainly follow. Grant's aggressive theories for conducting this campaign had already placed him at odds with General Henry Halleck, the overall Federal commander in the west.

Grant came to this command position with an undistinguished record, having graduated in 1843, 21st of a class of 39 graduates. By a series of strange and unusual circumstances the young West Point Lieutenant posted as a regimental quartermaster, he had only briefly been noteworthy during the Mexican War in the battle at the walls of Chapultepec and the gates of San Cosme. For those he had received two brevets. However, a series of alcohol related incidents, some fact and many fiction, starting at "The Point" and following him to duty in California after the Mexican war, eventually, on July 31, 1854, lead to the resignation of Captain Grant from the army that he loved. His letter of resignation was accepted by the then Secretary of War, Jefferson Davis. What followed for Grant were but a series of business failures.

When President Lincoln used the provisions of the 1792 Militia Act to call a 75,000 man volunteer army to serve for three months to put down the coming rebellion, Ulysses Grant, at age 39, applied for a commission. Because of his history of drink, his string of failures in civilian life and the circumstances leading up to his previous resignation, the commission as a Colonel of the 21st. Illinois Volunteers was quite slow in coming, but did finally arrived on June 17, 1861, primarily through the efforts of Congressman Elihu Washburne. During that lengthy waiting period, while Grant was becoming increasingly depressed at the delay, he was secretly contacted by officials representing the new Confederate nation about accepting a command in the Confederate army. He was eventually persuaded not to do so during a meeting in Springfield in the early spring of 1861, by his close friend, the U S Senator from Illinois, Stephen A. Douglas. The Senator had previously defeated Abraham Lincoln in the 1858 election for the Senate, but then had been defeated by Lincoln for the Presidency in 1860. With the Southern Democrats dividing their votes between Breckinridge and Bell, and the Northern voters between Douglas and Lincoln, Mr. Lincoln became President with but 39% of the popular vote, the lowest total in American history.

Grant was a Northern Democrat, and known to favor solutions other than war for the existing slavery problem. For example, the aims of the "Free Soil" party; keeping the western territories free of slavery and open for the settlement of free labor, with the ultimate aim of isolating slavery in the south. Confederate States President Jefferson Davis and Vice President Alexander were also both initially opposed to secession, but later followed the will of the Secession Convention in February, 1861.

Strangely, Grant had become a slave owner himself. Just prior to his marriage in 1858 to Miss Julia Dent, of St. Louis, he bought a mulatto, William Jones, but then freed him a year later. His new bride, however, owned three slaves at the time of their marriage, which property her new husband would sometime later returned to his father-in-law. Julia Dent was the daughter of a well-to-do Missouri family that were long-time slaveholders and strongly pro-southern. Thus, had it not been for Senator Douglas' friendship and persuasion, joining the Confederate forces might not have been an unexpected step for Ulysses Grant.

Among the other unusual ironies of this coming war was that each eventual opposing commander had been offered the opportunity to lead the army of the opposite side; immediately prior to the secession of South Carolina, Robert Edward Lee was offered the position of second in command to his mentor and his commander during the Mexican War, General Winfield Scott. General Scott was 75 years old and still commanded the Armies of the United States, although mostly in name only. Captain Lee, while flattered, said that while he prayed that Virginia would maintain her neutrality, he would not raise his hand against his homeland if she did not. Also consider, at the start of the war, the eventual commander of The Army of Northern Virginia, Robert Lee, did not own slaves, having freed them at his wife's request many years earlier. These two men would lead the largest armies ever assembled on the North American landmass, yet neither had previously led men into combat. During the Mexican War Robert Lee, then a Captain in the Corps of Engineers served primarily as a personal scout for General Scott and never led a combat assault. Lieutenant Ulysses Grant was assigned to the Quartermaster Corps and except for the two cannoneers he briefly directed in action at the Gates of San Cosme, he likewise had never commanded a combat unit.

Grant's new army was formed primarily with new volunteers, and to provide combat leadership, the veterans of other western army units, some of which were already late into their one-year enlistment. These units had been scattered throughout western Missouri and northern Arkansas. As the remote units and fresh volunteers were joined together for training at Jefferson Barracks, Missouri, Grant began to form his army for the western campaign ahead. Grant was most impressed with the development of armament in the period since the Mexican War, and was himself, a proponent of the .577 caliber English Enfield rifle for its accuracy and distance, although most of his senior troopers preferred the Springfield. The new Springfield's were a 'three-banded' rifle. It reminded the second rank, when it reached through the first rank to fire, to keep the front man's ears between the last two bands to avoid a concussion. Grant would later write regarding the short range and inaccuracy of the musket of the Mexican War period, "A man might fire at you all day without your ever finding out."

Immediately after the Confederate Commander Pierre Gustave Toutant Beaurgard opened the war on April 12, 1861, by the 34 hour bombardment of Fort Sumter in Charleston harbor that caused not a single causality, Confederate units under the command of General Johnston were led by General Buckner to occupy Hickman and Columbus in Kentucky and fortify them as strong points. These fortifications effectively blocked the Union's traffic on the middle Mississippi River by stringing an anchor chain across the river at Columbus and mounting cannon on the heights. This was the initial involvement by either side into neutral Kentucky. Governor Magoffin had pleaded with both sides, "Don't send troops into Kentucky!" Although Lincoln had only received a total of 1,364 votes for President in the entire state of Kentucky in 1860, the state would in the next four years produce 67 Generals for the Union cause.

The aggressive action by the Confederates caused Kentucky on September, 18, 1861, to drop its position of neutrality and join the war on the side of the Union. Grant quickly moved from his headquarters at the terminus point of the Illinois-Central Railroad in Cairo, Illinois, to occupy strongly Confederate supporting, Paducah, Kentucky. Grant then opened the campaign by sending troops by river steamer down the Mississippi to Belmont, Missouri. Next was the capture of Mills Springs, Kentucky, followed by the successful assaults on the partially completed Fort Heiman and Fort Henry on the Tennessee River. On February 16, 1862, by the surrender of

Fort Donelson on the Cumberland River and the capture of 12,000 Confederate prisoners of war, including four Confederate Brigadier Generals, Grant became the over-night hero of the Northern newspapers. They changed Grant's initials of "U.S." from "Ulysses Simpson" to "Unconditional Surrender" Grant. With his defensive line now severed, the states of Missouri and Kentucky completely in Federal control, and the heavy losses of manpower at Fort Donelson, General Johnston was forced to evacuate Nashville, Tennessee, and retreat south along the Mississippi and Tennessee rivers. Nashville was occupied by Federal forces on February 25, 1862, and became the first southern state capitol to fall.

Grant's successes and the resulting newspaper headlines caused him to be relieved of command on trumped-up charges by his jealous commander, Henry Halleck, while Halleck himself was being rewarded with command of all Federal forces in the west. Ordered to remain at Fort Henry while his troops advanced to the south, Grant was quickly promoted to Major General and restored to field command when General Charles F. Smith became gravely injured in a non-combat accident and died shortly after.

Grant found his command at Pittsburg Landing, Tennessee, a force of 42,000 men that had been moved by steam packet down the Tennessee River with the objective of pressuring Johnston at Corinth, Mississippi, and either capturing or destroying this key railroad center. General Smith had put this army ashore during the last week of March, 1862, at the small settlement landing selected by Brigadier General William T. Sherman. It was only one of two openings in the river cliffs where the boats could land men and supplies, and a few miles from the primitive Methodist country crossroad meeting house, know in the area as the Shiloh Meeting Church. Sherman's forces had been the first to arrive in the area on March 16.

Over night on April 6, after the first day of the battle, Grant was also joined by the 25,000 troops of Major General Don Carlos Buell, who had made a forced march overland from Nashville, and the 7,000 fresh troops of Brigadier General Lew Wallace. Their very late arrival at Pittsburg Landing however, nearly brought the Union to a disaster. If General Johnston been able to solve his armies' logistical problems and had attacked on April 4th. as originally planned, Grant's force would likely have been destroyed, his career put in shambles, and the course of the entire Western campaign changed….all for the two days lost to muddy roads.

Author's Note: The Civil War's initial encounter actually occurred three months prior to the firing on Fort Sumter. On January 9, 1861, four cadets from the Citadel in South Carolina while standing a battery watch on Morris Island fired on the ship *Star of the West* as she attempted to resupply Fort Sumter. After the *Star* was struck twice by the cadet's barrage, she withdrew without landing her supplies.

Author's Note: Jefferson Barracks. Jefferson Barracks was established on October 23, 1826 as the nation's first "Infantry School of Practice" and continued as an active major military installation until its closure in 1946. It would serve as a gathering point and training location for troops and supplies bound for service in the Mexican War, Civil War, various Indian conflicts, the Spanish-American War and both World Wars. The 2000 acre base, stretching for two miles along the Mississippi River, also served as a 3000 bed Union hospital during the Civil War. Jefferson Davis trained there in 1828 as a newly commissioned Second Lieutenant; First Lieutenant Robert E. Lee was assigned there in 1837 working with the Engineers to straighten the river's course, and in 1843 Second Lieutenant U. S. Grant's first assignment after West Point brought him there where he would meet his bride-to-be, Miss Julia Dent.

John Michael Kelley, III

John Michael Kelley, III, spent the first sixteen years of his life on a half section, black dirt farm in southeastern Iowa with his parents and two younger brothers. The farm was in the name of his pa, John M. Kelley II, but had been homesteaded by his grandfather while Iowa was still part of the Wisconsin Territory. The farm was located a few miles down river from the first white settlement and fort in this new territory west of the Mississippi. The fort was established to satisfy part of a Lewis and Clark treaty with the Indians. But because of constant attacks on the fort by the Winnebago Indians, it was evacuated and burned by the detachment commander in 1813. Never-the-less, John Kelley and his new bride were determined to homestead and settle the rich bottom land and make their home there.

John Kelley, Senior, at age 16, had sailed from Ireland in the bilge of a leaky vessel, driven to the new world by the ravages of the potato famine in his homeland. He had intended to go to Boston, where most of the Irish came in America. But the ship he stole aboard dropped anchor in the mouth of the James River, just off Norfolk, Virginia. John Michael Kelley, a protestant Orangeman like his father before him, was fortunate to arrive in an area settled mostly by non-Catholics and before the work notices began to appear with, "Irish Need Not Apply". He had knowledge and a skill for mathematics that helped him land a position as a surveyor's helper for the Norfolk-Washington Railroad Company.

Five years later his work contract satisfied, John and his new bride departed for the Wisconsin Territory and the life of a land owning homesteader. A life he could not even have imagined in his native Ireland. However, he found the promised 40 acres located in the flood plane of the Des Moines River, the Les Moin River as the French fur trappers had named it. John and his bride moved further up the Mississippi, to the Seven-Mile Rapids and the river village of Montrose to find the good crop land he was seeking. Even though not his to claim, he staked it, clear it, build a cabin, planted a crop and defend it against all those, both white and red, who would try to take it from him. He and Kathleen expanded and prospered in this new wilderness while raising five of their seven children to adulthood.

The eldest child, a son, was named John Michael Kelley II, but throughout his life would be called JM. He too had a love for the land and followed in his father's footsteps on the farm. They were hard working and successful and soon expanded their holdings with the purchase of another 80 acres from a nearby neighbor. That neighbor, like many new to the frontier, returned to the east following the third time his cabin had been destroyed by Indians. JM's life was devoted to the farm and their growing horse herd, and except for the 15 months he was in Mexico during the war, he never left it. He and his father felt they owed a debt to this new land that had been so generous to them. So, JM left Julia, his young bride, and their toddler son, and in 1845 volunteered with General Zachary Taylor at Palo Alto in south Texas to free Texas from Mexico. Because he knew how to build things with his hands and had his father's gift for mathematics, he was mustered to serve in the Corps of Engineers, under Captain Robert E. Lee, a gentlemen from Virginia. JM earned a battlefield commission at the Battle of Buena Vista, Texas. When Captain Lee was transferred to General Winfield Scott's command for the battle for Vera Cruz, he took young Lieutenant Kelley with him and they continued to serve together during the balance of the war. JM was invited to remain in the army after the war, his friend, Captain Lee encouraged him to do so, but his heart and his life were in the black dirt of the Iowa farm he worked with his father. JM left for home shortly after the Treaty of Guadalupe Hidalgo was signed in February, 1848. The tall, dashing hero of a foreign war would himself soon become a land owner. The prosperous farm and the horse herds passed to JM not long after his homecoming when John, Senior's health worsened from the consumption during the bitter winter of 1848. Though his father would live for some years, he would never again regain his strength, but he would see this new territory become a state and grow and prosper. By 1857 the Galena-Chicago Railroad was bringing 3,000 immigrants a month looking to establish homes in the new state of Iowa. During JM's absence in Mexico, John, Senior, befriended and supplied a young Mormon leader, Brigham Young. They met when Mr. Young led an advance party of Latter Day Saints over the river into Montrose to begin the task of setting up base camps and marking the trail for others to follow from Nauvoo in Illnois to their Zion, the Promised Land that would be found in the valley of the Great Salt Lake.

JM and Julia had three sons, the oldest John Michael III, by 17 had became increasingly restless with the life of a farmer and went off to join Mr. Lincoln's new army, even though regulations held the bottom age to be 18. John III went to 'save the union' though his dream was to go explore and serve in the great American West. So, his plan became to join the 7th cavalry and become a horse soldier out on the plains. In March of '61, he gathered with other Iowa farm boys on the Keokuk & St. Paul Railroad for their first ride on a train. However, through confusion about his place of his enlistment, he was mustered in at Keokuk, Iowa, as a twelve month infantry volunteer in the Iowa 14th and that same day boarded a steam packet headed for training at Jefferson Barracks, Missouri. As it turned out, his enlistment timing was good, a few months later, on May 3, 1861, the new volunteers in Mr. Lincoln's army were required to serve for a period of three years. But in March of 1861, no one in the north believed the south would fight well, or could fight for very long.

Even though disappointed, John took his $100 enlistment bonus and swore to serve out his twelve months. By then the war would be over and he could go west and pursue his dream to be a cavalry soldier, or maybe ride for the Pony Express out of St. Joe in Missouri carrying mail along the 1,950 mile route to Sacramento, California, even though the recruitment ads stated, "orphans preferred". At that moment, anything would be better than going back to be a dirt farmer and spending the rest of his life staring at the south end of a north bound team of horses. John belonged in the cavalry. At a very early age he and his brothers were taught to ride and shoot. As his grandfather was fond of saying, "the meek may inherit the earth, but none of it will be west of the Mississippi River." John, Senior, had tried in vain to impress that sentiment on the Mormon pilgrims a few years earlier when they had stopped by the farm on the way to their new home in Illinois, the place they called Nauvoo. They gathered from all over the east to build a city larger than Chicago, and then elected to abandon it the year JM returned from the war when their leader Joseph Smith was pulled from a Carthage jail by a mob and lynched.

In the next few months John Michael would see considerable action in the Boston Mountains of southwest Missouri and northwest Arkansas where he proved himself in battle and was promoted to Corporal. Then following their decisive Federal victory at the battle for White Mountain, his company and others were recalled to Jefferson Barracks, south of Saint Louis, to begin training with a bunch of new recruits for a newly commissioned Federal General, Ulysses S. Grant.

Author's Note: Iowa had became a state on December 28, 1846, only 15 years prior to the start of the Civil War. Yet during the next four years the state would provide 76,000 men to the Union effort; the largest percentage of eligible men to serve from any state…Union or Confederate. Thirteen thousand Iowans would die during the war, over half from disease.

Andrew Glenn McCord

Andrew was born the middle child of Angus and Lucinda McCord who came to Texas by two very different paths. Just before Andrew was born, their oldest son had died at age five of the croup probably brought on by a two-week dust storm in west central Texas. When Andrew was born his daddy named him after, "the greatest man whoever lived, Andrew Jackson, 'cept maybe for Sam Houston that is."

Angus had been born in middle Tennessee in very poor circumstance. At 15 he ran away from home to join up with Colonel Davey Crockett's volunteers for their trip to join the fight against El Presidente, General Antonio Lopez de Santa Anna. The Presidente had promised to uphold the Mexican Constitution of 1824, which granted 'Texians' the right of full citizenship, then he recanted and swore to drive all Norteamericanos out of that northern province of his Mexico. The disputed area was the Nueces Strip; the area between the Nueces and Medina Rivers on the north and the Rio Grande River on the south. Texans believed the border with Old Coahuila to be the Rio Grande River, while Santa Anna declared it to be the Nueces. A "misunderstanding" of but 150 miles.

In a way, Angus was fortunate in that Colonel Crockett and his 37 men had left for San Antonio De Bexar, Coahulia Y Texas two weeks before Angus arrived at the gathering place, the tavern in Lawrenceburg, Tennessee. Angus did whatever work he could find for his support while waiting for the next volunteer company to gather and follow Colonel Crokett. For a while he cut hickory and made charcoal at the Daniels' whiskey still in the nearby Tennessee hills. Young Jack was not much older that Angus when he learned the whiskey trade from his grandfather. Before Angus and the next group of volunteers reached the tent town of Texarkana to cross into Texas, the Alamo had fallen and all of their Tennessee comrades were dead. The volunteers then joined up with the army being gathered by Major General Sam Houston on the plains at Gonzales. Angus, who had never owned a thing in this lifetime, was attracted by the promise of 800 acres of Texas land and $24 in gold for those who stayed with General Houston until they won independence for Texas. And stay he did!

Lucinda was the daughter of a New Orleans cotton broker and had accompanied her father to Galveston, Texas, on a buying trip, following the winning of that new nation's independence. She and Angus saw each other when Angus brought his first bales to market. Their eyes met and locked and they were immediately in love. When the buying trip ended, Lucinda did not return to Louisiana, but instead over her father's strong objections, became the bride of Angus McCord. The young couple worked hard, and as others gave up to the difficult life in central Texas, they borrowed money, bought their land, continued to expand and began to graze Mexican cattle as well as grow cotton. By the time Texas left the Union, cotton was almost $50 a bale and the McCord's owned and grazed 3000 acres of free range in the Hill Country of central Texas. Along with their two surviving children, Andrew and daughter Suzanne, life was good and plentiful for the McCord family.

On February 1, 1861, following the failure of the "Peace Conference" called by former President John Tyler, Texas joined with the seven other cotton growing southern states in forming the Confederate

States of America. It was then certain that war with the Unionists would follow, and just as certain it would be joined by young Andrew Glenn McCord. Andrew planned to join his fellow Texans in the division being formed by General Hood and headed to the eastern campaign. But at the last minute Angus used his considerable influence to cause Andrew, to be assigned to the 6th Arkansas and remain closer to home. Like many others of that time during his mustering in Andrew's name was written in the record poorly, and since "Glenn" was all that could be read, he would from then on be Glenn McCord. While serving in the 6th, Glenn would serve with and befriend Mr. John Rawlands, who later in the war changed his name to Henry M. Stanley. Long before Mr. Stanley would lead his expedition to darkest central Africa in an effort to locate a missing British Doctor and missionary, he would be captured at Shiloh. Stanley would serve briefly in the Union army, but be discharged due to his poor health. He would then enlist in the Union Navy only to desert because of the extremely cruel punishment metered out by the ship Captains at that time. Besides, the Navy abolished the 'Spirit Ration' that year. Mr. Rawlands had intended to completely avoid any service at all, but being among the last eligible males remaining, the young ladies of his hometown sent him a dress. He immediately volunteered. His later, famous African expedition would end with the greeting, "Dr. Livingston, I presume?" Glenn would later also remember meeting a slight built, quiet fellow officer; Lieutenant George E. Dixon of Company E, 21st. Alabama Volunteers. Lt. Dixon would later in the war become Captain of the CSS H. L. Hunley, the first submarine to actually sink an enemy ship-of-the-line. At Shiloh, Dixon's life was likely saved when a Union mini-ball struck a $20 gold coin in his pocket, a parting gift from his intended bride.

General Hood's 1st. Texas division went to the eastern campaign and would lose 82% of its mustered forces at the battle of Antietam Creek. Yet in spite of that slaughter, the "last man" to survive this War would be from Hood's original division. Walter Williams of Hood's 1st would survive until December 19, 1959, when he would die at age 117. The 6th of Arkansas joined the forces commanded by General Albert Sidney Johnston and began moving from Corinth toward the showdown at Shiloh Meeting Church, Tennessee.

The Place

Shiloh Church, Tennessee (Pittsburg Landing)

Ironically, Shiloh, Tennessee was named for the biblical village, whose name means, "place of peace". It became the first of three battles for control of the railroad crossroads at Corinth, Mississippi; those three battles would include two future presidents, a world famous explorer, and an author.

There are many examples during the Civil War where the same battle was called a different name by each side. Generally the Confederates named their battles for nearby towns while the Federal army relying on their crude maps as they invaded the south, often named the same battle for a nearby body of water, a river, or other landmark. But then there was not even agreement by which name this war would be called. In the South it might well be called The War for Southern Independence, The War for States Rights, The Second American Revolution, or the War against Northern Aggression. In the North it was often referred to as The Southern Rebellion, the War Against Slavery, and the War for The Union. And as it grew and continued on, the citizens of both sides would call it simply, 'The War', as though no other had ever been fought before or would be again.

Both sides would depart from their normal naming scheme in this battle but still would not agree on the name. The Confederates chose as the name, the location where they first encountered the Union in force, around General Sherman's headquarters on the grounds of the little log country church. General Sherman would be wounded in the hand by buckshot at almost the opening volley of this battle. To the Federal newspaper reporters it became simply Pittsburg Landing. Each side would agree however, that this bloody two-day battle, by any name, had been the key to the western campaign and would change forever any belief of a short, clean war.

General Grant came to this field with a total of 68,800 troops, arriving at Pittsburg Landing, Tennessee, by steamboats and the forced march of two divisions overland. In two days, April 6 and 7, 1862, the Union army would suffer 13,000 casualties. General Johnston arrived from Corinth, Mississippi, with 45,000 Confederate troops and suffered 11,000 casualties in the two days. The 6th Mississippi lost 71% of the division's force. Almost 24 thousand Americans were casualties in this single, two-day battle, nearly 24% of the total forces engaged. True to Grant's concerns, Northerners were appalled by the terrible casualty count and tried to assign reasons. The rumors raised that Grant was drunk at Shiloh and thus, was surprised by both the location and the number of Confederate troops. However, Grant, who was reinstated late in the preparation following his being relieved after the battle at Fort Donelson, was then forced to execute the plan laid out by General Smith upon the latter's death. An excuse he never spoke. Had it not been for his sponsor, Congressman Elihu Washburne of Illinois, Grant might well have faced Court-Martial. With that, he was again temporarily relieved of command to defend his decisions, then for some time following Shiloh, General Halleck placed Grant in a role of reduced authority. Both actions ultimately contributed to the Union's failure to immediately pursue and destroy the retreating Confederate army. Congressman Washburne was moved to say on the floor of the House, "There is no more temperate man in the Army than General Grant. He never indulges in the use of intoxicating liquors, at all." Just a slight enlargement of the actual truth of the matter.

At a minimum, the Union grossly miscalculated the size and location of the Confederate force. The Union army was off-loaded from a fleet of steamboats in the late afternoon and encamped with the Tennessee River to its back, its right flank blocked by Snake Creek and its left flank up against Lick Creek. Grant intended to begin an offensive march to Corinth, where he expected to find the Confederates, and thus no defensive positions were ever established. To his complete surprise, the Confederate Army was not 25 miles away in Corinth, Mississippi, but only two miles away on his front, having advanced down the Corinth-Pittsburg road, and were awaiting the drier conditions of the Sunday morning dawn.

The initial day of the battle went very poorly for Grant's forces and they were nearly driven from the field. It went poorly for Grant, as well. It took some time for Grant to even reach the battlefield from the command headquarters General Smith had established at Cherry Mansion in Savannah, on the eastern side of the river. The battle started while Grant was at breakfast. Later that day, his horse slipped in the mud of the rain soaked battlefield and fell, pinning Grants leg. It did not fracture, but he directed the rest of the battle on crutches. In the afternoon of the first day, General Johnston was wounded in the leg and later bled to death on the field while refusing treatment as he continued to direct the battle. With General P.G.T. Beauregard now in command, a final assault on Union lines was ordered. However, unknown to either Beauregard or Braxton Bragg, a member of the staff, Major Numa Augustin had ordered a halt to the advance and a withdrawal for the night to the food and comforts of the captured Union camps. With that, the Confederate forces broke off the advance with victory in sight.

General Johnston was but one of the 24,000 casualties of this two-day encounter, but would become the American of highest rank ever to be killed in a direct battle, in any war. Overnight Grant was reinforced with fresh troops, and during the second day recovered all the ground previously lost. At dusk on the second day, the exhausted and severely depleted Confederate forces, now under the generalship of Beauregard, withdrew from the field toward Corinth, then later on toward Tupelo and Jackson. As they retreated, the Confederate forces would strip the Union dead of clothes, footwear and weapons. Loaded down as they were, escape became difficult and large numbers were shot down by advancing Federal forces. The Federal troops, however, were much too spent to pursue the retreat and without their field commander, the Federal army encamped. Grant would again be relieved of his command to answered charges. Again he would consider resigning, but Lincoln intervened with the public statement, "I can't spare this man. He fights." When returned, Halleck would give Grant a much reduced role. Halleck gathered an army of 110,000 men, but still he would not be moved toward Corinth, until finally the last day of May, almost 45 days following the battle. Halleck, it seems, preferred a desk to a saddle.

With Grant finally returned, the Federal army moved to occupy Corinth, Mississippi, at which point the Union found the city had been abandoned weeks before as the Confederate Army, now racked with dysentery and disease had retreated deeper into the south. At times Beauregard could field less that 65% of his men under arms.

In later writings, Grant would recall Shiloh thusly: "I saw an open field over which the Confederates had made repeated charges the day before, so covered with dead that it would have been possible to walk across in any direction, stepping on dead bodies without a foot touching the ground." He was referring to the old sunken wagon road the Federal forces would call the "Hornets Nest", so ably defended by Colonel Peabody of General Benjamin Prentiss' command.

This single battle would forever change all preconceived notions that the Civil War would be short lived. This war would labor on for another three bloody years with Americans killing Americans. More Americans became casualties in just this two-day battle than in America's three preceding wars combined. Yet five other battles in this war would be more costly than Shiloh (the name history would finally settle on). Though plagued by poor record keeping, an estimated 650,000 Americans would be killed and 486,300 wounded during the four years of the Civil War, far exceeding the nations' **total** losses from all of its wars from the Revolutionary through the Korean, combined. The Union would commit 2.5 to 2.7 million men to the war and suffer more than 370,000 casualties, while the Confederate States of America suffered an estimated 280,000 casualties from their 1.3 million men under arms.

But it was in this battle, of this war that Corporal John Michael Kelley, III (USA) and Lieutenant Andrew Glenn McCord (CSA), enemies at its start, would encounter each other and begin their strange adventure.

Corinth, Mississippi

Just prior to the start of the Civil War, Corinth was a frontier boom town built only 25 years before on what had been Chickasaw Indian land. 1857 saw the final completion of the two longest railroads of the same gage in the south, and they crossed at this remote location; the Memphis & Charlestown ran from the Mississippi River to the Atlantic Ocean, and the Mobile & Ohio from the Ohio River to the Gulf of Mexico. Originally called "Cross City", it was incorporated in1855 as "Corinth", Greek for crossroads. But by 1861 the railroad junction had become a liability for the citizens as both the Confederate and the Union armies brought havoc to the town and its residents. The majority of the residents opposed secession, but the community did raise a company called the Corinth Rifles which became apart of the Mississippi 9th Regiment.

General Halleck had termed Corinth as, "The second most strategic city in the south, and must be insured at all hazard". Three battles were fought for control of this railroad crossroad, the first being at Shiloh Church. The Union eventually occupied Corinth on May 30, 1862; won the Battle of Corinth in October against General Earl Van Dorn in the bloodiest battle within the state of Mississippi, then after setting it ablaze, abandon the town in January, 1864, as Union soldiers were being gathered in the east for Sherman's Atlanta Campaign. At various times as many as 300,000 soldiers from the North and the South had occupied Corinth, a town of but 1,500 prior to the war.

Chapter One

"THE ENCOUNTER"

The conscious world returned very slowly and brought with it sharply increasing pain to Corporal John Kelley, 14th Iowa Regiment, Union Army. The first pain message he became aware of was the intense pain in his forehead, just above the right eye and the star burst of bright lights behind his closed lids. Next was the difficulty to just breathe from the choking mud in his nose and mouth. With a mind in near panic, he could only reason that he was laying face down in the dirt. But, what dirt and where? When John tried to roll over onto his side to get his face clear, every spot on his body began sending intense pain messages to his brain; all except his left arm, which sent no message at all. He tried to open his eyes to get his bearings, to find out where he was, and what had happened. But, the command to 'open' was ignored, except for just a small slit from the left eye, and all that came back from that was darkness. John moved his right hand to his eyes and felt a wet, gooey mass covering his upper face. His mind jumped to the first conclusion, 'dear God, I've been shot in the head and I am here alone and blind.' He moved his hand up to the spot of the sharpest pain on his forehead and found the origin

1

of the goop; a long, ragged wound above his right-eye, toward the center of his forehead. The wound seemed to be caked with the mud of the clay he had been laying in, but was now mostly dry, only a small trickle of liquid was present to keep the mass damp. Between the sharp pain and the blackness panic was now running almost unchecked. By shear force of will, John commanded himself to lie back while he tried to come to some understanding of his situation. If he couldn't, he would certainly die here, alone….if he only knew where 'here' was.

John lay on his back for long minutes that seemed to him to be hours, staring sightlessly into the darkness of his closed lids, and fought to push back the fear now close to ruling him. His mind reached to recall even one small detail of what had happened here…..little came forth. But the effort of his concentration eventually helped, and small bits of memory began to float back…to take form. The fog of his mind slowly began to clear and as he shifted his position to make himself more comfortable, some of the pain in his body began to ease a little. The tingling in his left arm signaled the blood was now beginning to circulate on that side. He began to recall a trip down river on a steamboat…a gunboat named for a president. *Tyler* that was it, the *John Tyler*! When was that, maybe four or five days ago…maybe longer? Then the little rough log, country church standing at the cross- road, just like the one his ma took him to as a youngster. And those beautiful peach trees in full bloom they were in the orchard on the road as they marched toward the church, must have been at least 10 acres. It was such a beautiful and peaceful scene, like being home on his pa's farm in the Iowa spring. He remembered thinking then, 'this is so beautiful, surely the war will not find us in this place'. God, what could have happened between then and now to cause this? And the rain, he remembered the days and nights of never-ending rain when they first arrived, and the cooking, and eating, and sleeping…then fighting in the mud.

Slowly his memory of the details of the fierce battles began to take shape, how surprised their officers were at the strength of the Confederate forces they encountered, and that they were right in front of them, not 25 miles away as they had been told. That was it!

He was someplace close to Pittsburg Landing. That's where he and his squad had left the steamboat. They came up the gentle slope from the Landing onto the Pittsburg-Corinth Road and marched around to the old church. But General Sherman's boys were already camped there, so John's company moved back around by that orchard and Mr. Manse's cabin and found a spot to camp. John's mind began to slowly develop the sights and sounds of the battle, being first overrun and in a full panic retreat back toward the river and the steamboats. Past the pond that was red in color from the blood of the wounded men and horses dying standing right out there in the water. And the cannon, my god I didn't think the entire south had 62 artillery pieces, yet there they were, on one ridge, every black, smoothbore mouth open and yawning right at him! About 4 in the afternoon they all let loose and General Wallace's' entire line just broke up. John remembered clearly the smoke ring that each cannon produced as it fired. A perfect white smoke circle that just floated on the still air for almost 200 yards. He could see dozens of the white rings floating at the same time. He had led his squad back into the protection of the sunken wagon road and reported to Colonel Peabody, who told him, "Boy, you just find a hole, crawl in it and pull it in after you." When the barrage lifted, John's squad joined up with some of the boys from the Iowa 3rd, and a short while later when the sunken road was over run by the Confederates, they all escaped through underbrush so thick a rabbit couldn't run in it, and retreated with the others back toward the Landing. On the second day, with no sleep because of the all night firing from the gun boats, they stood shoulder-to-shoulder with the fresh troops and charged back through the Rebel lines. John's memory was now returning all too clearly and with it the horrors that he had witnessed and those that he had caused. The cries of the agony of death from the wounded men of both sides. The place on the sunken road where they had been the day before, now being called the "Hornets Nest", where bodies laid so thick that when they finally charged the retreating Rebs. their feet could not find the ground.

John's memory saw him later being ridden to the ground by the Confederate Captain who had charged his horse into their position when the squad ran out of lead and powder. His mind saw the bright sun-light reflected on the wide-blade sword being waved wildly over the horse's head. Then the head of the soldier in front of him was rolling away into the mud as his body continued forward for two additional steps, then ran out its life. It was John's instinct that he could not outrun the horse that caused him to turn and dive under the charging animal's front hoofs to avoid being beheaded. The last memory was the blow to the head as the horse stumbled on him and then fell over him.

Now, these many hours later, that's why it is so quiet and why he was so alone, the battle had ended and the remains of the two armies had withdrawn to where ever armies go after such a slaughter, the Union back by the Landing and the Confederates retreating toward Corinth. He had been left on the field with the dead and those not yet quite dead. Maybe he was here because he was already dead and that was why he felt so alone…. no, he hurt too badly all over to be dead and wasn't there supposed to be a bright, white light to follow? Wasn't death supposed to take all pain away? So he had been told when his grandmother had died in such great pain and then a moment later looked to be at such a beautiful peace. Made him think that death might not be so bad, once you finally arrive there. No, he wasn't dead; he hurt like hell and he still could not see…not bright light, not anything but darkness!

Gradually, with his mind clearing and in the night's quiet he heard the familiar sounds of a spring night in the middle south, the crickets, the frogs, the buzzing of mosquitoes, and the sounds of the night birds. Surely the battle must have ended; he had not heard a bird sing for four days. So peaceful, until he recognized that those pleasant sounds were also being punctuated by the sounds made by the men who knew they are dying and are faced with doing so alone and far from home. John couldn't tell from the cries of suffering and the calls for "God save me", or "mother help me", even which army the dying men were from. He decided that dying men from all armies' likely sound about the same when they see the end of their life so near at hand.

After he rested a bit and gained some control, John slowly sat up, reached around to his belt on the left side and found his bull's-eye canteen. He took a long drink even though the water was warm and stale in spite of the canteen's wool covering. John couldn't remember when he filled it last, hopefully not from that red pond. He splashed some in his cupped hand and took it to his forehead and eyes. Slowly and very carefully he washed the mud and blood mixture away, and his eyes began to open. For some moments his sight was blurred, even painful, but gradually with the full moon for light, his immediate world came into focus. A line from an old hymn, "I was blind but now I see" came from someplace back in his past. The night sky was clear and bright, the ground well illuminated. What was the full moon of April? The Planter's moon? His Indian pal from the "half breed tract" territory in Iowa had taught him the Indian meaning of each full moon when they had played together many years ago, now he could only remember "Harvest" and "Hunter". He thought that was September and October, not April. Eye of the Hawk, the child of a Sac mother and a white father, had been a true and wise friend to grow-up with.

Now his eyes began to focus on the world close around him; but his mind would not, could not comprehend the horror he witnessed. Hypnotized at the sight, he finally had to will himself to look away. But look where? There was no place of peace left to look; the carnage was everywhere his eyes came to rest. At all points were the bodies and parts of bodies of the dead, and a few of those not yet dead, but soon to be. Shadows of dead horses and others in such shock they just stood motionless with heads drooping. Broken and discarded weapons, packs and other military gear that became too heavy to carry or were no longer needed, broken and burned wagons and cannon carriages without wheels, and the small sewn bags in which each man had carried the few special belongings from home. Just five feet away was a headless body, too mutilated to even show which army he had fought for, but John knew it was his. A few feet beyond him a Confederate officer lay impaled on his broad sword, his horse just beyond with a broken leg. Perhaps John's attacker? This must be what General Sherman had in mind when he told his boys, "War is cruelty and you can not refine it." As John's senses tried to absorb the sights, the sounds of the dying, and most of all, the terrible smells around him, he was suddenly struck by the realization; he could never go through anything like this again. Would never! He had been to one major battle too many, had 'seen the elephant' one too many times. He had volunteered for 12 months, he had now survived far more than that, his time was up…had been up! He should not have even been here. This had not even been his fight, he should be home. Someone had just forgotten to tell him. Another major army mistake…happened all the time. They should have said 'thank you for your service' and sent him home long before this battle.

There would be plenty of needed things left here on this field, he could outfit himself from this devastation and go away…go to the new west where no one would know him and this war could be left far behind. He had always wanted to go west, maybe finally join that new pony express out of St. Joe. Perhaps go to Texas and learn to be a cowboy. He would do it; this was his chance, maybe his last. "Take it', his mind screamed at him; **'GO'** while you still can! Who's to know? I could be that fellow over there with no head attached. When it gets light, the squad will come and dump him in a hole in the ground and no one will know who he was, or even care. And his family will never know where he fell….or why.

As he was imagining his departure from this army and this war, John came to realize if he did this thing, if he left before they told him to, he could never go back home again. Would never see his ma, or his pa again, never see the farm where he had grown up. When the Army came looking for him, they would look there first. John's pa had been to Mexico in '46 and for awhile served with Captain Robert Lee. Would he understand his son's decision or would he feel disgraced by it? He could not even let them know he was still alive; maybe it would be best if they thought him dead. But if he didn't go, he would likely never see those things again anyway. This was his fifth major battle in just the last 13 months; no one could keep doing this and live long, or if he was spared in battle, keep from some day killing himself over the horror of it all. He hoped to never again hear that sickening sound of a lead ball cracking the skull of the comrade kneeling beside him. John crawled a few feet to sit against the broken remains of a tree, its top shredded by canister. After a brief rest, then slowly, he started to get to one knee and paused again. As his body became more steady and his head clearer, he stood. He had made the decision. He knew he was going to go! Having decided, it was now the time to get ready and to be gone before the daylight.

 John wet his bandana from the canteen, and tied it tightly around his head to cover the wound and try to stop the trickle of blood that had returned when he washed the mud away. The first essential was a good horse, if such still existed on this field. The Confederates always seemed to have the best horses. John picked-up a broken rifle for a walking stick and started moving slowly, unsteadily in the direction of their last retreat. Most of the animals he saw were in such shock they wouldn't last a day on the road. If the Indians had a horse like that they would eat him and then go on foot. He was becoming discouraged until he topped a small rise just beyond the shell of the church. There he saw a big gray mare, maybe 15 or 16 hands, grazing unconcerned. She raised her head as John approached and nickered in response to his voice. Catching up the reins John checked her over with his eyes and hands. Just the act of rubbing her down made both the horse and the man feel more secure. She obediently picked up her feet as John felt for wounds in her legs. Good, she was sound and, like him, seemed ready to get off this field and away from this place. That was easy, the first need was satisfied.

The next was to be armed, and the best arms would be found belonging to the Union. John wanted a revolver, one of those new fixed cartridge, .44 caliber models by Samuel Colt; he had seen some of the officers carrying them. Also a repeating rifle, if such could be found. He had heard about the new 7-shot Spencer repeating, breech-loading rifle that was being issued only to the cavalry. John had heard the story of how the Federal ordnance men had turned down the Spencer in 1860, 'because the soldiers would fire too fast and waste ammunition'. The horse soldiers bragged that, 'a body could load that rifle in the morning and shoot all day with out running out'. He led the big gray back toward the crossroad area and hobbled her in some good grass. This would be his base camp. As he found the things he needed, he would bring them here. He felt good fortune was surly with him in finding such a sound horse, especially one with such a good Mexican-style saddle and a bed roll with an oil cloth ground blanket still tied behind. And best of all, a good looking, English double-barrel scattergun was tied up in the ground blanket. Given that equipment, some Confederate officer had likely been shot off of this horse. Eye of the Hawk would have said this was all part of a good sign; this was the right thing to be doing. At least he wouldn't have to sit one of those Federal McClellan saddles. With that 11 ½ inch split in the middle, it was a true butt-buster. Good for the horse, but hell on the rider. Those things truly hurt your backside after a while, how did the horse soldiers sit them all day?

For the next two hours John used the light of the moon to scavenge the battlefield. At first he could not look for long at the wreckage of the men about him, in fact felt sick as he did so. But later it became so commonplace that he was able to continue his search and step over the bodies, almost without notice. Such was the nature of men at war; they steeled themselves against the ugliness of it. In the end, that was how they went on and, for the short term, stayed sane. It was usually some later in life when they had to deal with what they had seen and what they had been a part of. It took awhile, but he found the weapons he was seeking. Both were in good condition and cartridges for the Spencer came in two bandoleers. There were .577 caliber Enfield copies everywhere, but John wouldn't carry one across the yard! By comparison, they were so inaccurate and unreliable that John had directed his squad whenever they had an option on the battlefield pick up a Springfield model and throw the Enfield down. He had drilled his squad on the 9-step Scott manual of arms until they could load and fire at a rate of three times a minute with the Springfield, in battle that rate either went drastically up or down, but for certain, the 9-step method was quickly forgotten. He also has his squad wrap their rifle barrels in leather so they could be handled. At three rounds a minute the barrels quickly became too hot to touch, or hold to aim. Fortunately for the Union, many of the Confederates here had been issued those look-alike Enfield, or carried the old .69 caliber smoothbore they brought from home. The smoothbore, which fired four iron balls at a time, was a very effective weapon within 30 yards, but beyond that range, the greater threat was to the one holding it.

The patient, selective search had been well rewarded, he had the weapons he wanted, a wide brim hat, a small sewn bag of gold coins, some dried beef and hardtack, a spy glass, and a brass compass with which to find the way to Texas. It was easy to know which side was supplying his needs from the haversacks he found; the Union soldiers tarred theirs to waterproof them while the Confederates did not. He was on his last trip to return to the gray mare when he heard a weak voice call out. His first thought was it's the final earthly cry of a dying man. Then he became alarmed for he feared someone had been watching his preparation to leave the field. He stopped and waited, then it came again, "Over here, I'm hit, please, help me....help me". John's first reaction was to run for the horse, grab-up his gatherings, and ride out of here. But compassion for a fallen warrior pulled him in the direction of the call, in spite of the fact he could be putting at considerable risk his chance of escape. The call repeated and John altered his course toward the voice. While walking he chambered a cartridge in the Spencer he carried in the crook of his left arm. About 40 yards off of the pathway John saw him; a Confederate Lieutenant. John stopped in a shadow a short distance away while trying to decide if he should just shoot this enemy, or walk away and leave him. His sergeant had been heard to say many times, "the only good rebel is a dead rebel." Finally compassion won out and he did neither, but was drawn closer to the fallen man.

"Please help me, I've been hit twice and I'm gonna' bleed to death before they come for me at morning light. If you've seen any war a 'tall, you know any wound can be a death sentence, and I've got two...bad ones it appears. If you don't help me my next ride's likely to be in the 'dead wagon'."

9

"I don't have the time or inclination to help you, **Sir**", John replied. "I am about to get on that horse yonder and leave this war."

"And go where?"

"I'm heading for the west and away from this; my muster period is up over a month ago! I shouldn't even be here"

"The west? That's a big place. Just where in the west you thinkin' of going, Corporal?"

"I believe I'll give Texas a try, my pa was there on his way to the war in Mexico and thought it a fine place, a place worth fighting for."

"That's where my home is, I'm from central Texas, area they call the Hill Country. Tell you what Corporal, you help me and I'll not only not tell anyone you're leaving, I'll show you the way to Texas. You help me get home to Texas and my pa will surely give you a reward."

"Why do I want to be slowed down by the likes of you? I don't need you, Texas is a big place, how hard could it be to find?"

"You're gonna' travel over 800 miles, all of it through Confederate territory, wearing that rag-tag Federal uniform, avoiding the 20,000 troops General Holmes has waiting in Arkansas, and them Sons of Liberty and American Knights who are collecting a bounty dead or alive for deserters like you on the border. And if you get by all that, wind up smack dab in the middle of the largest state in the Confederate Nation? Corporal, you've got to be smarter than that to have stayed alive this long. Why you're dumber than a mule if you think you can pull that off alone, you won't even see the big river before they get ya'."

"Deserter is it? I served my time...more 'n my time. And what's that make you? Don't recall you saying anything 'bout being mustered out. Could be those Son's of Liberty would be interested in the likes of you as well." Then John fell quiet for a long time as he thought over what he had just heard. He hated to admit it, but there was more than a little sense there. If he could trust the Lieutenant to show him the correct way, they might could do this thing together, but neither could likely do it alone, and if he couldn't be trusted, well he'd just kill 'em. That Reb. Lieutenant will most likely die on this field by morning before his people could even find him, and by noon John would likely be captured by some Reb. patrol and on the way to a Confederate prison, or an exchange point. If that happened he'd be back in this army in a month, marching to yet another battle....perhaps that one to be his last. Or worse yet, just slung over a saddle...shot by some damn bounty hunter. No, this thing needed a second thought.

Finally he ask, "How bad you hit?" He saw a large amount of blood on the coat front and pants leg.

"Hard", was the pained response.

John eased him back down on the ground and opened his coat and shirt. From the amount of blood on the right side of the chest, John figured he would soon be dead either way. He opened the tunic, washed away some of the blood with the canteen he was carrying and felt for the wound. The ball had hit in the middle of the rib cage, struck two ribs and been deflected to exit out the side below the arm. Looked worse than it probably was given all the blood, but certainly at least those two ribs were cracked, or broken. The wound in the right leg was a different story. The ball must have been partially spent as it entered the front, missed the big bone, but it was still in there buried deep in the muscle in the back of the thigh. John pressed the upper muscle on the leg making the Reb. suck-in a lung full of air. He could feel the ball move under his fingers.

"Here's what I can do. By-the-way Reb. what's your name anyway... I'd like to know who you are before you die?'

"Andrew Glenn McCord from the Hill country of central Texas. At home I'm called Andrew after Andrew Jackson, but in this Army I somehow wound up being called Glenn".

"Well Andrew Jackson Glenn McCord, **Sir**, I'll wrap those ribs so you can ride...gonna' hurt like hell with every step the horse takes, but if you true want to go, you can suck it up and ride. That ball in your leg has gotta' come out. I'm not gonna' build no fire, but we can use some whiskey to clean the wound and my knife."

With that said, John got up to go fetch what he needed. Concern entered Glenn's eyes. "You gonna' leave me here to die and just take off?"

"It is a pleasing thought, but no, we'll start this thing together."

"How do I know you'll even be comin' back?"

"Cause you just heard me say it, and that's all you need, or get." With that John turned and walked away to pick-up what supplies he needed. He was about 10 yards away when he realized he had left the rifle, with a round chambered, leaning against the tree stump by the Lieutenant. John suddenly turned and looked back and saw Glenn smiling. "That's just in case anyone tries to bother ya' while I'm gone. There's a round chambered, just don't shoot yourself in any new places, I've got about all I can do to save you now," John added as though he had just planned to leave the rifle handy. Then he turned his back and walked away. That was mighty careless! If I'm gonna' be that careless, it's good I am leaving the army, cause I'm soon dead anyway.

About an hour later John returned leading two horses, carrying more guns, and all the items he had collected on his earlier trips. Glenn had been sleeping and was startled when he heard the horses.

"You been gone awhile, I begin to wonder"

"No need. I told you I'd be back"

"I don't usually put much stock in the word of Yankee Corporals."

"I usually don't make promises to Reb. Lieutenants, but them I make, I keep. And from this moment forward, no more rank and no more Sir. If we're going...we're going as equals."

"Agreed. You've got a good eye for horse flesh for a Yankee, that gray mare is a sound looking animal".

"That's why I picked her out for me. Yours is the bay." John smiled for the first time in days.

By the end of the next hour, John had removed the spent ball in Glenn's leg, while Glenn nearly bit clean through the leather strap John had put between his teeth. He bathed both the leg and the chest wounds in whiskey, what they didn't drink as both worked up their nerve, then bound up the wounds with strip bandages from the medical bag he had found. They cleaned up as best they could, finished the whiskey and rested. John gave Glenn a Colt, London .36 caliber revolver he had found and some shells.

Glenn confided, "I was never much on drinking whiskey. Pa enjoyed it, but wasn't too keen on it for me."

John replied, "That's about 150 proof, so it's a good way to learn. My family's Irish going way back. Hell, we even use whiskey for teething babies. The Irish figure that what whiskey won't cure, there just ain't no cure for."

The sky was getting pale in the east when they mounted up and started off of the battle- field. Glenn had needed lots of help just to get up on the bay, but finally made it without crying out. Took some considerable guts, John figured. Both men had slept longer than they intended, but it had been three days full of misery with damn little chance for rest in-between. Soon the "Medical and Burial" details from each army would be returning to this field. The teams from each side would cooperate and help the other locate and sort the dead and the body parts of the dead, just as though they had no idea what had caused all of this. Probably even trade some coffee and tobacco before departing again for their own lines. Damn strange war John thought with Americans killing Americans, and then stopping to trade goods over the dead bodies.

"Come on, we're burnin' daylight", John growled as he pulled the gray's head around to the west.

13

As they topped a rise before dropping down into the bottom of Owl Creek, the two soldiers reined-up their horses and these enemies sat side-by-side in silence and looked back at the destruction each, in his own way, had helped create. The still battlefield had acquired a quiet peace, there was little moving or crying out now, the wounded having died or just given up expecting help. Each place where the men's eyes could find light enough to see, the field was littered with the strange shapes of broken men, animals and equipment. Each distorted by the shadows caused by the dimming light of the late night moon, meeting the pale light of the dawning of another day. These two young warriors, who came to this field as enemies intent on killing each other, were leaving now knowing they were completely dependent on each other for their very survival. If they could get through the mistrust, and focus on the mutual need, this adventure might have a chance. If they could not, each would likely die, or one might yet kill the other.

Chapter Two

"THE WAY WEST"

Glenn took a last, long look at the field of death and destruction laid out before them, then not being able to comprehend the sight any further, turned the bay gelding and eased him down into the rocky bed of Owl Creek. The tree growth was heavy along the rain swollen, quick running stream and the still weak, pale light of the morning was quickly shut out. Each step his horse took brought a new message of pain, seemingly from a new location in his body. The bandage around his leg was already blood soaked from the pressure against the saddle. He wondered again if he could possibly keep up with this Yankee Corporal for the next few hundred miles, and if he could not, then what? Would he just be left to fend for himself? This Yankee was very intent on escaping to the west, would he allow Glenn's wounds interfere with that...to slow him down? Two days ago this man would have quickly and efficiently killed him given any opportunity, now Glenn's very survival depended on his ability to trust this enemy, not a comforting thought. True, John had left his loaded rifle close and then had provided him with a side arm.

But, Glenn could find only limited comfort in these facts. But the only other choice open to him was to find a Confederate patrol and surrender them both....then he became the traitor to their pledge to help each other, and John either went to Libby Prison to die, or would just be killed outright. At this moment Glenn's world was full of what looked to be, only very poor choices.

John continued to sit quietly on the big gray and, though he knew they should be leaving, he could not take his eyes from the sight before him. He had been in many major battles in his last months of army service, but nothing had prepared him for a sight such as was before him now. By comparison, the other battles had been "clean", or at least the army had moved on from the field of battle and he did not have so much time to witness, to absorb the graphic results of war. But here, he couldn't even count the bodies just in the small area in front of him. In full daylight it would become a sight unbelievable. He knew again, that having served out his promised time, leaving was the thing for him to do, but still, he just didn't feel completely right about it. Probably because he knew his Pa would not have left and would not approve of his leaving. What worried him most was the Lieutenant! Would he really serve as a guide as he said, or would he surrender him to the first patrol they encountered? And what about his wounds...they looked bad and he was bleeding again after but a few minutes ride...could he survive them? If he took worse, should he leave him and go on to the west? Could he even get there through so much enemy territory without his help? Glenn was probably correct, John could likely never safely find his way through hundreds of miles of enemy country...it had sounded so easy before he had been forced him think it through. That was a lot of trust to place in a man who only two days ago was definitely trying to kill him, or that he would have killed if he came into his sights. He would have to be very watchful of Glenn and just try to focus on one day at a time.

John looked in the direction Glenn had departed; he was falling too far behind so he pushed the gray down into the tree covered creek bottom. He heard Glenn moving away to his right as his horse stepped into the water, then on to a rock. At least there would be good cover and concealment while following the creek back upstream. John moved to the opposite bank, the gray stepped over the deadfalls and quickly caught up. Glenn moved up on the bank in front of John and they fell into column. John looked up and smiled at the view in front of him. He had left the farm because he grew tired of each day looking at nothing but the south end of a north bound team of horses, now here he was again…different location…different purpose…but the same view. It occurred to John that if you're not in the lead, the view just never changes. He wondered if sled dogs ever noticed that.

The sun rose and became warm upon their backs, even being filtered through the spring leaves overhead. It was the first time in days that either man had been warm and dry. The momentary comfort and the quiet broken only by the spring birds and the creaking of the saddle leather caused each to relax and slump in the saddle. The lullaby sound was that of the horses' hooves on an occasional stone or a splash of the stream as they maneuvered for easier walking. With slack reins the horses set their own pace and found their own trail moving on upstream. John concentrated on the singing of the birds around him and tried to identify some by their song, then heard nothing as his eyes close and his chin fell to his chest. From years of training, his body quickly adapted to the rocking movement of his horse, and horse and rider became as one. Glenn's slumber was more troubled as each of the bay's movements was telegraphed to his wounds, especially his damaged ribs. But exhaustion finally prevailed over pain and Glenn relaxed and also fell into a deeper slumber while trusting the horse to follow the creek bed. For more than two hours they proceeded at the slow rocking chair pace, warm and seemingly secure. At least at that moment, no one was trying to kill them.

John was the first to snap alert, startled when he realized the horses had stopped. Where they had stopped, or for how long, he had no idea. They had arrived at the headwaters of the creek and with it, the last of their concealment and the last of their tree cover. The horses had found a small grassy area, still under the overhead canopy of big Oak trees, where two hearty springs flowed freely from the limestone formation. This was where Owl Creek had its birth and where it began its journey toward Pittsburg Landing and the Tennessee River. Satisfied they were still alone, John stepped down and stretched to work out the kinks, then pulled the rifle and took it with him. After a quick look around, he helped Glenn dismount and move to a spot where he could sit with his back to a fallen tree. The horses were grateful for the rest and began to graze close by in the sweet blue grass. That damn war was already a far piece away, for both the horses and their riders.

"This is it," John announced upon his return, "The end of our cover. You have any idea where the hell we are?"

"We came close by here coming up from Corinth, on our way to take positions above the Peach Orchard. But you're right, there is no more undergrowth cover to be had, it's bare as the West Texas prairie out there."

John moved to the edge of the tree line for a closer look at the open countryside beyond. "Where do we go from here?"

"We'll head on up this hill, then we'll pick up a wagon road heading west that will take us to the tracks of the Mobile & Ohio railroad. We can follow the rails to the southwest and they will take us around Corinth on the west side. Yankee, you have any idea which way is gonna' be southwest?"

"If I'm not, this here compass is", John said as he reached in his saddlebag and withdrew a fine brass instrument and snapped open the lid. Glenn noted the engraving; "Captain Jonas P. Markum, CSA" on the back. Seeing the troubled, disapproving look on Glenn's face, John quickly added, "Captain Markum wasn't going to be needing it any more."

During the next hour they ate some dried beef sticks and hardtack, also from John's saddlebag, and washed it down with fresh spring water. Glenn may have objected to the compass, but did not choose to question the source of the food…he just did not want to know where it had come from. John filled the canteens, watered the horses, then stripped off his shirt and washed in the pool fed by the cold spring water. His head wound had dried, so he washed out the bandana and returned it to his neck. Using his newly acquired wide-brim hat, he brought water up to Glenn and helped him clean and then re-bandage his four wounds…two entries and two exits, one of the latter created by John's battlefield surgery of the night before. John thought the wounds looked some improved, even though all were still leaking. Not knowing what else to do, he splashed them with some of the contents of his bottle of mash whiskey for good measure. "May not cure, but it sure won't harm", he thought.

John finally broke the silence between them, "you know we could likely encounter a patrol from either side once we get up on that west bound road. We're square in the middle of the land between the two armies and both are going to be very watchful and more than a little trigger-happy."

Glenn was otherwise distracted by the extreme burning of his wounds. "John that damn whiskey burns like hell do you have to keep doing that?"

"I'd a lot rather drink it, so appreciate the sacrifice I'm making to keep you alive. Now what's to be our plan for the patrols?"

"I agree with you, much as I hate to; we could see a patrol from either side from here on. We'll avoid 'em if we can, and if we can't, we'll ride right up like nothings wrong. Which ever side is patrolling, that's the one of us in charge and the other is his prisoner. We'll just have to play-act our way through. If we don't, one of us is damn sure going to spend this war as a prisoner."

"I can't think of anything else and we sure as hell have to get out of this creek bottom and out from between these two armies, besides I think our chances of bluffing a patrol on the road is better during daylight, patrols can be a mite touchy at night."

Glenn nodded his agreement, "It will be dark by the time we get to the railroad and then we should be beyond Corinth before it gets light again. Being there at night will help us spot the picket fires and steer clear cause the entire Confederate Army of the West should be around there somewhere."

Neither man was anxious to move out of their cover, but slowly they collected and repacked their things, and remounted. Glenn led the way out of the undergrowth into the cleared pasture field beyond, up the grade before them and toward where he expected to find the westerly heading wagon road. Likely wouldn't take long before they would find out if this really was a 'no-man's land', or if they had company….and if so, from which side would they be? But at the moment, no matter…Glenn was going home and John, at long last, was headin' to the new west of his dreams.

Chapter Three

"THE PATROL"

After being beneath the canopy of the trees all morning, the sun now seemed unusually bright in their eyes and warm upon their backs. The great expanse of the pasture before them was a solid dark green, sprinkled with the all the bright shades of blue and yellow colors of the wild spring flowers in full bloom. Each man saw this and had their quiet, private memories of their homes in the spring...the Mississippi River valley of southeastern Iowa, and the Hill Country of central Texas. It was near impossible for them to see this beauty, to feel the silence, to be at such peace and then put that in context what had happened just a few miles from this spot. Neither man spoke as each, in the quiet of his mind, absorbed this new world God had put before them.

The horses now grazed, watered, and rested were ready to move out and kept trying to pick up the pace. It was if they also were anxious to quickly leave what was behind them. That was okay with John, but Glenn, who was hurting with each step the horse took, held the bay in check. John moved a quarter mile ahead up the hill to a split rail fence that separated the field from the rutted, westward wagon road they had been searching for. He dismounted to lay the rails down. As Glenn came by he picked up the reins of the gray and led her through the opening, while John re-stacked the rails.

"Why bother with that, don't see any animals left around here?" Glenn asked.

"Just the farm boy in me I guess, can't stand to see a fence down."

"You better take that wide brim hat off and wear your Yankee forage cap. You're going to have to at least **look** like a soldier if we encounter any other riders."

At that moment, Glenn was beginning to wear a little thin on John's nerves, perhaps he should just ride on alone, but the advice was sound so he kept that thought to himself for later, hung the wide brim over the pommel horn and pushed his uniform cap down on his head. Regulation or not, it did not feel nearly as comfortable. "Its called a Cappie, John said."

"That's cute…a Cappie is it? What's that brass thing on top?"

"That's a French horn, all the infantry wear them."

"Why on top where it can't be seen?"

"Worn properly, the Cappie is mashed forward so the horn shows. Like this."

"I still think its cute!"

They eased the horses up on the road and side-by-side started toward the west and the railroad right-of-way that would take them away from this place. In another hour the sun had moved enough to be full on their face and in their eyes, but still John thought he saw movement and a dust trail ahead and quickly pulled up. Glenn was slumbering in the saddle and rode a few yards on before the bay came to a stop. He came full awake with a start.

"What happened…what is it….what's wrong?" When he turned, John had a small brass telescope extended and tight to his right eye. "Now where in the hell did you get that thing?"

"Out of my saddle-bag! But that's not important now, what's important is we've got company, and they have definitely seen us and are headed this way at the trot."

"How many and, more important…which army?"

"Three. There's a Captain, a Sergeant and a non-com. Looks like you're going to get to be my prisoner first, cause they're Union."

"What you want me to do?"

"Take your revolver out of the holster and tuck it in your waistband where you can get it quickly, and pull your jacket over it so the butt doesn't show. Then slump in the saddle, head down. Look humble like a prisoner, instead of some wise-ass officer."

"Okay, but what's your plan….you're not planning to try to shoot our way through…are you?"

"No. I'm going to try to talk our way through just like we planned. But if that fails, you need to know, I am not going back! From what I can see, the only experienced fighter in the group is probably the Sergeant. I'll be on him. The Captain's uniform is too pretty…he's definitely a politician, not a soldier. Likely seen nothing of the war and the non-com is probably his aide, so he's the same. If I start something it will be with the Sergeant, then you take the other two. Don't blink, don't hesitate, just take 'em down! Just think of them as your enemy, cause that's what they are. We've got one chance and that's surprise. They are not going to expect a prisoner to be armed and that's our advantage. You got that?"

"I've got it. I don't think I like it…but I've got it."

"Well, you best do it and do it right, or expect to spend this war in some damned unpleasant place."

23

John reached forward, pulled the rifle from its boot and chambered home a cartridge. He laid it across the saddle in front of him, cradled in the bend of his left arm. "Watch my right hand. If I go to the trigger guard, you come up shooting, and for God's sake, don't miss! They won't expect you to be armed, so their attention will be on me. Now move up in front of me, off to the right. I want them on the left side as they approach so this Spencer doesn't have to move much to come to bear, and remember, you're a prisoner, look like it!"

As the distance closed, John and Glenn moved to the right side of the road and the approaching patrol, as if on signal, moved to the opposite side…John's left side. John tilted the rifle muzzle slightly down so as not to appear too menacing. The Captain held up his hand and the five halted facing each other. The positioning was just as John had planned it would be, with the Sergeant on his front, left quarter…about six inches forward of the muzzle. As John looked the trio over he knew he had assumed correctly; only the Sergeant had seen any of this war, the other two were definitely rear echelon…way in the rear. Both the Captain and the non-com were washed clean and fresh shaven this morning, neat and tender cheeked, while the Sergeant's face and uniform looked like five miles of well traveled road.

"Corporal, who the hell are you and what are you doing out here?" The Captain barked.

John sat straight, rendered a salute, and held it until the Captain was forced to acknowledge it, and it was returned, then responded, "Captain Sir, I am Corporal Kelley, 14th of Iowa. I was sent out yesterday by my Sergeant not to return without a prisoner who could still talk, and I've got me an officer, by god! Took me all night, but I've got 'em!"

"Where is your outfit now?"

"You must have passed close to 'em up by the railroad. Now sir, bye your leave, I'll be on my way."

"Hold up Corporal, you were **not** dismissed. I would like to know how's a scruffy Corporal of the likes of you came by a rig like that. Sergeant, I do believe I see a CSA brand on that mare's rump and that's one of those new repeating rifle he's holding. I suggest you relieve the Corporal of that rifle, causes me some concern the way he continues to wave it around. I also believe I'll take that scattergun in the bed-roll too, looks English from my perspective. It'll make a grand souvenir for after the war. You must either be a spy or a deserter to be so well equipped by our enemy. Sergeant Porter here will relieve you of your prisoner and then you can, "bye my leave" and return to your Company."

"With all due respect sir, that's not going to happen. I liberated this here mount and this rig in keeping with our battlefield orders of conduct. I've done nothing wrong here and I've showed you no disrespect, **Sir**. You have no call to disarm me or to take my prisoner. I am operating under specific orders and, with all due respect, **Sir,** I fully intend to carry them out. My Sergeant was very clear...don't return without a prisoner that can talk. Should I, he'll just send me back out again and I've already been out there all damned night as most of the likely prisoners are already dead! This here is my prisoner...and I'll be taking him back! You want him, you go take him from Sergeant Mullins, cause that's where he be headed, **Sir**. But I should warn you, **Sir,** Sergeant Mullins is a mean son-of-a-bitch that few ever cross twice."

During the exchange, Sergeant Porter attempted to ease his horse to John's right, to reposition himself more in the front of John and away from that rifle he was holding so casually. Without shifting his eyes from the Captain's face, John sensed the movement and gently applied pressure to the gray's flank with his left heel. The big horse moved away from the pressure and squared around just enough for the muzzle to come to bear directly on the Sergeant. All of this occurred with out John ever interrupting his response to the Captain, or looking at the Sergeant. John's right hand moved slowly, almost casually, up the stock of the rifle he held as if in a moment of caress, then it stopped just shy of the trigger guard. Glenn had not moved during the exchange, just slumped with his head down.

He saw the hand move and then stop short of the trigger guard. He flexed the fingers of his right hand as he thought, "this crazy Yankee bastard is about to reopen this battle".

 The moment of truth was near at hand! Sergeant Porter saw and immediately understood the position he was in with this rag-tag Corporal…if the Captain pushed this or started anything, he was the first one going down. At this range that damned .44 would lift him clean out of the saddle. He couldn't take his eyes from the muzzle opening….it looked big enough to hold a man's thumb. It would sure put a hell of a hole in a man, and it was plain, this battle-crazed Corporal had already made up his mind who that man was to be.

Sergeant Porter became desperate to gain control over this exchange. "Captain if I may sir, we don't need this damned Lieutenant as a prisoner, he don't look like he's gonna last long anyway. He's bleeding from at least three places. If you want a prisoner sir, I'll go get you one that will last at least until we return and you can meet up with the reporters. There's little glory to be had from showing up with a dead prisoner draped over the saddle."

The Captain's face flushed. He was not used to having his commands disobeyed by a lowly Corporal half out of uniform, or over-ridden by a damned Sergeant, who's job it was to support him. He sputtered, but realized that without the force of the Sergeant, he could not make this work. Besides, he didn't have to have **this** prisoner; he just wanted one to show off. Could be worth a lot of votes later on after the war.

"This is your lucky day Corporal, keep your damn prisoner and your contraband rig and pass on!"

"Thank you sir. "You're very correct Captain, **Sir**; it is certainly a lucky day for all of us."

With that, John and the Sergeant made eye contact for the first time and a look of full understanding of what had just happened here passed between them. John knew he would never want to meet Sergeant Porter again, without first having the drop on him. He pulled the gray's head around, nodded to Glenn and as the trio parted, they rode through and on down the road. Quietly John instructed, "Don't look back, keep your head down and just ride slowly away."

After a few yards, John picked-up the pace to a slow trot, and keeping Glenn in front of him, moved on down the road. Just as the road turned to the left, John looked back and saw the three in the same spot. There was a lot of animated conversation coming from the Captain, mostly directed at the Sergeant. Then the two made the turn and moved out of sight. Shortly Glenn pulled-up and turned to face John.

"You crazy son-of-a-bitch, were you really going to shoot that Sergeant?"

"You know I think that's progress in our friendship....that's the first time you haven't called me a Yankee. I wouldn't have wanted to, cause I think that Sergeant is a good soldier stuck with a worthless piece of crap for a Captain. But I would have, and what's most important, when the Spencer came to bear on him, the Sergeant knew I had made up my mind. That's what made him suddenly so helpful. Otherwise, they would be dragging your sorry ass back to see some reporters from the Captain's hometown newspaper, and I would be wondering around trying to find that damned railroad by myself."

Truth be known, at that moment Glenn felt very fortunate to have hooked-up with John, but he just shook his head and rolled his eyes toward the late afternoon sky. "Come on, let's find that railroad before it get's dark, and before you decide to take on both Armies." But as they rode he silently wondered if he would have been prepared to shoot someone in a butternut uniform, had the situation been reversed. Might well be a question he should answer for himself, and early on.

They rode on side-by-side until after the sun had left the sky. John was finally able to get his hands to stop shaking, but the few sips of the sour mash did the most good. For some ten miles, however, John frequently looked over his shoulder at their back trail, almost expecting to see the trio. They had spotted only one other mounted group of about ten Union cavalry, but they just cut over the road about a mile ahead. The two men stepped their horses in to the scrub timber beside the road and waited until the patrol cleared their intended trail. Just before it got so dark that the ground was hard to see, they came to the tracks of the Mobile & Ohio Railroad. They moved up on to the road bed and with Glenn again in the lead, turned southwest toward Corinth, Mississippi. John felt a moment of satisfaction…even without the sun or the compass; he knew this was the direction to turn. This was southwest! It did occur to him, 'hell I likely could have made Texas without dragging Glenn along'.

They made good time on the railroad bed as it was easy footing for the horses and there seemed to be no one else around. The only problem was the trestles. The horses would just not venture out on the ties, especially in the dark, so they forded each of the streams along the way, and that used up some time. It was probably a little after midnight when they reached the outer railroad yards at Corinth. John had a pocket watch in his saddlebag that he had picked up on the battlefield, but didn't care enough about the time to search for it. Besides, Glenn wouldn't like where the watch came from either. It was now four days beyond the full moon, so the moon was beginning to flatten on one side and withdraw some of the light it had so generously given to John as he roamed the battlefield. John had also noticed the gradual building of haze over the moon's surface as more clouds moved in from the southwest. There was definitely a spring storm out of that direction, and not so many hours away.

Glenn pulled up and with John beside him; they studied the landscape before them.

"Damned strange there ain't more fires to be seen," Glenn observed out loud.

John agreed. "Our Captain had told us just before disembarking; we would be facing over 40,000 men. An army that size should be showing thousands of cook fires and picket fires. Course we did thin that number out a bit, but there can't be a hundred fires as far as we can see."

"That's both good and bad," Glenn offered. "It's good we haven't stumbled into Beauregard's entire army, but if they ain't here where they're supposed to be….just where in the hell are they?"

"Beauregard? We were told General Johnston was in command."

"General Albert Sidney Johnston was killed in the afternoon of the first day's battle."

"So that's why your side broke off and withdrew, when you had us on our butts? That cost you the battle, you know. We were in damn sorry shape just before that happened, but then we got reinforcements over night. When I went back to get more powder for my squad, The General was talking about callin' the boats back to the landing!"

"Yes, it's strange the seemingly small things that a major battle can turn on. He was only shot in the leg, but bled to death because he had sent his medical people to treat your wounded. Not for that, we would have taught you Yanks to swim…in the Tennessee River."

"Then who would you have found to wet-nurse you home? Come on, let's move out of here!"

They again fell into column with Glenn in the lead and moved toward the outer rail yard. They found a west heading road and left the Mobile & Ohio, then again turned south crossing over the Memphis & Charleston rail bed, then again west, away from the small town. They past the darkened Corona College and then out into the open countryside.

"This don't look like much of a place," John observed out loud. "What's all the fuss about?"

"May not look like much, but this is the most significant rail center in all the west. The two longest railroads of the same gage in the Confederacy cross right here."

The picket fires were now safely to their back and falling further behind with each step of the horses. John looked up for guide star he had been using, but instead saw that the moon was now almost complete hidden behind the gathering bank of clouds. There was considerable lightening on the horizon directly ahead. They would need to find cover before this night was very much older.

Author's Note: General Beauregard had been forced, as much by the dysentery within his army as by the extensive losses to the Union at Shiloh, to abandon Corinth and retreat on toward Jackson, Mississippi. General Hallack, jealous of the publicity showered on Grant, relieved him of command on trumped up allegations. Halleck was not interested in exposing his army by moving forward into Corinth. So, with nearly 100,000 men, the Union encamped through another month while the beaten Confederate army escaped. This left Glenn and John making their way west in the "no-man's land" between these two limping armies.

The Confederate forces, under the command of Major General Earl Van Dorn did finally counter attack the federal positions in Cornith on October 3, but were soundly defeated with over 5,000 killed.

Chapter Four

"THE STORM"

Glenn again slumped in the saddle as fatigue and pain took its toll on his body. John moved the gray up ahead so the gelding would have something to guide on. The storm was now almost on top of them and each flash of lightning illuminated the roadway as it turned night into a moment of day. The roadway was deeply rutted…. For certain this was a road that had recently been traveled by many, heavily loaded wagons. Given where they were, it was definitely the armies of the CSA, but which way were they headed….to a battle, or away from the same one they were leaving behind? John reasoned, since they had failed to find the cook fires and picket fires they expected around Corinth, it was probable the army, or some major part of it, was moving away from Shiloh Church and could be just ahead of them. This was a hell of an arrangement, trapped between the Union's probing patrols and the retreating and regrouping Confederate Army of the West. Either one would likely be inclined to shoot first.

John's deep thought was interrupted by an extremely bright lightning flash. Silently he began the slow count, one thousand one, one thousand two, just as Eye of the Hawk had told him. At only four the massive thunder rolled over them. Glenn snapped alert, "what the hell?"

"We're caught out in a damn bad storm and its coming right at us. Best find some shelter while we can. You ever been on this road before, you know of anyplace close at hand?"

"No, we didn't come this way; we formed up in the area down around Tupelo and came to Corinth that way."

"Keep your eyes open, we need a building, or a cave of some sort, and we'll be needing it soon!"

They rode on in silence using the brief flashes of lightning to examine the sides of the road for a shelter. Both horses became skittish and started dancing sideways along the road. John fought back the urge to pick-up the pace in the face of the storm which was now right on top of them. The badly rutted road held him back. All they needed was a horse with a broken leg, or worse, a rider with one. It would be difficult enough to do this with two sound horses, but impossible riding double. During a flash, John imagined he saw a silhouette of a building, a barn he thought. He called Glenn's attention to the location, and they waited for the next flash. While they waited, it began to rain, first a few gentle drops, then in sheets driven by a suddenly growing wind coming directly at them. Both horses lowered their heads to attempt some protection, but the men had to keep staring into the night, seeking some form of shelter.

"There! It's a barn", Glenn shouted over the wind, "and I didn't see any other buildings around."

"I didn't either, let's move over there. There is a little foot bridge over that drainage ditch about 25 yards ahead".

They pulled up the horses' heads, moved to the edge of the roadway, and quickened the pace. The horses sensed shelter and didn't even shy from the hollow feel of the narrow foot-bridge. The sliding doors to the barn were missing so they rode directly into the black opening.

There both horses stopped quickly, unsure of just where they were or what footing they had. The men used the fierce lightning flashes to inspect their surroundings. There were three box stalls along one side and a small milking area along the other. The center area had been left open for hay storage. There was a lot of debris, both metal and wood, scattered about, some of the barn's side-boards were missing, and also a small pile of hay remained in the center section. The place had not been used as a barn for some time. With the next flash, John looked up to find the roof reasonably solid, so they would be dry, and could wait out the storm, hopefully without company from either side.

John helped Glenn down, and then stripped the tack from the horses. He turned Glenn's saddle upside down and laid it back on the hay. Then helped Glenn to lie down so his back rested in the underside of the saddle. "If you're real lucky this day, there won't be any blacksnakes in your bed, or rats either." With hands full of hay, he wiped down the horses, and then turned them into a box stall. He found some hay that did not smell of mold, and threw some to the horses. They seemed to think is was eatable and took after it eagerly. Glenn was already settled in and breathing heavy, so John took the rifle, moved to the door and sat on his haunches with his back to a pole to watch the storm. Ever since he was a child he had always been fascinated by storms and would usually leave his bed at night to sit and watch until they passed. The rain was intense, still being driven in sheets, but the violent lightning had settled down some. The steady beating on the barn roof and siding was like soothing music and soon John's butt slid to the ground and his chin again found his chest.

John's sleep was troubled as his mind relived and further confused the events of the last few days. He again saw the Captain waving the sword and charging toward him, only this time the face was Glenn's, and when the man in front of him lost his head, it was John's face on the head that rolled away. Then he was standing in the barn at home and his pa was scolding him for running away from the war. "But pa, my time was up."

"No matter, no one told you to go; Grandpa and I are shamed by you."

"But Grandpa's dead and I'm doing good, I'm keeping this soldier alive, he likely couldn't live without me!"

The answer came back, "are you so sure he is still alive?"

John came awake with a start and was relieved it was a strange barn he was sitting in. He immediately got up and went to check Glenn. Hell yes he's still alive, I won't let him die, his mind shouted! John found the saddlebags and the supply of sour mash. A couple of pulls later he replaced the cork, stretched and felt better. He stacked broken boards to start a fire, not only for the warmth, but he needed to see some light to drive the demons of war further away, out into the stormy night.

When Glenn finally awoke, he was at first not certain where he was, but was certain he felt more rested than he had in weeks. He couldn't remember his last full night of sleep. As his mind gave recognition to his surroundings, he looked around quickly for John. He didn't see him, but his saddle was still where he had laid it the night before, and John would not go far without his saddle. He could tell from the flickering light on the underside of the barn roof above him that there was a fire going. His body still hurt, not only the wounds but now in addition, he was just plain stiff and sore. Then he remembered he had gone to sleep in clothing soaked by the rainstorm. Not a smart choice, but in his condition, he could have made no other. As he rose to a sitting position he saw the gray light of early morning through the open doors, and that it was still raining hard. He heard the rolling thunder and knew the storm had not left the area. Looking toward the fire, he saw John sitting on a log; he also saw a spit with something cooking over the fire. "Tell me that's not a barn rat," he said.

"No, that's a rabbit that got too curious. I skinned him out and he is about ready to be our breakfast, or whatever meal this is."

"What's boiling in the tin cups?"

"Old Indian nourishment, boiled corn soup. I found some field corn still on the cob in the crib back there, ground it between two flat stones and put it in water to boil. It was kind of old and kind of dry, so we may not be able to eat some of the larger pieces but we can drink the soup. Grandpa was never very fond of rabbit cause he said they were too lean to do a body much good; what you need is bear fat. But I was just too damned tired to fight a bear last night. This one should at least fill our bellies, and even that will be different."

"Anything that doesn't taste like dried beef and hardtack! I saw you sitting in the barn door last night with your Spencer. You expecting trouble on a bad night like that one?"

"My Grandpa taught me years ago to always expect trouble to find you in any situation. And since this war started, I've not often been disappointed."

Glenn got up from the saddle and started to stretch out the night's soreness, but his ribs pained him so that he saw bright lights flash behind his closed eye-lids. He wanted to ease back down, but did not, because he wanted John to think he was getting better. He moved slowly to find a spot close to the fire and sat very carefully. John was busy finishing their meal and pretended not to notice the pain in Glenn's face. John got up and returned to the fire with a bottle of sour mash, eased out the cork and said, "Take a pull of this it will ease the soreness. Did you know God invented whiskey so the Irish wouldn't rule the world?" Glenn smiled at the humor but started to protest that he didn't use much whiskey, but thought what the hell, John's probably right, it can't hurt. Actually it turned out to be considerable help. After the second pull he felt much warmer inside and the pain and stiffness did seemed to ease some.

John moved the boiling cups off of the fire to begin cooling and each man knifed off a piece of the roasted rabbit. It turned out to be a grand feast! Neither young man could remember one they had enjoyed nearly this grand in many weeks. The milled corn had cooked up in the boiling water and they drank it all. The rabbit was tasty and between them it nearly disappeared. To John's surprise,

Glenn reached for the bottle of mash almost as often as he did to wash down the food. Could be reason enough to believe he might make an Irishman out of him yet. After they finished the meal, John moved to the barn door to catch water to wash out the cups and moved the rest of the rabbit off of the fire for later. He added some broken boards to feed the fire and sat back at his spot by the barn door to watch the coming of morning and the continuing storm. Glenn stripped off some of his wet outer clothes and placed them by the fire to dry, and sat close to the heat source to dry the ones he was wearing. At this moment life was good for each man; reasonably dry, rested, well fed, bellies warm with good sour mash whiskey…. and for now least, no one was trying to kill them.

Staring off into the last of a stormy night, alone with his thoughts, John finally broke the silence, "do you mind if I ask you about something about this war that I don't understand?"

"No, not at all."

"I don't understand this slavery thing and why you folks in the south want to fight this damned war just for the right to keep another people in chains. You're obviously a Christian man, how can you believe the teachings of the Bible and still think its right to make a slave of someone?"

"If you're going to go live in the south…in Texas, there are some things you need to understand. In the interest of expanding your limited Yankee education, I am going to give you not just one, but many of the arguments favoring slavery…arguments you've not likely ever heard up north! First, in spite of what you call the teachings of the Bible, races have been enslaving each other since before the words of the Bible were even written down. Even God's chosen peoples of the Bible were slaves, and then found their freedom and they in turn kept slaves, we can presume both with God's approval. In the south we do not find that the Bible says anything that makes the act of slavery a sin against God. Quite the opposite, there are many passages in the Bible that actually support slavery, and specifically the enslaving of the black race. You should read Genesis

9:25-27 where Noah cursed his son Ham's descendents into eternal slavery and those descendents became the southern tribes of that region of the world. Then there's Leviticus 25:44 where God said you should not enslave your own people, but that slaves are to come from neighboring lands."

"This is not a new cause that your northern abolitionists just uncovered. The very first Negro slaves were brought to this country not two years ago and not by southerners, but by the Dutch, to Jamestown, in 1619. All of the Founding Fathers who got together to write the Declaration of Independence owned slaves, including Thomas Jefferson and Benjamin Franklin. Their Constitution is completely silent on the subject of slavery. When they wrote…"All men are created equal"…they were referring to **their** demand for equal treatment and equality, between the American Colonists and the rest of the subjects of the British Crown. They made no attempt to stretch that net to cover all the races of the world; the blacks, the browns, the yellows, and certainly not the red man. At that time, none of them were the concern of the writers…in fact; some of those races were the enemies of the Colonists. The problems they were addressing were just between themselves and the King of England… that's the people they were seeking equality with. Even the Chief Justice of the United States Supreme Court stated in his ruling of the Dred Scott case in 1857 that the Founding Fathers who wrote the Declaration of Independence and the Constitution had been thinking only of white men."

John listened intently to Glenn and saw the passion in his face as he had framed his answers. True, these were new points that he had never heard before. "But does every white man in the south own slaves…does your pa own slaves?"

"Not by a damn site, at the time the war started there were about 4 million slaves in the eleven states of the Confederacy. Fewer than 1 in 10 southerns' actually own even one slave and the ones that do are all rich plantation owners. In the last 13 months of your war you have probably not yet fired your rifle at a slave owner in the Confederate army, they seem to have ways of staying out of this thing. Slavery is an essential factor in the economy of the south. For example, it takes seven field workers to support even one acre of cotton, add their families to that number, and that's too many people to hire and pay for what cotton will bring on the world market, and cotton is the **only** cash generating crop the south has. But there are other, even more practical issues; the south has a capital investment of over $4 billion in slaves...how would that be recovered? If the 4 million slaves were freed, who would feed and clothe them, they have very few employable skills...who would hire them? Not the southern planters, they have no money. My pa never held slaves. When he and mamma first started out, it was mostly because they had no money to buy them. It was pa, mamma, and two Mexicans who worked the cotton for shares. Later when they could afford it, pa figured out what he said everyone else would some day figure out; it cost more, a lot more, to produce a bale of cotton with slave labor than with paid labor. Paid is better labor, works harder, and cares more about the crop. As for cattle, working cattle with slaves is out of the question. One last thing that perhaps you can help me understand; four of the Union states held slaves when this war started and have been allowed to continue to hold slaves. So why is slavery right and just in the four Union States, but needs to be abolished in the eleven Confederate States?"

"You're correct; I've never heard those points before. You're obviously a well educated man, not a dumb sod buster like me."

"You're not a dumb sod buster...a dumb sod buster would not have the questions you do about what this war is for. Even most of the soldiers in our army don't understand, or even care what the war's about....its the adventure, the glory. Many of these were the things my pa and mamma talked to us children about as they saw the war coming, so we would understand what was going on. Also, I was "one of the privileged few" to attend the Agriculture and Mechanical College of Texas for the better part of two years and these things were debated at great length as the threat of war began to grow. It was a military school and because of that my regiment elected me a Lieutenant."

"Who is this 'us' you mentioned?"

"My little sister, Suzanne."

"Just how little?"

"She's about a year and a half younger than me."

"She married?"

"No, not even serious about anyone when I left. Too damned strong willed for any of the men she's met. No man in central Texas could catch her or tame her."

"Pretty?"

"She's a beauty, dark eyes and dark skin...looks just like our mamma's Louisiana folks."

John's voice took on a different tone as he said, "interesting."

John filed the little sister information away for later, then looked back at Glenn and asked, "Well if it's not about slavery, what's this war being fought over?"

"Most of the thinking people in the south believe it is over states rights...the right of the people to decide what's best for them, through their elected state government. Not being told what's best for them by someone from Illinois that now happens to be in Washington; someone we didn't even elect as our President. We elected Mr. John Breckinridge of Kentucky and others voted for the Whig, John Bell of Tennessee. But you had more people to vote for Lincoln than we did to vote for Mr. Breckenridge or Bell. So now Lincoln believes it is his duty to tell the people of the south what's best for them....he's never even been south of Kentucky, so how does he know what's best for us? Lincoln jumped all over the passion behind the slavery issue as a way to get elected President, but his cause was not really slavery. His cause is about not having the Union break up while he is the President. He even wrote in a letter, '....if I could save the Union without freeing one slave, I would do that'. As a lawyer, Mr.

Lincoln never stood tall for the rights of even the free black men in Illinois. Fact is, Fredrick Douglas urged the people to vote for Mr. Gerrit Smith, not Lincoln. Does any of that sound like a man with a first passion of freeing the slaves?"

"You mean this whole thing is over whether the Union stays together, or not?"

"Mostly. Slavery may be the torch that first lit this fire in the north, but now the south is saying you can not tell us how we will live, and the north was saying keep the Union together and we'll work out the slavery issue."

"Is it possible to work out the slavery issue, sounds like the leaders on both sides are well dug in?"

"Sure it's possible. It would eventually work itself out when cotton growers finally get as smart as my pa. Cotton takes a lot of land, good loamy soil with natural fertilization, and as I just explained to you, it takes a lot of hand labor. As a crop, cotton is very hard on land…just uses it up if you don't properly feed it and rotate the crops. Either do that, or eventually it won't even produce a crop. That's why the rich cotton growers need to expand slavery into the western territories, for fresh cotton land and to keep the balance in Congress between free and slave states. As for the labor, slave labor is very expensive unless you're farming huge holdings. The cost to buy and maintain a slave makes slave labor much more expensive than freeman labor, pa proved that. Besides, someday soon someone will invent machines that will do a lot of that hand labor…do it faster, do it better and do it at a much lower cost. Then where will the slave holders be? Just like Mr. Cyrus McCormick did with his mechanical reaper for you folks on the northern plains. After all, we're all at this work to make money and if a man can make more money without slaves, then why have 'em?"

"Then why are people like you and me in this war, I don't know if I even have an opinion about the Union breaking up?"

"Well you should have because if this nation breaks in two, neither part will be as rich, neither will be as secure, nor will either be as able to defend itself; and remember England, Spain and France would still like a piece of this new world. You and I are here for the much the same reasons young men have joined in every war since the beginning of time…the adventure. The chance to leave home and see what's over that next hill, the excitement, the glory…at least before Shiloh Church those were my reasons. War didn't seem quite as damn glorious after the second day as I lay bleeding to a slow death. After that, I am not so sure I know what it's about either. And I guess because you and I no longer know what those reasons are for us, just might explain why we are now leaving Mr. Lincoln's war. Besides, since the beginning of time old men have started the wars that young men then have to fight and die for. It's just the way things are."

"If you didn't own slaves and you seem to be saying the Union should stay together, why are you personally in this war?"

"Mostly because Texas is and she called her sons to fight. But I very nearly did decide not go when in 1859 Texas deposed Sam Houston as Governor just because he refused to take the oath of loyalty to the Confederate States of America. They threw out the greatest hero that Texas ever produced because he remained loyal to the Union he loved and believed in. Without Sam Houston there might not have been a Texas, except as the northern province of Mexico. I can tell ya', that did not go down at all well with my pa."

John looked out into the continuing rain, and after a time turned to Glenn, "You know no one can win in this war. As long as the homes being burned are all homes of Americans, the land being blown up is all American land and every soldier who dies is another American dead, neither side can win the war regardless of how it turns out. That's the tragedy of this war and the reason we should no longer be apart of it. I think I would have loved the war with the Mexicans, or the English. Its not war I hate…it's the killing of other Americans that I can't do anymore. The dead men, from both armies, were so thick in places at Pittsburg Landing that it was impossible to walk on the ground, yet every mother's son fallen there was an American. They weren't Federals, they weren't Confederates...they were Americans. Brilliant men have invented some extraordinary weapons for us to efficiently kill each other; canister, torpedoes, mines, repeating rifles. After Pittsburg Landing there is one thing of which I am very certain, this war is going to last for a long, long time, not the few short weeks we were told. From what I've already seen, the slaughter will be well beyond anything any of leaders could possibly have imagined at its start."

John had absorbed about all the political discussion he could handle for one day. Without further comment he got up, stretched, added some wood to the fire, and then went to check the weather before moving to lie down in the hay. The late afternoon sky was still dark and heavy and the rain continued at a heavy pace. In spite of that, John announced that the rain would stop after dark and they could travel on in the morning. Then, laying back into his saddle, he pulled the wide brim down over his eyes and was shortly asleep. This time complete exhaustion and the comfort of a fire, food and sour mash kept the war demons at bay, and he fell into a deep, untroubled sleep. He did manage one brief dream about a dark-eyed beauty, but she never did become his. Glenn threw some more hay to the horses, and then took up a position at the barn door, close by the rifle and the fire. His ribs still felt like they were coming through his side, but the wound in his leg had dried some since he had not squeezed a saddle for about 12 hours. He stared into the rain and the declining light and thought about home, the battle just past, but mostly about John and this new understanding that was developing. He certainly is no dumb sod-buster, Glenn thought that man is deep with strong beliefs and guts enough he'll back 'em up, anyone who fails to see that would make a bad error, maybe a fatal error, in judgment. There was a time in the last few days that he was certain that John would pick a time to leave him behind, now he believed they might stick it out together. The incident with the patrol had helped change his mind. He was certain John had been fully prepared to shoot their way through that road-block, if it had come to that. Glenn still questioned himself; would he have reacted the same way to protect John's freedom?

He looked over at the now sleeping enemy soldier, seemed strange now to think of him as his enemy. They looked enough alike to be mistaken for family. Both were over six feet tall, big shoulders and arms from a young life of hard work, a little thin from their army rations of late, with light hair. The difference was in the color of the eyes; John's were bright blue from his Irish blood lines while Glenn's were dark and flashing like his mother's. These two boys had grown up and grown together in the last few days. Would that be enough to carry Glenn home and John to the new life he dreamed of? John turned slightly in his sleep and the wide brim hat slid away. Glenn saw the slight smile and pleasant look on John's face and knew that whatever he was dreaming of at that moment had little to do with his old life as a soldier, or the battle just left.

Glenn stared out into the deeping night sky and noted that the rain indeed had stopped; they would travel in the morning. He stirred the coals before returning to his saddle to finish his night's sleep; perhaps his dream might be as pleasant as John's.

Chapter Five

"THE GREAT RIVER CROSSING"

Glenn could barely see through the foggy, gray light of early morning and the wet haze that hung in the air. He could just make out two Union soldiers digging in the dirt ahead of him. It was a grave… they were digging a grave! He knew he did not want to see the grave or look down into it, but like a magnet it drew him closer. His steps were slow and labored as he pushed aside the undergrowth and moved along. He could not get too close as the wet ground might cave and pitch him forward into the hole. The soldiers had stopped digging now and watched him approach. They leaned on their shovels and begin to laugh loudly at him as he stumbled forward. Glenn stopped and peered down into the gaping hole. It was him…he was the body laying in the bottom of the grave, eyes wide open, searching for someone to help. Glenn looked at the Union soldiers and shouted, "I'm not dead, I'm not dead! I have a new friend who is taking me home." Then their two shovels full of dirt covered his face and his protests were silenced.

"Your friend has gone on and left you to us, he won't be helping you any more." The dirt began falling on him and he could not get away. "Now you are dead," they laughed. Glenn was thrashing wildly, but the dirt kept falling, he could look down and see his body being covered.

Wait! Someone had come to help him…he felt a tapping on the sole of his boot. He tried to move away, but the tapping followed him and continued until he forced his eyes open. It was John towering over him kicking the sole of his boot, "come on get up, you're burnin' daylight!"

Glenn blinked himself fully awake, relieved to see this friend in the dim light of morning, even if he was kicking him, "what the hell does that mean anyway?"

"I don't know, but my Grandpa used to call my brothers and me to do chores that way in the mornings. That was his favorite saying, anytime he thought you were wasting time and should be working; he had you, 'burnin' daylight'. You were having one hell of a dream, I was afraid you might hurt yourself."

"It was no dream; it was a full-blown, raging nightmare."

"Could you see yourself dead in it?"

"Yeah, you too?"

"Yes, a couple of times, why do you suppose that is?"

"I don't know, maybe we're surprised to have been in such a slaughter and still be alive…maybe we think we're supposed to be dead…and feel guilty we're not while so many others are. Anyway, I'm glad to see the fire built up. What's that cooking?"

"More Indian corn soup, that's all we have the makings for, and the rest of the rabbit. We need to breakfast and get moving before a Union patrol stumbles on us."

"Any idea what time it might be?"

"No, the pocket watch ran down. But it's got to be at least half-past four anyway."

They ate everything they had, cleaned up their leavings, then mounted up and moved out into the coming dawn. There were but a few streaks of yellow and gold in the east when Glenn turned his back on it and headed the bay into the slowly retreating darkness of last night. The sky had cleared, just as John had forecast. It would be a good day for travel, providing they could do so alone. Even the roadway was better; the rain had smoothed out some of the wagon ruts, the grassy strip in the center was mostly well drained and dry, and the footing good. Through the morning, Glenn kept them working to the southwest by first taking a westbound road and then a southbound road and always the many wagon tracks stayed ahead of them. The air was crisp with less humidity and both men and horses felt like traveling. John, content to follow Glenn's lead, entertained himself watching hawks making lazy circles in the sky as they hunted for their next meal. It was fascinating just watching; their wings were so strong they were capable of catching rising currents of warm air and soaring on those invisible columns. He remembered as a child laying on his back in the tall, sweet grass and watching them. Eye-of-the-Hawk had told him that his people believed that to see a hawk in flight was a sign of a good day ahead. John hoped that friend knew of what he spoke. How they maneuvered on the up-drafts and seemingly never needed to flap their wings. John wondered what it would be like to soar high above, without a care. Certainly would be a handy way to spot patrols ahead.

When the sun reached high overhead they stopped by a small spring for a noon rest. Glenn drew a map in the dirt to explain his intended route. He was going to swing south of the heavy forest that was now in front of them, and then continue well to the west and south of the town of Oxford. There was a small college there and they were certain to have some kind of armed militia about the campus. If you're shot, it doesn't matter if it's by a snot-nosed school boy with a rusty smoothbore, or a first line regular. Shot is still shot! After passing Oxford, Glenn said they would travel more west than south to reach the Mississippi River just to the southwest of the small town of Cleveland.

John wondered aloud, "How we gonna' get us and the horses over that river?"

"As my pa used to say, 'before you can cross a river, you've first got to walk up to it'."

A few years back Glenn and his pa had been ferried across the river there, just below where the Arkansas River empties into the Mississippi on the western side. They had been on their way to Memphis to attend the Cotton Exchange auction, and had crossed there, then again on the return trip. Glenn figured the ferryman might remember him, and if so, might carry them over the Great River into Arkansas. It was worth a try as there were not any places to cross that were not both heavily traveled and well observed by one army or the other. It was just over 200 miles, and Glenn figured that if they were not interfered with, and the weather held, they could cover it in about five days of moving steady. With the noon meal of dried beef and hardtack over, and the horses rested, they mounted up and headed south toward the town of Oxford. Finally, the wagon ruts they had been following continued on to the west into the great forest. That was one army out of their way, or was it, since they were now to the south of **both** armies. John saw as they mounted, Glenn's leg was leaking again, this time on both front and back…the bandage and his trousers were again soaked through.

The sun was just an hour from being gone on the seventh day, when they reached the high bluff above the great Mississippi River. They had lost almost one full day hiding in the woods from a Confederate patrol. The patrol hung around so long that it appeared they were specifically looking for the two riders. The young men were well hid in the woods, but the concern was that the horses would nicker and give away their position. Each man stood by his horse's head with his hand over the animal's nostrils. The horses didn't care for that much, but it did keep them quiet. Later the patrol gave up on whatever they were searching for and rode away back to the north.

Glenn led them down beyond the crest of the bluff and about 50 feet down the hill so they would not be silhouetted against the late day sky. As he strained his neck for a view along the riverbank, he said, "This might not be the exact location. It looks familiar but I don't see the ferryman's cabin."

John reached into his saddlebag and withdrew the spy-glass he picked-up on the Shiloh battlefield. "Here, try with this."

Glenn looked with disdain at the instrument that John offered in his extended hand. But John quickly added, "I told you, the gentleman was through using it." After a hesitation, Glenn reached and took the scope from his hand. Extending it, he held it against his right eye and began his examination of the riverbank, both up river and down. "There, I see a cabin, but there's no ferry raft at the river bank." As Glenn studied the cabin, a man emerged, picked some wood from a pile by the door, looked around quickly, and returned inside the cabin. "Damn, that sure enough did look like I remember him, but where's the ferry?"

"How many years ago were you and your pa through here?"

Glenn thought a moment, "oh, about four or five."

"Sweet Jesus, after five years do you expect to be able to tell what the place and the man look like, especially from this distance? And why would he remember you?"

"I think he would remember pa, they struck up quite a conversation since both of them were originally from the same area of Tennessee. I think I just need to go down there and see what's what, and you need to hide your Yankee ass in that grove of pines till I come back for you, unless you intend to show me that with your attitude you can simply walk over the river! It's already been done once before."

"So its back to Yankee again, how soon they forget who saves their hide and keeps them fed." With that, John eased the mare down into the trees and dismounted to get comfortable. He watched Glenn work his way down the bluff toward the cabin. Through the scope, John saw Glenn stop before the cabin and a short time later the man they had seen before came out. They obviously exchanged some words, and then the man extended his hand toward Glenn, who shook it with enthusiasm. Glenn dismounted painfully and with a decided limp, followed the man into the cabin. John squirmed around to find a smooth spot, pulled his wide brim over his eyes, and quickly dropped off to sleep. John's grandpa always said, 'that boy could fall asleep lying on a rock pile'. He smiled thinking about his grandpa, he had been a wise and wonderful man, worked the hell out of him, but John loved his memories of the two of them together, and besides, he never knew he was working...he just thought he was having fun.

Sometime after dark John was awakened by something, a man he thought, moving slowly through the trees just below his position. Deliberately, quietly John withdrew the Colt and eased the hammer back. With the left hand he moved the wide brim up until his eyes were clear. He strained into the darkness looking for the shape of the thing moving below him, and waited. There, it moved again, just off to the left...it was definitely a man; John could just make out the head and shoulders. He brought the gun hand up slowly to bring the Colt to bear on the shape. He held his breath and waited...waited for identification, or a clear shot, which ever came first. Then...

"John! John! Where in the hell are you?"

"Glenn for Christ sake, I was ready to blow your head off! Where's your horse?"

"At the bottom of the bluff, I came up on foot. Come on our crossing over the river is all arranged."

John exhaled, eased the hammer down, re-holstered the Colt and rose to follow Glenn. He caught up the reins of the gray from where she had wondered off and followed Glenn down the hill by the noise he was making. In spite of the cool night, John's face was wet with perspiration. "Does this guy know you're bringing a Union soldier to his home?"

"Yes, I've told him the whole story."

"And that's okay…we are in Mississippi you know?"

"He's not feeling too good about the Confederacy right now, seems a Confederate patrol came by two days ago and destroyed his ferry so the Yankees couldn't use it to move troops across the river."

"Well if the ferry was destroyed, just how in the hell are we going to cross?"

"He has a smaller log raft hidden downstream that he can skull over."

"How small, can we take the horses?"

"Yeah, just room for the two of us and the horses. Come on, his wife is going to feed us before we go."

As the two young men approached the cabin, a short, solidly built man emerged. He stopped and looked John over very carefully, taking particular notice of his holstered Colt. Then he stepped forward, smiled a slight smile that was missing many teeth, and extended his hand. "My name's Seth Miller", he said, "this here's my wife. You can wash up there, then come and sit. We'll eat some before we cross over the river."

John's hand was completely swallowed up in the handshake. He felt that if Mr. Miller had squeezed, he would have broken every bone. As the man turned back toward the cabin, John noticed his shoulders were about two axe-handles across and his upper arms were as big around as John's legs. No doubt he had the strength to skull a raft with two men and horses over the river.

John washed as best he could and slicked back his shaggy, sand colored hair; fortunately there was no mirror so he didn't have to see his appearance. He hung his hat on a peg by the wash stand, and then as an after thought, unbuckled the holster and hung the Colt there also. When he entered the cabin the good smells said, 'home'. There were onions and potatoes fried dark with the skins on, a big iron skillet filled with biscuits just slightly brown on the top, on the hearth a haunch of venison cooked slowly, and to top it off real coffee....John couldn't remember his last taste of real boiled coffee. The room was about 15 feet square with the only the light from the cooking hearth at one end and the coal-oil lamp on the table. It was furnished with a rough-cut lumber table, four chairs, each different from the others, a rocker in the corner and a cupboard with faded curtain for the covering. There was a second room behind a drawn curtain, which John assumed was for sleeping. If there were children, they were not seen, nor heard, nor mentioned. There wasn't much conversation as they ate, there wasn't much need. Glenn had told Mr. Miller everything he wanted to know, and John was a lot more interested in the meal than he was in tellin', or hearin' a life story. Also, it seemed that while Mr. Miller could tolerate John in his home in a Union uniform, he had no great wish to engage him in conversation. After the meal, John went to his saddlebag and returned with a half-bottle of sour mash, which Mr. Miller, true to his Tennessee background, seemed to considerably enjoy, but it never loosened his tongue for small talk.

They thanked Mrs. Miller over and over for the meal, but unfortunately had nothing to give her as a gift that wasn't already critical to their own survival needs. Seth Miller disappeared down the path leading to the river and then south along its bank. He told Glenn it would be about two hours before he was back with the raft. So the young men checked their gear and tended to their animals, then settled down to sleep off the feast. The next thing they knew, Miller was hollering Glenn's name to get aboard. They led the horses to the raft, but the animals had no intention of walking aboard. Glenn said it was just like the railroad trestles, they wouldn't walk on those either. John took off his bandana and blindfolded the gray, and after she got used to being sightless, led her aboard, but with lots of conversation in her ear. He had some sympathy for the horse's feelings, the raft was small, about the size to accommodate a team and wagon, and rocked with each movement of man or animal. John didn't like the feeling of it either; he kind of wished he was blindfolded. Glenn followed John's lead with the blindfold and eventually all were loaded, but none were comfortable.

Miller pushed off into the dark, muddy water and as he rocked the single oar, pointed the raft slightly up stream. The river was high and boiling from the heavy spring rains in the northern plains. It was full of debris, including some large trees, all being carried fast on the strong current. Miller told both men to keep a sharp eye for anything large coming at them, and showed them the poles they could use to guide the trees around the raft. John hoped that none came at them because he felt if he relaxed his tight grip on the big gray's bridle, she would lunge and go overboard, probably taking him with her. As it was she was stamping and pawing with her front hooves. Miller's course was to skull almost straight across to the islands on the opposite side of the main channel, around the islands on the downstream side, then over the last open water to the Arkansas shore. It was a very nervous crossing for the passengers, both two and four legged. But for Miller it was a routine run and he skillfully held the small raft pointing slightly up-stream as he moved almost straight across the dark, angry body of water. Fortunately the debris that found the raft was small and did little to alter Miller's course. It was still long before moon-rise, but John was surprised how light it was on the surface of the river, for such a dark sky. It was as if the water collected and amplified what light was available from the night, and then reflected it on the surface. John had been raised just above the seven-mile rapids on the Mississippi River, so he was not a stranger to this Father of Waters, but this would be counted as his first night crossing on a small, log raft with a nervous horse and a wounded companion.

They were now about 100 feet from the first group of islands, where the current seemed to be the strongest. Miller strained to keep the bow of the small raft pointed up-stream into the current, and then let the raft slip sideways toward the first island. The island was tree covered, dark and foreboding as it became silhouetted against the night sky, causing John to alternate between starring at the island and looking up river for debris that might impact the raft. On one of his quick glances at the island he saw what he thought was a muzzle flash, followed quickly by the echo of a musket report. He heard the ball whistle through the center area of the raft, just past his head, and instantly the sickening thud of contact with something solid. Reacting as a soldier who had been through considerable combat, John grabbed the Spencer from the saddle, dropped to one knee and spaced four quick shot about a foot apart around the area of the flash. He had no way of knowing if he hit anything, but there was no return fire. Suddenly the raft lost heading and began to fall off into the current. John looked back to see Miller crumble as he grabbed at his chest and then his body slide off the stern and into the dark water. John hollered to warn Glenn as he grabbed for the gray's bridle to try to settle her down. From the corner of his eye he caught the last movement of the big tree trunk just before it plowed under the turning raft. The up-stream side of the raft was lifted high into the air and the deck pitched downward sharply. Both men and horses were thrown wildly down the slanting deck, through the log rail and into the dark muddy water churning by. John realized that he was still clutching the rifle in his right hand and the gray's bridle in his left...he was determined not to release his grip on either. The raft and tree sped by and away from him. He called out to Glenn and heard the reply come from further downstream. "Grab anything on the bay and just hang on, he will find the shore. Watch the hooves; he'll kick the hell out of you!" John moved back to hold on to the pommel horn and give the gray her head. He had pushed his wide brim hat off the back of his head when they boarded the raft and now it was full of water and the cord was getting tighter on the front of his neck. He couldn't move it over his head and he couldn't let loose of anything to free a hand. He tried turning his head and neck sideways to take a little pressure off of his windpipe and to not drink the muddy water, as he fought for air.

Later, John would not be able to recall how long they were in the river, or how far down beyond the islands they were swept. The big gray seemed to have a sense of which way the shore lay, so John continued to struggle to hold on to the horse and the rifle, while she floundered and snorted, but continued to swim. Eventually he became aware that she was rising up out of the water, she was standing on the bottom. Tentatively John put his feet down and touched the sandbar....welcome to Arkansas, he thought. He let loose of the saddle horn, struggled the last few feet up to the bank to collapse in the sand, then quickly slipped out of the hat. If it was strangling him in the river, it was a killer now hanging around his windpipe, full of water.

John retched again and again as his stomach repelled the last of the muddy water he had swallowed. The only thing he could think of was he losing that wonderful meal of just two hours earlier. When he could catch his breath he called out for Glenn, but there was no response. He waited a few minutes for some strength to return to his limbs, and then rose to go catch-up the gray mare. She kept backing away as John slowly approached, as though she wanted nothing to do with anyone who would blindfold her then put her on that raft, finally to pitch her into the wild river at night. As John took a few steps forward, she would take a few steps backward, keeping the distance between them constant. But John continued to talk to her and eventually she stood and waited for him, as though she had now made her point. He put the rifle in the boot, mounted and headed off down stream, staying near the river's edge. He continued to call Glenn's name, but still no response. When he stopped to listen, he heard the bay nicker just up on the bank ahead. He moved up to him and dismounted to search for Glenn. He kept walking ever-widening circles calling out his name, but without success. When he finally turned to go back for the horses, John heard a sound down next to the water, and moved in that direction to investigate. Glenn was lying on a sand bar, about half out of the water, nearly drowned and not moving. John pulled him up clear, put him on his back with his head turned to the side and began pushing on his stomach, mindful that his patient also had two broken ribs. Glenn coughed and expelled a considerable quantity of the river. Then, whether in pain from his ribs, or in relief of the river water, said, "For the love of God man will you stop pushing of my busted ribs!" At that moment John was so relieved he could have hugged Glenn, but thought better of it and just smiled into the darkness. But he did clap him warmly on the shoulder.

"Who in the hell fired that shot, and did you get him?" Glenn asked.

"Don't know the answer to either question. I assumed it was Confederate though because Mr. Miller had said there was no Union on the western side. As for getting him, all I know is after I fired, he stopped."

"Speaking of Mr. Miller, what happened to him?"

"Got to be dead. He took the round squarely in the chest, I saw him clutch himself and then fall backward into the river, just before that tree turned over the raft."

"You think they were shooting at us?"

"No. I think whoever it was hit what he was shooting at. He likely figured the river would take care of the rest of us."

"But why?" Glenn puzzled.

"Could be it was part of the same renegade Confederate bunch that destroyed Miller's ferry They probably thought we were the first contingent of Union making the crossing. How's that make you feel, to be mistaken for a Yankee? The thing that worries me, I wonder if they thought we were Union because they had already seen some Union forces in this area? That might could give us more company than we can avoid if both sides are over on this side of the river."

They each thought on that for a while, then Glenn said, "Let's gather the things we can find and move back into a more sheltered area and build a small fire. We need to get organized and dry out; we're damned fortunate just to be alive."

"You're right about that, if it hadn't been for the gray mare, I'm not sure I would have made it to the sandbar, but damn, I do hate it about Mr. Miller. He was a good man just trying to help us. He truly deserved better than he got!"

Chapter Six

"THE MEETING OF SARAH"

John extended a hand to help Glenn slowly, painfully gather his feet under him. As the two young men stood facing each other, John on impulse, reached out and hugged Glenn to him. Then immediately embarrassed at the burst of affection he felt for this enemy, without a word turned away to catch up the horses. They mounted and Glenn led them a short way up the bank to a grove of soft maple trees now nearly in full-leaf. "I think this will do", he said. "The leaves will scatter what smoke there is from a fire and we're still close enough to the river to have a ready supply of driftwood for fuel. It burns fast but gives off good heat and not much smoke." John gathered some wood and after a considerable effort, Glenn got the damp flint to spark and a fire started. They spent the balance of the evening drying out their gear and clothes. The uniforms were in bad shape… full of holes and showing rot and mold from being wet so much of the time over the last few weeks, and all of the leather was green with mold. There was just enough smoke trapped under the trees to keep the flying bugs away, but venture a few feet up the bank, and they would feed on you with a vengeance. Because of what had happened at the island, the men agreed that someone should be on guard tonight. John was too on edge to sleep so took the first watch. He picked up the rifle, checked the sticky action, then moved just to the outer edge of the protective fire-light and smoke and set-down with his back against the tree. Glenn eased his tired body back on his damp, upturned saddle to try to get some sleep.

John watched as Glenn tried to find a comfortable position, but seemingly could not. Finally he observed, "You hurtin' pretty bad after that swim?"

"I'm okay 'cept for all the muddy water I swallowed, just too worked-up to sleep I reckon."

"If your not gonna' take advantage of my watch to get some sleep, can I go back to our conversation in the barn, some thing's you said are still troubling me?"

"Sure." Glenn moved around so he could see John in the fire-light.

"As I think on it some more, I don't understand just how you in the south figure this nation would be better split-up. You said yourself we'd be much weaker against foreign powers."

"This effort by the south to set itself up as independent Confederate country was not a mad enterprise, or even a great break with past history. In the first place, you need to understand the word 'Nation' never appears in the constitution. That's because our Founding Fathers never set out to create 'a Nation', they were building a federation of sovereign states each of which in itself was the sovereign nation. Their only intended purpose was the mutual protection from foreign invasion and to encourage trade with the other nations of the world. James Madison, our third President and a writer of the constitution, even said that just as the states volunteered to join the federation, they could also volunteer to leave it. And with that as the understanding, thirteen of them decided to try it. Before South Carolina exercised its right to volunteer to leave that federation, there had been eight other attempts at secession, the first was called the

Whiskey Rebellion in 1794 and was eventually put down by Robert E. Lee's father. The next was when President Jefferson made the Louisiana Purchase. The New England states were going to leave over that. In fact, all eight of those secession attempts were among the states located in the north, not in the south."

With his lesson over, Glenn again settled back against the saddle and John moved off to gather wood, still wondering if he had ever really understood what this war was all about. Didn't make any difference now, it wasn't his war any more. But as much as he had hated it...he knew he would also miss the excitement and the danger, and the men he had served with. But his new pledge was to keep Glenn alive and see him home, and with God's blessing he was gonna' do just that. The driftwood burnt so fast, that most of his watch was spent gathering wood along the riverbank. It seemed so peaceful now down along the water's edge. The river was still dark and ominous, but in this cove with only a little current running, it no longer seemed such a violent threat. John stared off into the dark waters and found it hard to recall all of the details of what they had survived this night, and then Seth Miller came again to his mind. It just wasn't right that Mrs. Miller was left to sit in that cabin waiting for a man who was not coming back, but what could they to do about it in their situation?

The men traded off in a few hours and Glenn kept the fire burning with the wood John had gathered. John was exhausted and slept until after the sun was well over the height of the bluff behind the eastern riverbank. When he was full awake, Glenn reported, "I've been looking over our supplies and our gear, and friend we're not in very good shape. I assume the weapons will work okay, at least for now, but we've not much left in the way of food. The hardtack was in tins, so we can still eat it, but soaking that moldy dried beef in muddy river water did not improve its taste. And just to keep the score accurate...you're the one now burnin' daylight!"

"Yes, and I'm hungry as hell after losing all of that meal Mrs. Miller fed us. If you think the guns are okay, I'll try my hand at hunting us up a meal."

"I field stripped 'em and wiped 'em down while you were sleeping and the action on each seems to work smoothly for now, if rust doesn't set in before we get some animal fat to put on them."

With that John got some brass loads for the scattergun, checked his colt, pulled on his wide brim hat and got ready to walk out of camp.

Glenn looked intently at John, "you've been asking me a lot of questions about this war from the southern point of view, if you'll take a minute, I've got a question for you."

John found a place to sit with his back against the soft maple tree, "I don't know much about the politics, but I'll try to give you my best thoughts on the subject."

"You are a good Christian man; you said you were raised by a God-loving family. From that learnin', why do you think God has allowed this war and suffering to go on?"

"From what I've been taught, I think God hates this war…hates all wars, as much as you and I hate this one. Although if we're gonna' go and have one anyway…having one to free some of his people from being slaves is likely a better reason than most. And, I have to tell you, I don't really believe all you were saying about slavery being all right with God…I don't believe it is! Read Exodus. God went to great lengths to free his chosen people. Maybe Mr. Lincoln did come late to the slavery issue, but he came…how do we know but what that's not the work of God after He found the right man, kinda like Moses was? Slavery is a man-thing, not a God-thing and having some of his people in chains, owned by someone else, can just not be all right with the God my ma introduced me to."

"But He is all powerful. If He hates this war so much, why doesn't He just stop it?"

"What my Pa believes is when God made this world...this Garden, for us, He had to surround it with some natural laws so as we lived here we would learn that some things will just happen the same way

60

every time, not just when God is watching, or not watching. There's a high cliff on the other side of the Mississippi River from our farm, it goes straight down maybe 50 feet on to rocks and then into the river. If you took a hundred people up there...God-loving people, and they prayed for hours to be saved, prayed till the blood ran out through their skin, when they jumped off that cliff they would all still die when they hit the rocks at the river's edge, not just the ones that didn't pray hard enough. That's the natural law of gravity and it works every time, equally, for both the good and the bad. If it didn't, we wouldn't know if this was the time we could jump off the cliff, or not. It's the same in a battle. I believe in God, I believe God loves me and I love Him, but at Shiloh Church if I stepped out from behind my cover, one of your boys would still put a ball in my head...maybe you; and I would still be dead! God's likely thinking, I put those wonderful brains in their heads and gave them the ability to use logic and reason, I gave them the ability to communicate with each other and pass on the lessons of history...and this is the best use they could make of My gifts? No, I think at night after that second day of battle at Shiloh Church, when God looked down on us and saw how we had used His gifts and what we had done to each other for the past two days...He cried."

John was finished; he'd said all he had to say. He picked up his hat and pushed it down on his head, slapped the dust from the seat of his pants, and with his scattergun in the crook of his arm, strolled out of their camp.

"You know that hat looks some better after spending time in the river, it didn't fit you worth a lick before. I hated to tell you that cause you seemed so proud of it. You gonna' take the gray?"

"No", John replied, "She's too noisy to hunt with, besides I think they could use the rest and the grass. There's some good grass up on that levee, you might tether the two of them up there while I'm gone." With that John moved out and headed off through the trees along the base of the levee and this time it was Glenn who was left to ponder what had just been said between them. 'That Yankee boy, that sod-buster never ceases to surprise me!'

It was a beautiful day, the sun was bright and warm on John's back, and there was just enough breeze to keep the tall grass stirred and the bugs away. Just being over here on the western bank of the Mississippi River made his heart feel light and gave the belief that this adventure was going to work out. The few puffy white clouds sailed by like the ships of the sky. When John was a small boy his grandmother and he would sit on the cool grass in front of their cabin, watching the clouds and describing to each other the pictures they saw there. At least, he sat on the grass, grandmother was by then confined to a wheelchair. They both had active imaginations and would entertain each other for hours with stories about the pictures they saw in the clouds. John had almost forgotten his mission as he became wrapped up in the cloud pictures and wished he could again share them with that wonderful lady. She was a fine, lovin' person. But the sudden intense buzzing very close at hand, like a large dried gourd full of seeds, froze his blood and tensed his muscles. He knew it was a rattler and he knew it was close. John fought the impulse to look, afraid even the slightest movement would cause a strike. The buzzing was on his left side and almost straight out from his left boot. John wondered if a rattler could strike through a boot, he also wondered just how complete a job Glenn had done cleaning and reassembling the scattergun. He was surely going to find out the answer to both of those questions…and soon! Again the angry buzzing, but still John resisted the natural reaction to try to jump away. He turned his upper body very slowly to the left with his lower parts remaining as if spiked to the ground. He strained his eyes as far left as they would go trying to pick out the snake. Then he saw it, about five feet straight out from him, it was tightly coiled with the head and tail erect. John could not turn his head any further to the left as the shadow of the wide brim would pass over the snake. If the movement of the shadow caught him, that snake would either retreat or strike and John didn't like the odds on those two choices. He considered his options and set his plan, he would jump straight back with both feet together, swing the scattergun and fire…but it had to be all in one smooth motion. The snake's head came up and moved from side to side as the heat began to radiate off of John's clothing. John jumped backwards. The snake lunged at the spot where he had been standing. As John hit the ground, both barrels of the shot-gun erupted catching the rattler just below the head which just disappeared into a red mist. Stretched out the snake was easily six feet long, even absent the parts now missing, and as thick as John's wrist. He remembered when he first caught a glimpse of it from the corner of his left eye, he felt somewhat secure as he was certain it could not strike far enough to hit him, yet there it lay in the tromped down grass where he had just stood. So much for his working knowledge of rattlers!

Glenn heard the extra loud blast of the scattergun and thought, 'we eat' and started pulling more wood up to the area of their fire. Two hours later John still had not returned, but Glenn had heard two more shots, both times from further up the river…it was either going to be a feast, or John had started his own private war in Arkansas, and with John, it could just as easily be either one. When he finally returned to the camp, John was carrying a skinned and cleaned rabbit and a squirrel. "Guess you're not the great white hunter you thought to be, Glenn chided, I heard you fire both barrels first."

"Just as good as I had to be" said John as he reached into his pocket and tossed a bloody set of rattlers at Glenn's feet.

"Damn that thing must have been a big one, he didn't hit you did he?"

"No, but he sure had it in mind. By the way, thanks for the cleaning job on the scattergun, otherwise you'd likely be heading on alone."

John made a small grill of woven green willows and laid the game out over the hot coals of Glenn's fire. "Glenn, do you think we should try to do something to tell Mrs. Miller her man is dead and how it happened?"

"I'd like to, we sure owe them, but how?"

"Well, I found a flat bottomed boat with a set of oars high up on the bank about a mile up river, we could row it over to the eastern side.

Up home we call them jonboats and they are so stable they're used for huntin' ducks on the river, in some often bad weather too."

"How big is it?"

"Oh probably 10-12 foot long. Big enough for the two of us to make a crossing, if you've a mind to go."

"You'll have to do the most of the rowing, my ribs are a might sore after our unplanned swim last night. What about the horses and our other gear?"

John thought a moment, "we'll move the gear out of sight from anyone passing on the river and tether the horses in that good grass. We'll be over and back in a day, everything should be alright here for that long."

"Okay, let's do it, we owe them that much, but can we eat first? I am beginning to feel some hungry!

"We'll go tomorrow at first light. When we finish eating this feast my skills as a great white hunter have provided, I'll go up and bring the boat down so we can leave from here."

They finished the rabbit; some of the squirrel and some of the hardtack, and then John hiked up the river and returned with the jonboat. By the time he got back, Glenn had already thrown-up his meal. "Is my cooking that bad?" John asked.

"I don't know what it is, ever since we were in the river I've thrown-up everything I put down, even water. I'll be okay, you get some sleep, and I'll take the first watch tonight."

The men traded off after midnight, and at the first hint of light in the east Glenn felt the now all to familiar tapping on the bottom of his boot. "I know, I know...were burnin' daylight!"

As soon as it was light enough to see the surface of the river, they loaded up and pushed off. John sat in the middle seat with his back to the bow so he could pull the oars through the water. Glenn sat on the stern seat facing forward with the Spencer across his knees. The river was about a mile wide in this location, and they could plainly see the eastern bank, but then anyone on the eastern bank could just as plainly see them as well. The river did not seem nearly so threatening in the light of day, but still running hard and just as muddy. No wonder Glenn was still throwing up, if he swallowed much of that brown liquid. John pulled heavier on his left oar and kept the small boat headed slightly upstream, just like he had seen Miller doing. He worked smoothly and efficiently, just like the old days of huntin' ducks with his pa on the upper Mississippi. It took about two hours, with a couple of short rest breaks to reach the eastern side. John would have liked to rest more, but as soon as he stopped, the boat would lose headway and the bow would swing downstream, sending them further away from the Miller cabin.

When they reached the eastern bank, the water was more protected from the swift current, so John could turn the boat upstream and row easily against the milder river force until Glenn pointed out the Miller's cabin just ahead. They beached the boat, tied it off and stepped out just as an old smooth-bore muzzle poked through the opening of the cabin window. "Hello the cabin, its Glenn McCord, we were here two nights past."

"What did you boys do with my husband, he didn't come back home?"

"We came to tell you what happened, can we come in? Please Mrs. Miller, put the rifle down, we mean you no harm."

"Alright, come on up, this old gun don't shoot no how." The two men looked at each other with unasked questions in their eyes, and then started up the path toward the cabin, each beginning to wonder if this was still the correct thing to be doing. Nothing had changed in the cabin since their last visit. Mrs. Miller made some coffee, and they each took a place around the rough-cut table. For the next hour they told her about the night crossing, the shot that came from the island, Mr. Miller slipping into the river, and then the loss of the raft. Her only comment was, "Those renegade bastards, may they rot in hell! Seth never did them no harm and left alone, he never would have sided with the Yankees." She dabbed tears in the corner of her eyes, but managed a slight smile when Glenn told about John's returning fire. At that moment John pulled a small draw-string bag from inside his shirt, opened the bag and laid a Yankee Eagle gold piece on the table in front of Mrs. Miller. "This is the toll we agreed to for the crossing, we just never got to pay it to Mr. Miller", John explained. "So it is owed to you." Mrs. Miller just stared at the shinny gold object as it reflected the light from the coal-oil lamp. She never had seen that much money, let alone owned it. "Seth never charged that much for a crossing in his life, you boys are just making that up cause you're feelin' sorry for me."

"No madam", said John, "We agreed to more than the usual toll because of me being a Yankee and there might be some trouble involved if we were seen."

She wiped her eyes on her apron, examined the coin, took it to her mouth and bit down hard with two of the few remaining teeth in her head, then satisfied that it dented, dropped the gold coin casually into her apron pocket. "I know you boys have to be hungry." John eagerly agreed, while Glenn's face took on an ash gray color. But it was decided she would give them some fresh bread and smoked deer meat to eat on the return crossing, as it was getting on into the afternoon. But first, John had another cup of coffee and a thick slice of bread with cold butter. That would be his last of either for awhile.

She carried their food in an old flour sack down to the boat as they got ready to return, and handed it to Glenn after he found his seat in the stern. They all said their words of thank-you and good-bye, and the young men pushed off into the muddy river. John hollered back, "Don't trade that coin for any Confederate dollars." Mrs. Miller waved again, turned away from them, then cried openly into her apron. She couldn't decide if it was over the loss of her Seth, or the kindness and concern of these young men. No-one had ever shown much charity toward her before, and him being a Yankee at that.

Since they were well up-stream from the location of their camp, John could row west awhile, then let the boat drift downstream while he ate, he wished he had some more of that coffee to wash it down…or maybe a little sour mash. There was one bottle that had survived the fall into the river, but it was back with their gear. He noticed that Glenn took just a few small bites of the bread, but that was all. "You know, that was a real good deed you did for Mrs. Miller back there. You're a good man, for a Yankee", Glenn offered.

"You know, what you said just now really worries me? Sergeant Mullins would always reminded us that, 'no good deed will ever go unpunished'."

The return trip was smooth and trouble free, and Glenn soon spotted the bandana he had tied to the tree at the river's edge to mark their camp. John pulled the boat well up on the bank to protect it, should the river get any higher, and they returned to inspect their camp. All seemed to be as they had left it and the horses still grazed in the tall grass next to the levee. The sun was casting long shadows from the western bank, and the young men gathered wood to prepare for their last night next to the mighty Mississippi. "We best be on the move again in the morning", John said. "You know where to head from here?"

"We'll take much the same trail that pa and I took; at least as best I can remember it." Glenn smoothed out the sand and with a stick, drew a crude outline of southern Arkansas. "We'll head straight west to cross the Bartholomew River north of the Devils' Swamp, then southwest over the Saline and the Ouachita Rivers. We'll stay north of the town of Warren and then swing south of Camden, that way we should be able to avoid most all the towns. Then finally we cross the Red and the Sulphur Rivers and we're in Texas! I figure six or seven days if we're lucky."

"I thought the Red River was the northern boundary of Texas, I remember pa talking about crossing it on his way to join General Taylor.

"It is the border between Texas and the Indian Territory on the north, 'The Nations', as we call it, but not between Texas and the part of Arkansas we are passing through. We're damn well going to avoid crossing into The Nations. North of the Canadian River are the Creek, the Cherokee, the Seminole and the Pottawatomie. South of the river are the Choctaw, the Chickasaw, and roaming where they damn well please are the Comanches, and the ones who call themselves *The True People*, the Kiowa. Once they were called the "Five Civilized Tribes", but they became damned 'uncivilized' after they were relocated by force off of their home ranges. I hear the Kiowa and the Comanche have become especially unfriendly towards whites since the army pulled out of Fort Richardson and Fort Belknap to go fight in Mr. Lincoln's war. The Comanche are the most feared of all the plains Indians. Magnificent warriors, they'll ride a week on nothing but pemmican, fight a major battle against superior numbers of better equipped forces, then ride another week home. If their horses drop, they will stop and eat 'em, then go the rest of the way on foot." Returning his attention to the map, "and right about here on the border is a little tent village named for both states."

"Looks like you do know the country," said John. "I'll just follow you straight to your daddy's barn-yard."

John settled down to a tasty meal of deer meat and bread, washed down with some of the last of the sour mash. Glenn ate just a little, and then a short time later went off into the gathering darkness to again throw it all up. When he returned in to the firelight, John thought he looked like death warmed over. "Warm a little water and whiskey in that cup and just sip some."

"Will that really do any good?"

"Well it just might. Besides…."

"I know, its whiskey, it may not cure, but it can't hurt."

John had taken the second watch, so he had the horses saddled and ready before it was light. He noted the leaves of the soft maple trees were now all blowing such to show their silver underside. Grandpa had always said that was a sign of a bad storm coming, but then when Grandpa had pointed that out; it was the cottonwood trees, not the soft maple. John had seen enough of the river and this place to last him for quite awhile, besides, he was anxious to be on the way to Texas, so he was unnecessarily noisy in his chores, hoping to get Glenn up and moving. Glenn heard the activity and awoke…before he had to hear again that thing about 'burning daylight'. As soon as the first rays of the sun came down the eastern river bluff, they had the camp cleaned up, were mounted and easing their mounts up over the levee, heading west.

As they came up over the rise, they had their first look at the gathering storm clouds in the southwest, a sight that would stay with them, and over them, for the next three days and nights. The wind was tearing up the leading edge of the storm clouds, causing long, dark, ragged funnels to cling on the under side. In an hour the early morning sun was already covered and shortly the wind and the rain started, heavy and never ending. John would remember that Grandpa's sign of a coming storm worked with the silver maples trees in Arkansas just as well as with the cottonwood trees in Iowa.

Three days later the storm was still in progress. There was no protection, or shelter to be found…no barns or abandon buildings like before. They tried stopping under bridges, but as the stream level rose the horses would be standing in water. They had the ponchos that doubled as ground covers and shelter-half's in their bedrolls and they put those over their shoulders, but in two hours they were soaked through, and became steamy inside like a spring plant house. There was no relief, no way to make a dry camp, so mostly they just stayed in the saddle and gave the horses their head. When they stopped to give the animals a rest, they tried to do so under big trees. But after three days of rain, the tree leaves stopped nothing. If there was one good feature, it was that the weather was so miserable no one else was out either, so they ran little danger of detection, and by riding into the night because they couldn't sleep, were making better than 30 miserable miles a day.

By the dawn of the fourth day, they had passed to the north of Warren and turned southwest to find a road between Camden and El Dorado. The good news was that there actually was a dawn on the fourth day. The rain had finally stopped just about first light and the sky was clearing. During the night John had led them under a cottonwood tree, but the leaves continued to rain on them and each horse just stood quietly with their heads and tails down. When they moved out into the open, the first rays of sunshine since the river fell warmly on their backs. Glenn had taken much worse in the last few hours and John had begun leading the bay so Glenn could hold on to the saddle-horn with both hands to keep from falling off. Their clothes were nearly rags; they had no food left and had not had much but rain-water for the last few days. Like the horses, the young men were also exhausted. John doubted any of them could go through another day. Without help in some form, this adventure was about over. He reasoned that in this part of the country, help probably meant capture and a prison camp for him. But if he tried to keep pushing forward without food and a dry place to rest up, Glenn would be dead. His wounds were much worse and he had not kept even the meager rations down since being thrown in the river. If the horses didn't get some rest and a chance to graze, they would drop, and being afoot the men couldn't possibly survive. John sat there feeling the warmth of the sun on his body, but no warmth of the spirit from within.

"Glenn ol' friend, were going to have to chance it, and pick a likely farm house to stop for help. If they decide to turn me in, so be it. You're about finished and both horses have given all they've got to give us, frankly so have I. This was a great adventure and we about pulled it off, but we've just used up all our luck...and that's a hell of a thing for an Irishman to have to admit!" To all of that Glenn raised his head and tried to smile, but could not manage much of one. He knew he was hearing the truth of their situation, so he nodded and put his chin back down on his chest and again closed his eyes.

John held the horses quiet in the tree line, their heads drooping, and continued to watch the farmhouse. It had been a solid house at one time with board siding and glass windows, but now the whole farm was badly run down. With the spyglass, he could see the shingles missing from both the barn and the house, there were gaps where siding was missing off of the barn, weeds in the small door-yard garden, and the milk cow was tethered, that probably meant the pasture fence was down. As he watched, a tall, young woman came out of the summer kitchen, pumped a bucket of water, and carried it back to the house. It was just possible that there was no man in residence here. John's study was interrupted by a groan from Glenn. "Okay my friend, this looks as possible as we're likely to find. Let's try to talk our way through…once again!"

John moved the horses slowly up the weed overgrown ruts of a wagon path toward the door-yard gate, still leading the bay. As they approached the yard gate, the door to the summer kitchen opened and the young woman John had seen earlier stepped forward into the yard. She looked much more menacing though from this distance with the double-barreled scattergun held tightly in her two hands and pointed in John's general direction. But when John looked at her, he found it difficult to concentrate on the shotgun. John observations from afar were correct; she was tall, about 5 and1/2 feet, with hair in the morning sunlight the color of summer straw and pulled up in a bun at her neck. Wisps of hair at the side of her head had worked loose from the bun and the slight breeze danced them over her face. She didn't take her hands from the scattergun to brush them back, but just turned her face into the breeze to let them blow clear. When she looked back at him, John saw the most beautiful, deep green eyes he could ever remember. Her face was long and John had thought her too thin to be pretty, but that same breeze that blew her hair also moved the washed-out blue dress tight against her body and John saw how wrong his last thought had been. No, she might well be the most beautiful woman John had ever seen, but then it had been awhile since he'd actually seen one up close. And while he entertained these lovely thoughts of her, here she was menacing him with a shotgun.

She squared herself and those green eyes bore straight at him. "Who are you and what are you doing on my land? You're not welcome here, Yankee!"

John touched the brim of his hat as he introduced himself. "Ma'am, I am Corporal John Kelley, late of the 14th of Iowa, and I have the honor to present at the other end of this lead rope, Lieutenant Andrew Glenn McCord from Texas, also late of the 6th of Arkansas. We met at Pittsburg Landing in Tennessee, and I am attempting to return him to his home, but we've run down on our luck and are sorely in need of some true Christian charity."

Ignoring his plea she responded, "The Arkansas 6th was my husband's regiment. Did you shoot this man Mr. Kelley, is that why you're taking him home, or are you both just renegades?"

"I don't believe I shot him ma'am but then there were thousands of people shooting at each other for the better part of two days…a lot of Americans, that is. Perhaps Mr. McCord knew your husband."

"Not likely, my husband was not with his regiment at Shiloh Church. Do you know, was Mr. McCord at the battle of White Mountain some time back?"

"No Ma'am he was not. But I was."

Her voice lost a bit of it's strain, "Mr. Kelley I don't trust you or your intentions here. You come uninvited into my door-yard, a scrounge of a man in the worst looking Yankee uniform I could imagine, riding a beat down horse with a CSA brand, heavily armed, and leading a Confederate officer more dead than alive, that you say you didn't shoot!"

"Ma'am, we desperately need help. If you don't want me here, I understand and I'll ride on looking for help somewhere else, but please consider helping my friend. He can go no further and live to see another dawn."

During all of this exchange the shotgun was held steady on John and the deepest green eyes John could ever remember, never wavered or left his face. In this moment of silence, while she tried to decide what to do next, Glenn lost his grip on the pommel and with a groan, slid to the ground under the bay's hooves. The horse nervously danced sideways, but John held tight to the lead rope. He looked at the shotgun and again into the deepest green eyes he had ever seen, decided she was not going to shoot, at least not at that moment, and stepped down to go to his friend. She paused, then her decision made, she leaned the gun against the yard fence, and moved with him to check Glenn's wounds.

"He'll likely not make night fall, Mr. Kelley. Bring him into the summer kitchen, there's a cot you can put him on, but first, strip him down to the long johns. I'll not have those vermin infested clothes in my house." Relieved at her change of heart, John quickly did as instructed, carried Glenn to the house, and eased him onto the cot. He then moved back through the door-yard, scooped up his reins, and was stepping to remount, when she spoke through the screen door. "I don't abide a Yankee on my place, but I don't abide using up good horse flesh either, especially good southern horse flesh. You may find a place for your horses in the barn and there is some of last year's corn. They could use a meal. You can find a place in the barn for yourself as well, Mr. Kelley, at least for tonight. My husband's clothes should near fit you. I'll send you a change out with Mathew, along with soap and a razor. There's a horse watering trough behind the barn, I strongly suggest you could use all three."

John wiped down the horses with hands full of straw and had just finished feeding some corn to the starving animals when he heard a young voice behind him say, "Mr. Kelley, Mamma said you'll be needing these. She also said for you to take this shovel and bury the clothes behind the barn, yours and Mr. McCord's."

"And who would you be?"

"I am Mathew Graham, I am 6 years old, and I am the man of this place while my pa is gone to the war."

"Well Master Graham you sure do look like your mother, and since you're the man of the place, my friend and I do most appreciate you letting us stop and rest for awhile. Is it all right with you if I call you Matt, that's how my brother is called?"

73

"My mother only calls me Mathew but I like to be called Matt. Sometimes people call me Matt when my Mamma can't hear, so I guess its okay. Mamma says when you get to looking better and smelling better, you're supposed to come to the back door for some food, and mamma said, 'do not wear them guns to the house'." Having said his piece, the man of the place turned on his heel and left the barn.

The water in the trough had been warmed just enough by the sun to feel mighty good. John couldn't remember his last true bath...with soap. He soaped and rinsed, and soaped and rinsed again. The razor hadn't been used in awhile but John brought up a new edge on the harness leather, and with a piece of broken mirror probable used by the last man who shaved there, started the clean-up process. Since he had such a good start, John decided to leave himself a mustache. He had started once before but his Sergeant, who had a big, bushy handlebar of a mustache, had made fun of his effort. So John had shaved it off. This one was a little darker and some thicker and John thought it made him look older, so it would stay, at least for now. John dressed in the clothes Matt had brought, and found them a fair fit. Then he dug a hole behind the barn and buried the tattered remains of the two uniforms together. If only their whole experience could be done away with that easy. He went to the back door without hat or guns and took a seat on the wash bench. Shortly, the beautiful lady with the deepest green eyes he had ever seen handed John a plate of food and a big tin cup of steaming coffee. As he stood, he noticed that the loose wisps of hair had all been recaptured and pulled back into place. "Sit, eat. Mr. McCord said it had been a few days since your last meal."

"It has been that ma'am. How is Glenn?"

"He has some seriously bad infections in his wounds, the one you made taking the ball out and poured the whiskey on looks the best. I cleaned him up and fed him some bread soaked in hot soup. He opened his eyes and talked some. He told me about how you two met and the journey so far. He also told me in some detail about the river crossing, you going back to tell Mrs. Miller, and especially

74

about the encounter with that Yankee patrol. He still wonders if you would have shot them to protect him. Frankly, so do I, Mr. Kelley."

"I don't know either Ma'am, cause when I saw what a greenhorn the Captain was, and then got the drop on the Sergeant, I was certain I could talk our way through."

"You two are a strange, unlikely pair, but he sure does have faith in you getting him home."

"That's surely my intent ma'am, I promised him I would!"

"Now Mr. Kelley, eat 'fore your food gets cold."

"Thank you Mrs. Graham."

"How'd you know my name?"

"I don't ma'am, just Matt told me his family name was Graham."

"His name is Mathew….and mine is Sarah, Sarah Graham."

John stood and offered his hand…and after a moment, she took it. Her hand felt small and delicate, yet strong in John's big paw. John looked into her eyes, like emeralds he thought, and for the first time there was a softening and the slightest smile in the corners. Then just as quickly the softening went away, the frown lines between her eyes returned and she withdrew her hand. They went nervously to her hair, even though every strand was still in place, and she looked at the horizon with those beautiful deep green eyes. John found himself short of breath, as though he had been running up a hill. He sat quickly to concentrate on the food and the coffee.

He said, "Thank you Mrs. Graham", without adding, thank you for what.

She turned, gave him a long, serious look, then moved back into the security of her summer kitchen and closed the screen-wire door behind her.

The food was life-giving to this starving man, but later in his bed roll, all John would remember was the cool strength of her hand in his, how well it fit and the brief smile he had seen in those deep green eyes…the color reminded him of the water in the lake formed where the Mormons had quarried the stone for their temple. Like none he had ever seen before.

Chapter Seven

"THE MILLERS GET SOME REVENGE"

The rest of that first day at the farm went by quickly for John. He made a pallet in the barn for his use that night; it remained to be seen if he would be allowed to stay beyond that. Then made up a tether for the horses so they could get out in the good grass, and started to look over the farm and the many needed repairs. It was obvious that the place had been without a man's hand for some time. John knew he could help Mrs. Graham catch up the work if she would let him stay on while Glenn recovered. The thought made John smile outwardly; here he had joined Mr. Lincoln's army to get away from a much better farm than this one, now he wanted to stay on this one for awhile. He reasoned it could have something to do with the deepest green eyes he had ever seen. During John's walk around the perimeter of the pasture he had found a number of places where fence posts were missing and the wire was broken down. He would fix that tomorrow then the milk cow and the horses wouldn't have to be tied. While he was contemplating tomorrow, John looked down over the pasture toward the house, the summer kitchen door slamming caught his attention, and saw Sarah….Mrs. Graham walk to the tethered cow and start the evening 's milking. He knew he should go do that for her, but for the moment he just sat down in the sweet grass and watched her. While he was watching and daydreaming, she finished, took the bucket and stool, and returned to the house. 'The production from that cow must be way down for her to finish so quickly'.

John continued to relax in the rich grass and enjoy the view. Next Mathew headed for the barn calling his name. John stood, answered and started walking toward the barn. "Mr. Kelley, mamma says to wash up for supper, and come to the summer kitchen door…. and no guns around the house." John just got seated on the wash bench when Mathew pushed through the door and handed him a tin plate of boiled potatoes, corn, red beans and rice. He just got his disappointment under control from being served by Mathew, when Mrs. Graham pushed through the door and handed John a steaming cup of coffee. "Mathew go on back inside and finish your supper." With a "yes ma'am" the man of the place retreated.

"Mr. Kelley I saw you up inspecting the pasture fence, some of the posts are gone and it's been torn up for some time."

"If you'll allow me ma'am, I could fix that. The production from your milk cow would go way up if she was free to pasture."

"The place could use a man's hand alright and I would appreciate some help. I know you want to stay on until your friend has recovered enough to travel on home. You may just be working for the taxman, however. There are no cash crops on this farm any more, it hardly even feeds us, and the war has caused the taxes to be raised to the point I don't know how they will be paid. Another item Mr. Graham gave no thought to. I would guess they are up to $40 now. I was in hope that I could hold this farm, poor as it is, to give Mathew something to start his life with."

"I would appreciate you letting me stay and for you caring for Glenn. I'll work off our keep and think it a good bargain, don't concern yourself about that. How do you think Glenn is doing?"

"Mr. McCord's wounds are badly infected, mostly from the river water. Tomorrow I want you to go gather some moss and the bark from a tree I'll show you. I'll make a poultice and try to draw some of that infection out; otherwise it will spread through his body and soon kill him."

"Yes ma'am, first thing. I promised to get Glenn home to Texas and I'll help do that any way I can. There should be plenty of moss in that timber beyond the pasture. What kind of tree bark do you need?"

"I'll show you, I have a small piece left in the house. It's called Peruvian bark and it was used as a poultice by Mr. Lewis and Captain Clark when the journeyed to the Pacific Ocean."

They both fell silent. Then, "Mr. Kelley, when you arrived you said Mr. McCord was not at the battle of White Mountain, but that you were."

"Yes Ma'am, that I was."

"I would like you to tell me about the battle. My husband, Mathew's father, not only fought there, he was killed there. That's why he was not with his regiment at Shiloh Church."

"Ma'am I'm awful sorry about your husband's death, but I don't know what you want me to tell you."

"I want to know about the battle, so I can tell Mathew something about his pa when he's a little older and will want to know. As for being sorry, you don't need to be. John Henry Graham was a very hard man; hard on his animals, hard on this farm, hard on his family, and especially hard on his wife. He did not have to go to the war; he left because he wanted to go. It gave him an excuse to walk away from this farm and away from his growing responsibilities! His father and uncle had some influence in Little Rock so when he was elected to Captain's bars; he took off and never looked back. That was almost two years ago and you can look around to see how we've all done since."

"All I can do ma'am is tell you in my plain spoken way how it was there on that mountain. It was an ugly, bloody, stupid battle and the telling of it won't make it anything else."

"Don't soften it for my sake; I want to know how it is that my six year old no longer has a father."

"My regiment had been operating in southwestern Missouri, around Branson and Springfield, for some months and we had just about driven all the regular army Confederate forces out of the state. A patrol came back one evening and reported that a large Confederate force was getting ready to move north out of Rogers, Arkansas, to occupy the heights at White Mountain in northwestern Arkansas. That was a critical location for controlling that part of both Arkansas and Missouri. Who ever secured those heights would be very difficult to dislodge. General Samuel Curtis had us immediately pack up all the gear we each could carry and marched us through the night and for the next 12 hours, almost without a break, and we arrived on the mountain heights ahead of the Confederates."

John stopped to take a sip of his lukewarm coffee and to see if Mrs. Graham wanted him to continue. The expectant look on her face provided the answer.

"We started digging redoubts and cutting pine logs for our defense positions and to give us a clear field of fire. About two hours later three of our six-pound Parrott cannons came up, and about an hour after that our Studebaker wagons and the rest of our forces. Shortly then our scouts made the first contact with the Rebs..., I'm sorry, the Confederate forces. As soon as they saw us, they just started that blood curdling screaming and started charging up the mountain, right into the front of our positions. We just fired canister and musket into their ranks, until the charge finally broke. Those going back down the mountain tried to drag or carry their wounded, but there were almost as many on the ground as standing. We relaxed thinking they were broken and the battle was won, when they came again the same way and with the same result. They charged us three more times that afternoon, each time with fewer people than before. They never probed with patrols for any weakness in our lines, they never tried to flank our position, they never brought their cannon up, they were so certain they could dislodge us with their rebel yells and much superior numbers that they just kept charging up that mountain into withering fire. It was both the bravest and stupidest thing I had ever seen! The last charge late in the afternoon got stalled because they could no longer run through the piles of bodies from the previous attempts. As they started to retreat again and retrieve their dead and wounded, some of the younger ones from our side wanted to keep firing but the older veterans made them hold up. A little later a senior officer, a Colonel I believe, rode out of the Confederate position alone. He stopped his big black horse in the middle of the battlefield and while facing our lines, took off his hat and swept it low in front of his horse in kind of a salute of honor. It was a big triangle kind of hat with a long gray feather plume out of the side that almost touched the ground. I looked up and down our line for some officer to stand and return the honor, but none would risk the showing. I was so taken with the gesture; I laid down my weapon, stood at attention on the top of our redoubt and snapped him a salute that I held for the count of five, just like we had been trained. That old gentleman put his fancy hat back on, turned his horse toward me and returned my salute. We just stood there looking at each other for the longest time, and then he lowered his arm, turned slowly and rode back into the pine trees. The troops around me cheered him as he rode away....from all I've seen in this war; I've never seen anything quite like that."

"We waited until dusk but they didn't return. The next day at dawn I was ordered to take out a patrol to make contact with the remnants. The men said I was sent out because I had embarrassed our officers by standing and taking the Confederate Colonel's salute while they hid below the redoubt. But there just weren't any remnants of that Confederate force to be found. Almost every man in that regiment became a casualty on that mountainside, well over a thousand walked up there together but only a few walked away! It was both brave and crazy, but either way, damned poor leadership."

"What did your people do then?"

"The patrol found where many of their wagons had burned from our cannon fire and where the few remaining wagons had pulled out down the mountain to the south. We followed them on down the mountain, but were not able to make contact. I finally halted the patrol and sent a messenger back with a report and requested orders. When the messenger returned he said we were being recalled, and the main body was being returned back to Springfield in Missouri. I could not believe it. I had assumed the army would move on to Pea Ridge and Rogers, then occupy Fayetteville. Even with vastly smaller numbers we could have controlled all of northwest Arkansas, but we didn't. We just let the chance slip away and moved back the way we had come, back to our base camp. We marched in with colors unfurled to the music of the cornet band, just like on a Sunday parade. After that many of us were marched on to Rolla in Missouri to the rail head. Then sent by train on to Jefferson Barracks below Saint Louis, to help form General Grant's new army."

"But that seems such a waste, all those men killed and neither side wanted the territory? What was it all about?"

"That's what makes this war so senseless. It's not been about gaining, occupying and holding territory. It's about slaughtering the other side and destroying the countryside to his use, wherever and whenever you can! The Confederate forces soon raised up another army and that very same battle was fought again in early March this year, this time at Pea Ridge, your folks called it Elkhorn Tavern, and the Union won again. That's the reason eventually the North will win this war; they have more people and materials and they can absorb more of such senseless losses than the south can."

"Why do men do that? Why did you go to the Army, Mr. Kelley?"

"The military and the war are about the only way open for a young man to take the measure of himself. You can't do that by livin' comfortably on your pa's farm. I had to know what kind of a man I was, or could be. They say that battles allow you to establish your value system. Pa says that people know what you really care about by what you are willing to die for. Besides, I always wanted to see what was over that next hill. Recon I still do."

Mrs. Graham picked up the empty cup and tin plate then stood and stared off at the horizon and the retreating light of day. "How many times do we do this to each other, Mr. Kelley, before someone says, 'Alright, that's enough'? Is there a greater meaning to it all, that as a widow with a child to raise alone I just can't understand; is it some will of God that we destroy ourselves, some Divine punishment of the human race? Yes Mr. Kelley, you can stay here and help out till your friend can travel on." Then, without a word, she disappeared through the summer kitchen door. John sat a moment trying to understand what had just happened here, and then went to find his pallet in the barn. This was the first night for longer than he could remember he was not either the hunter, or the hunted. But again that night in his fitful sleep, he would be forced, against his will, to revisit the slaughter known as White Mountain.

The next morning John saddled the gray mare, and with Mathew riding up front, they went to gather moss and Peruvian tree bark. Later, under the very specific instructions of Mrs. Graham, John pulverized the bark, mixed it with the moss and the white of three eggs; and helped apply the mixture to Glenn's wounds, which were then bound. John thought Glenn looked very bad. His eyes were sunken and dark, his skin was very hot and a pale gray color, except for the wounds. They were red and angry looking over a large area with red streaks running up under his arm, and leaking a yellowish, green mess. When John said, "Friend, you're laying here burnin' daylight", Glenn opened his eyes, smiled faintly and then closed them again. He was clearly sinking.

The balance of day two, John cut replacement fence posts, and stretched and nailed fence wire. By evening the pasture was once again enclosed and after milking, John turned the cow and the two horses out. Mathew came to call him to wash up for supper with the usual instructions, "remember what ma said about no guns around the house!" The meal was much the same as last night, except Mrs. Graham had used the left over egg yolks in some fresh from the oven corn bread. As they sat on the wash bench and talked, John asked about her husband. She got kind of a far off look in her eyes and replied, "As I told you he was a hard man, a man with something he needed to prove if only to himself. When things went his way, he was fine, but when he was challenged; either by people, by animals…or just by the events of daily life, he could quickly become violent. One night he came home from some heavy drinking, it was well after dark, Mathew's dog heard him before he could smell him, and began barking and raising a fuss. As he came charging up to John Henry, my husband grabbed an iron bar from the gate, knocked the dog down and then proceeded to beat him to death. You never heard such howling and agony from a dying animal and all the time John Henry is screaming and cussing the dog at the top of his lungs. When the dog was finally dead, John Henry charged into the house and grabs Mathew out of bed to drag him out to see his dead pet. I jumped in the way to try to protect Mathew and John Henry beat me to the floor, pulled me up and beat me down again. Then he put Mathew under his arm, carried him into the yard and made him look at the dog. He was screaming, 'that's what happens to anything that doesn't obey me'. Now Mathew's hysterical and runs back into the house, only to find his mother on the floor bleeding from the nose and mouth. It was quite a time. It was weeks before the swelling left my face and my eye opened again, but that was not the first time he had hit me, nor would it be the last. At first light, while John Henry slept off the liquor, I pulled the dog's carcass up behind the barn and buried it, then scrubbed the blood off of the stones on the walkway. To this day Mathew has never asked about his dog."

John sat in stunned silence, not certain what to even say…he has just never heard of such a thing. He secretly hoped that he <u>had</u> been the one to kill Captain John Henry Graham on White Mountain. But he just softly said, "Sorry" and turned his eyes to the cold plate of food in his lap.

Over the next few days, John and Mathew rode up to gather more moss and bark, replaced the missing shingles on the house and barn roof, repaired the siding on the barn, and caught a nice mess of bullheads from a close by stream. John was feeling better than he had felt in a long time; he was enjoying the farm work and the feeling that he was doing some real good for someone. He would look forward all day to his evening conversations with Mrs. Graham on the wash bench by the summer kitchen door, and later his daily cool down bath in the horse trough before he went to his pallet. He was only invited into the house once during that time to help treat Glenn, but that was okay, he knew his place and stayed in it. John was just grateful to be allowed to remain and sleep in the barn while Glenn was getting help. And over the next week of having his wounds treated twice a day, Glenn did seemed to be getting some better. The wounds were less angry and as they improved, Glenn's color and spirits seemed to improve some as well. Perhaps soon they could continue on to Texas. John knew he would be real torn when it came time to plan their leaving. He wanted to get to Texas and start his new life, and he had given his word to see Glenn home, but he imagined leaving Mrs. Graham and Mathew was going to be some more difficult than he had ever considered when he first rode up that wagon lane .

Two days later while John was going through his morning clean up and shave behind the barn, he heard a group of riders in the door-yard, then men shouting loudly at the house, "get out here you damned deserters." He quickly pulled up his suspenders, toweled the remaining shaving soap from his face and ran through the barn to look through the half open door of the horse stall. What he saw made his blood run cold. Four mounted Confederate soldiers, unshaven and in very shabby, dirty uniforms were confronting Mrs. Graham as she stood by the gate to her door-yard. The same spot where she had confronted Glenn and him a few days earlier. As John watched, the leader dismounted and moved directly into her face shouting in a rage. Even from this distance, John could make out enough to know they were searching for the two of them. They were bounty hunters, for certain. "Been trailing those bastards all the way from the river, know they came here. Had a shot at them as they crossed the river, should have drowned....killed one of my men...damned deserters...reward dead or alive." Mrs. Graham, hands on her hips, was defiantly shaking her head 'no' and denying whatever he was accusing her of. As she did so, the leader kept pressing his filthy beard covered face closer to her and becoming louder and more animated in his questioning. She set her jaw firm and continued to stand her ground and shake her head. The renegade leader reached out and grabbed her by both shoulders and shook her hard enough for her head to snap back and her hair started to fall from the neat bun on her neck. But she toughed it out and would not take that first step backward. She brought her arms up quickly between his and brushed his hands away from her. At that point he shoved her backward by repeatedly hitting her on the chest with the heel of each hand. John stepped away from the door and grabbed the Spencer from beside his pallet. As he returned to the doorway he chambered home a shell. He looked back to the yard, the leader had just flipped something golden and shinny into the air in front of Mrs. Graham's face. It turned over and over as it climbed, with each turn catching the sunlight as it arched high above her head. While she was watching its flight and the start of its decent, he struck her with the full roundhouse swing of his open right hand. The blow popped as it caught her square on the left side of the face, between her eye and ear. Her head snapped back and she crumbled over backwards. Like a rag doll that had been thrown aside she tumbled into the dirt of the door yard, at about the same place where years earlier another crazy man had beaten a little boy's dog to death. Sarah struggled to come to her hands and knees, the blood and spittle dripped from her nose and open mouth, her undone summer straw hair now hanging down in a ragged pattern hiding her face. The leader looked down on her with a sneer, then put his boot on her hip and pushed her down on her face into the dirt. Again, she started to struggle to rise, and again the boot and the shove.

In a blind rage, John kicked open the lower half stall door and charged through screaming, "try that on me you renegade son-of-a-bitch, I'm what you're looking for if you're man enough!" The leader turned away from his prostrate victim to face toward John. He started the reach toward the holster on his right hip, but John, on a dead run, raised the Spencer and fired taking him through the middle of the chest. His body was lifted upwards then flew backwards from the force of the .44 slug on his body, and he was dead when he hit the ground. Still of the run, John chambered a new shell, raised and fired at the mounted soldier closest to him. He went flying backwards over the horse's rump, causing the four horses to dance and snort. Still coming on, John tried to again chamber a round, but the empty casing had split and the chamber was jammed. He jacked the lever twice, to no avail. John automatically reached to his hip, but no holster…the words, "and no guns around the house" rang in his head. He turned the Spencer like a club and continued to charge toward the remaining two, but each was already clearing leather with their side arms as they fought to control their horses. The furthest one came around in a full circle and when he turned back toward John his gun was up in his hand, coming to aim. At that moment a pale, sickly looking young man dressed only in his long johns and bandages, without boots or hat came through the summer kitchen door with a Colt in his right hand. Glenn took two steps into the yard, stopped, aimed and fired twice. Suddenly all four horses carried empty saddles. One of the soldiers rolled over and tried to bring his gun to bear on Glenn, but too late. As Glenn fired again, the soldier's face turned bright red and his head snapped backward into the dirt. The fourth man was trying to rise as John arrived on the run and hit him in the side of the head with the Spencer, now turned club. That quick, the fight was done.

John bent and carefully lifted Mrs. Graham, cradling her gently in his arms and wiping the dirt and blood away with his bandana. Glenn hobbled to the four fallen soldiers to make certain the fight was done…it was! John carried her into the house, he was surprised how light she was, and carefully laid her on her bed. Then he called Mathew to fetch some cool water from the spring-house. As he carefully bathed her face, neck and swollen left eye with the cool water, she groaned and opened her good right eye briefly, giving John the warmest smile anyone had ever sent in his direction. John noticed the deep green was flecked with little brown specks, then she closed her eye and went into a deep sleep. John left Mathew to watch his mother, and moved to help Glenn back to his cot on the summer porch. "You saved my life friend, when the Spencer jammed they had me for certain. But I don't know if you shot them or scared 'em to death, you did look damned strange coming through that door!"

"Well I hate to travel alone, besides you got a good bargain. Your butt was saved and you didn't even have to pretend to be a Yankee prisoner. How's Mrs. Graham?"

"She was hit damn hard, her cheek is cut and her eye is swelled shut, but she is out of it now and Mathew's with her. If you're okay, I'll go dispose of our guests before someone else shows up"

"I'll be okay, go. What you gonna' do with them?"

"Bury 'em behind the barn if there's any space up there not being used. That's where everything else seems to wind up here."

When John returned from the first trip to the barn to drag the last two bodies up to their final resting place, his eye found in the dust the shinny gold object the renegade had flipped into the air before he hit Mrs. Graham. When he held it in his hand he was looking at the same $10 Eagle that he had given Mrs. Miller for the crossing toll. It had her opposing teeth marks where she had bit it to test if it was real gold, or just another Yankee trick. As John thought about the Millers, and what this group of worthless renegades must have done to her while trying to claim the 'deserter's bounty', his breath got all caught up in his chest and moisture formed in his eyes. It made the digging of a mass grave more of a labor of satisfaction. John turned the four horses out with the others, kept the best two saddles and bridles, and buried every other item that came with the renegades. As a last thought before rolling the four bodies into the hole he had dug, he searched the bodies and the saddlebags, found $150 Confederate, a large bundle of good cigars and in a saddlebag, a full bottle of homemade whiskey. He saved these valuables and covered everything else in the hole.

John made some coffee, and then returned to sit by the side of Mrs. Graham's bed to watch her sleep. Her left eye was swollen, probably completely shut, and an ugly bruise was coming up on the side of her face around the cut. John imagined he could see the outline of the renegade's handprint on her white, pale skin. In spite of her wounds, or perhaps because of them, John thought she was the most beautiful woman he had ever seen, and as he watched her he noticed his breathing, once again, became more difficult. She finally stirred as if she could sense that she was being watched and opened her eye, at first with a look of panic, then when she saw John, she relaxed and smiled at him. "Mrs. Graham, it's alright, the renegades are dead 'n gone and you and Mathew are safe. You took a nasty blow to the head and you're gonna' hurt for awhile, so please, just rest."

"Mr. Kelley, after what we went through here this afternoon, I think it would be considered proper if you just called me Sarah and I called you John. Don't worry about the blow to the head; I've been hit much harder."

"But you won't ever be again, Sarah. That I promise you!"

"John, I'm so sorry, I almost got you killed by my silly instructions that you couldn't wear your gun around the place. I heard your rifle jam and I knew that you were not wearing a holster because I had said, 'no guns'. All I could think of was Sarah you fool, you just got that nice young man killed and all he ever did was try to help you."

"Actually, it was you saved me. You did such a good job fixing up Glenn, that he was able to come through that porch door and end the fight. We both thank you for that." Then he told her how strange Glenn looked comin' through the door-yard in his long johns. She started to smile at his funny story, but a look of pain suddenly came to her face.

These two young people who had come so close to death just hours earlier, said little more, but just quietly looked at each other for a long while in the soft, flickering light of the lamp. My God, but she was beautiful! Finally John stood, touched her hand and said, "You need rest, I'll see to Mathew and whatever else needs doing. You sleep."

With that said he took her hand in his, held it open, and then folded it over $150 Confederate and a $10 gold coin with teeth marks. "Hold tight to that Sarah, that's the future for you, for Mathew…and for this farm." Then with a happy heart and a light step, turned, walked through the kitchen and into the cool spring night. He needed a bath, some sleep and, now that he again had some whiskey, a stiff drink. Perhaps just not in that order.

Author's Note: The Battle of White Mountain described in this chapter is a figment of the Author's imagination, but was typical of the numerous conflicts waged in northern Arkansas and southwestern Missouri as the Federal forces attempted to secure the critical border state of Missouri for the Union. Missouri was important, not only for its resources and manpower, but because it controlled the major waterways of the Mississippi and Missouri Rivers, both critical to the support of the war in the west.

The Battle of Pea Ridge (the Confederates termed it Elkhorn Tavern) was for real. That battle was fought on March 6, 7 and 8, 1862, in northwest Arkansas between 16,500 troops under the command of Confederate Major General Earl Van Dorn, including 800 Cherokee Indians; and the 10,200 Union troops under command of Brigadier Samuel Curtis. Before the War, Curtis had been a congressman and one of the founders of the new Republican Party which had nominated Abraham Lincoln for President. Curtis had been informed in advance as Van Dorn moved out of Fayetteville and had secured his Union forces behind solid defensive positions. The result was a solid Union victory with over 4,000 Confederate casualties to about 1,900 for the Union and the action successfully secured the state of Missouri for the Union.

Pea Ridge was actually the third battle in this critical struggle. The first two; the Battle of Carthage (MO) on July 5, 1861, which was the first land battle of the Civil War, and the Battle of Wilson's Creek (MO) on August 10, 1861, both were Confederate victories, but cost the Confederates men and supplies that could not be replaced.

The last major battle for control of Northwest Arkansas was on December 7, 1862, at Prairie Grove, Arkansas, between Confederate General Thomas Hickman's 9,000 men of the Trans-Mississippi Army, and Union General James Blunt's 8,000 men of The Army of the Frontier. The hard-fought battle resulted in a solid Union victory, with each side experiencing a greater that 15% loss of forces in a single day. The Iowa 19th Regiment lost 49% of its men in this eight hour battle.

Chapter Eight

"THE PATROL, II"

John stepped out into the door-yard, looked into the night sky and stretched. It had been one hell of a day for each of them, and though light of spirit, he was more exhausted than he could ever remember. He hoped he could stay awake long enough for that drink and bath that he had promised himself. As he started through the dark night toward the barn, he took note of the heavy cloud cover growing in the western sky. Gonna' be some kind of weather before dawn, he thought, but the animals were secure and he was too weary to worry about weather…couldn't do much about it anyway.

Sometime, much later that night John was awakened abruptly by the wind banging the old siding on the barn. He rolled over to look upward through the hay-mow door, but saw only blackness; not a star was visible to his limited viewing area. As the wind sang its way through the barn, John was suddenly very cold…strange for so late in the season. He reached to pull up his extra blanket, and then thought, that house will be cold without a fire. Best go start one…. besides that would give him a fine excuse to look in on Sarah. As he stepped through the barn door the full force of the storm descended upon him. The small ice crystals stung his face as they were being driven on the wind sweeping down the slopes of the Ouachita Mountains to the north. He grabbed up an arm load of split wood on the way to the house. Glenn was up and held the door for him. "I just assumed that even in my weakened condition, I was going to have to go out in this storm and get that wood. First I have to save your Yankee ass in a gun fight you started but couldn't finish, then have to do your chores too?"

"By my count, you still owe me at least one more saving…probable more. First one was on the field at The Landing then a day later with the Union patrol….likely a lot more than that, but in the interest of our friendship, I just quit keeping score."

Then from inside the house Sarah was heard from, "John would you please quite picking on that poor wounded Southern hero and build us a fire before the good people in here freeze to death?"

The three of them drank hot black coffee and talked beside Sarah's bed until the storm passed and it started getting light. Sarah's eye was still swollen shut and the bruise on her face was turning dark purple and angry, but she was feeling better and her good spirits matched John and Glenn's. As they told stories about their previous lives, she told them about her older brother trying to physically attack her when she was eleven years old and her pa sending her off to live with an aunt in Little Rock. She was still mad about the injustice…her brother had done the wrong, but because he was needed to work on the farm, she got sent away. Her aunt saw to it that she was able to get some education while she helped in her family's boarding house. Then she met John Henry Graham when he was a guest there. He was thought by her Aunt to be quite a prize, and later when he ask her, she married him and never went back to her Pa's house again. Her mother was now dead and she didn't know where her pa or brother were, nor did she much care. With that, she shooed them out to get cleaned up while she got out of bed and made breakfast for all. John knew in his heart, he had never seen a more beautiful woman, swollen eye, bruised face, and all. She fairly made his heart sing!

After breakfast, John announced that since it was a day of celebration in his family, he was going to saddle the gray mare and do some scouting around the wagon trails, but would be back in time to do chores tonight, so both Sarah and Glenn should try to get some rest.

Sarah paused in deep thought. "A day of celebration? What's being celebrated, we just had the fourth of July?"

"My family are what's called in Ireland as 'Orange Irish', that's Protestant rather than Catholic Irish. My grandfather came from Waterford, Ireland as a young man and while he was alive, we always celebrated every 12th of July and he would again tell us the story of the great victory. That is the day in 1690 when William III of Orange defeated King James II at the Battle of Boyne to preserve Protestantism in Ireland. Otherwise we Irish would all be serving the Pope."

"Well since it's such a widely celebrated holiday John, by all means, take a day off!"

John and the big gray headed down the lane and turned toward the west; they'd both seen the East and there was certainly nothing back there that held any interest for either. The mare was very frisky from her long rest and good pasture and John put slack in the reins so she could set her own pace. They had gone about a mile and a half when John spotted a farmhouse setting back off to the right. It looked well-tended and friendly with a recent coat of white wash, so John eased the mare up the lane toward the house. As he approached he heard a woman's voice from the side garden, "Hello stranger, what can I do for you this fine summer day?"

John turned toward the voice and removed his hat, "Good morning Ma'am, I'm trying to find me a new pup for a fine young boy who recently lost his dog. Would you be having any pups on the place looking for a good home?"

"No. I'm sorry we don't. But it's a good mission you're on; every young boy should have a pup to raise up. I heard tell they recently had pups up at the Purcell place."

"Thank you Ma'am, just where might that be?"

"I didn't think you was from around here just from the way you talk."

"No Ma'am I'm not. Now just where did you say the Purcell place was?"

"Maybe I shouldn't be telling you…you being a stranger and all."

"Well I would be sorry about that Ma'am, and a little boy would be heart broken. I thank you for your time and trouble, and good day to you."

As he put his hat back on and turned the gray back down the lane John heard, "It's about two mile to the west on the south side of the road." John waved back over his head and shouted, "Thank you Ma'am. I won't tell 'em who told me!

John was enjoying the pleasant change in the weather and the dogwood trees covered in full leaf now with just a few remaining white blooms along the roadway. While alert to what was going on around him, he was none the less relaxed and allowing both the mare and himself to enjoy this pleasant day far from the war. It gave him a chance to think about Sarah and Mathew, and to wonder how all of this might turn out. He would like them to stay in his life, of that he was certain, but there was the promise he had made to Glenn and thoughts of that kept getting in the way of any plans he might make that included Sarah. As John rounded a bend in the road he spotted a four-man mounted patrol about a half-mile ahead. He quickly moved the gray into the tree line and pulled the sight glass from his saddlebag. They were Confederate for damn sure, and the four of them led by a Lieutenant, green from the appearance of their mounts and their uniforms, and headed this way. No question, but they had seen him as one was now pointing in John's direction. Well, the bluff worked once, let's try it again. But just in case it didn't, John moved the holster around on top of the saddle so he could reach the Colt with either hand, then pulled the Spencer from the boot, chambered a shell, and laid it across his left forearm. Now set for whatever their mission might be, he put the gray back onto the roadway and headed toward them.

As the distance narrowed, John could see the Lieutenant trying to look more official. He moved to sit very straight in the saddle and re-buttoned the top button of his tunic. He turned and snapped orders to the other three and they also sat straight and fell into single file. John moved again to the right side of the roadway to put the Spencer's muzzle close on the leader, without seeming to do so. The patrol halted on the Lieutenant's command and waited for John to approach. John moved the gray mare into a position that had the Spencer's muzzle about six inches in front of the Lieutenant and enjoyed watching his obvious discomfort at the arrangement, but not knowing just how to get out of it.

"Good day to you sir," offered the Lieutenant. "Who are you and where might you be headed?"

"I am Captain Jonas Markum of the 6th of Arkansas, and believe my mission this day to be one of my own keeping."

"I am authorized to inquire of your mission Captain, Sir."

"Just by what authority would that inquire be, Lieutenant?"

"I am Lieutenant Samuel Hicks of the Arkansas Headquarters Company out of Little Rock."

"I thought so; you all just look like rear echelon people to me, the total of you haven't seen five minutes of the real war. Where do you get off stopping me? Just what is your mission, anyway, and be quick about it Lieutenant? I am without uniform so I don't expect your salute, but by god, I will not tolerate your disrespect." John was truly beginning to enjoy his new role. Maybe he should have held out for a commission.

"Captain, Sir. We are sent to spread the word about the new conscription law just signed by President Davis and to look for candidates for conscription to the army under that law."

"I haven't heard it, what's that all about?"

"After the heavy losses in our victories at Forts Henry and Donelson, and then again at Shiloh Church, President Davis signed into law the Conscription Act requiring three years of military service for every healthy, white male between the ages of eighteen and thirty-five. Also, all one year musters have now been extended to a full three years."

"Lieutenant I'd be cautious about calling those three engagements victories, you just might be talking to one who had been there. What are the exceptions, with this government there are always exceptions?"

"Yes Sir! Certain occupations are exempt, like teachers, civil officials, and the overseers of twenty or more slaves."

"That must be real popular with the poor white folks who are doing the fightin' and diein' of this war so others can stay safe and tend their slaves!"

"Yes sir, it's been termed, *'The Twenty-Nigger Rule'*. But I reckon everyone is also rightfully concerned about hundred of thousands of unsupervised slaves running loose through the south. Captain, I beg your pardon sir, but do you have any identification. You are after all not in uniform and while your horse carries a CSA brand, I judge those to be Yankee arms you carry."

"Lieutenant you should be begging my bye-your-leave, not my pardon. I'm not in uniform because mine rotted away from the rains during and following the battle at Shiloh Church, clearly yours has never been so abused. I carry Union arms as they are vastly superior to those issued to us by our own new government. While I am not carrying any papers, I do have a compass, a gift, inscribed with my name." With that, John made a move to his saddlebag to retrieve the compass he knew was there. As he did so, the Private who had moved his mount to the right side of John made a jerky, faltering move to his right hip. John stopped and quickly swung the Spencer in a wide arc, catching the startled Private across the bridge of the nose with the barrel. The blood and the Private both flew. In the same motion, his left hand pulled the Colt, cocked it and brought it chest level on the startled Lieutenant. "Lieutenant one more stupid, clumsy move like that and you will be out here conscripting just to refill the ranks of your detail." John looked down at the startled Private on the ground; his nose was clearly broken with blood flowing freely. "Get up Boy." He was probably a year younger that John. "You'll live this time, but don't ever make a jerky move like that again. If you're going to draw your damn weapon, do it! Don't try to decide in mid-motion. Next time you'll most likely die while in debate with yourself."

"Now then Lieutenant, do you want to see my inscribed compass, or not?"

The Lieutenant responded with wide eyes and a less than firm voice, "yes Sir. If you please, Sir." Somehow his respect had returned.

With that, John withdrew the instrument, turned it over, rubbed it on his shirt to polish it up and handed it to the Lieutenant.

He examined it, "yes Sir, 'Captain Jonas P. Markum, CSA', thank you Captain Markum." And with that returned it to John.

"Now then Lieutenant, I suggest you and your detail go on about your mission. I'm going to sit here and watch you go till you're out of sight, just to be certain no more stupid moves get made. One last thing Lieutenant, about five miles up this road, on the right, is the farm of the Graham's. In that house is the widow of a brave Confederate Captain killed at White Mountain, and a man wounded twice at Shiloh Church, who is trying to recover sufficiently from his wounds to journey to his home. I would suggest to you that neither would be interested in your story of conscription or the *'Twenty-Nigger Rule'*. My advice to you is to pass the house by, because both of those good citizens of the Confederacy can be as unfriendly as a hornet's nest and are damned good shots."

"Yes Sir. Thank you Sir. Now bye-your-leave, Sir."

"Carry on."

With that, the patrol moved out and, as promised, John moved to the side of the road and watched them out of sight. Just before they turned the corner, the Private turned and looked back to see if John was still there watching. He was. While he waited for the patrol to make the bend in the road, John thought about the new conscription law that Davis and the Confederacy had placed in effect. It certainly did not affect Glenn, what with his bad wounds and all. But what if the Union had done that? Would he still feel he had done his full duty by serving almost 14-months on the 12-month enlistment? Would he have felt he was as justified in riding away from the war, his duty done? He'd have to think on that some more…or perhaps not.

John found the Purcell place just as directed. As he started up the lane a short, square built man with a full salt 'n pepper beard came out of the barn and waved a greeting. John waved in return and moved the gray toward the barn. "Fine looking mare you got there, son."

"Thank you sir, as you can see she is provided to me by our President, Mr. Davis."

"Don't usually see many riders out this way, and now you are my second visitor of this morning. Just had a young Lieutenant and a patrol stop by to see if we had anyone living here to conscript into the army. Is that not the stupidest thing? I thought that was why we were a fightin' this war to keep the government from telling us everything what we had to do. Well ma didn't want to go in the army just now, and I'm too old, so they went on their way."

"Yes sir, I had a little discussion with them up the road a ways back. Since I'm already in the army, they felt they couldn't use me either. Don't believe they were having a very good day."

"Well I know you didn't come here to hear me jaw about the damned government....not the one in Washington City and not the one in Richmond, so what can I do for you young man?"

"I'm looking for a new pup for a boy who recently lost his and I was told back up the road that perhaps you had some might be looking for a home."

"Matter of fact I do have four, that's the mother over yonder. I think I can just fix your boy up." John turned in the saddle and saw a big shepherd looking female. Turning back he said, "Its not for my boy sir, it's the son of a friend of mine."

"Who might that be?"

"Mathew Graham, John Henry and Sarah Graham's boy."

"You know John Henry do you?"

"No sir never had the pleasure. Mrs. Graham is tending to a comrade of mine who was badly wounded at Shiloh Church, and I'm doing some work around the place to pay for our keep."

"As I recall that place needs more than just some work, John Henry never was much for farming. Well step down and let's look at the animals, then the Mrs. can fetch us some coffee."

"I welcome the coffee Sir, but if it suits you, I'd just as soon let the boy come make his own pick. Then we'll be sure it'll be just the right one."

The two men sat in chairs placed under a big cottonwood tree in the side yard and enjoyed their coffee with fresh cream, and the cigars that John produced from his saddlebag. They spoke of many things, the weather, the war and the wartime prices, spring crops, some of Mr. Davis' policies, and that long, tall fool in Washington City. Eventually Mr. Purcell got back to John Henry Graham. "I heard tell Captain John Henry got himself killed up there on White Mountain."

"Yes sir, he sure did that."

"Just could not have happened to a more deserving person. If that pretty Mrs. Graham had any close kin worth a damn, John Henry would have been dead long before now."

"I don't follow you sir."

"Yes, I think you do young man, the look around your eyes gives you away. He beat on that pretty young woman a whole lot. My Mrs. was up there when the boy got sick three, four years ago. Said she was covered with bruises, lip split, and her eye blackened. Reckoned the Yankees did her some kind of a favor." John took a long drink from his coffee mug to cover the smile on his face.

Needing to change the subject away from Sarah, John said, "That's a fine looking crop of spring calves you got coming along there, must be 25 or 30 of 'um, but I've never seen those markings before."

"I think about 27 survived, now comes the chore of weaning that many and getting them on pasture. They are Black Angus and Hereford, each of blood-lines that are new here from Scotland and England. But thanks to the war and the blockade, cattle ain't worth much and no one I know in the south's got money to buy calves now anyway."

"What do you wean them on?"

"I just put them on pasture when its up well enough, but for a few weeks I feed them a mixture of milled oats and skim milk. Thin mixture at first, then gradually thicker, then in a few weeks just grass."

"I'm not familiar with the breed. What's their strength?"

"Much heavier beef cattle. They get heavy faster and the meat is leaner than the Longhorn or those Brahman cattle up from Mexico. Not as hardy on the trail as the Longhorn, but their tough enough, just drives slower."

"What would a good heifer calf bring, if you could find anyone with money?"

"At this stage, ready to start the weaning, I'd be pleased to get $5 in Mr. Davis' paper money."

"What would a $5 gold piece buy?"

"I'd be tempted to throw a second calf into a deal like that, if'n I knew anyone with a $5 gold piece, that is. We was supposed to turn in our gold some months ago."

"I just happen to still have one that my ma gave me before I left for the war. I believe we could strike a deal if you'd let me pick the calves, and throw in a couple of bags of those milled oats to see them through to pasture."

"You know son, I've got more calves than I can use and raise up, but I've got no $5 gold pieces. I'll also throw in a drink of good whiskey to seal the bargain, if you'll throw in another of them cigars."

They grinned at each other and shook hands. "Mister Purcell, we've just made ourselves a bargain!"

They drank and smoked, talked loud and laughed until late in the afternoon. Mrs. Purcell came out on two occasions to see if they were alright, and clearly they were, if you call getting a little drunk in the middle of the day, alright. John gave over the $5 gold piece over Mr. Purcell's objections that he shouldn't pay until he picked up the calves. "Hell", John replied, "I might get conscripted on the way back to the Graham place, and then you'd be out your only $5 gold piece."

"I have some considerable doubt one man, or a green Confederate patrol could get that done, face-to-face. Now Mr. Kelley, we've made us a good bargain and had us a good drink or two, with your permission I'd like to ask you a personal question."

"Yes Sir, you may ask me anything."

"From the way you talk, I knowed right away you're not from these parts, but I've come to believe perhaps you were wearing the blue, not the gray in this war. That be true?"

"That's the truth. I was in the Union army for 14 months; left after the slaughter at Pittsburg Landing, the battle the South calls Shiloh Church. I'm nursing a badly wounded former enemy home to Texas. As for the mare, she wasn't being used at the time I found her. If any of that bothers our deal Sir, I'll be pleased to let you out it."

"Not a chance. I haven't seen a damn gold piece since Mr. Davis called them all in. You seem like an honest man and if you can help that nice Mrs. Graham and that boy of hers get on their feet again, I'm all for you. Just don't think you're fooling too many people. How about that patrol, did they accept your story?"

"I don't know. They decided to ride on rather than push the issue. You know it's gettin' on in the day, I best be riding on too."

The two men stood and shook hands again, this time, for a long while. Finally Mr. Purcell asked, "How you gonna' get them calves?"

"The boy and I'll be back in a day or two in a wagon to gather 'em all up."

As John was mounting, Mrs. Purcell came out with a big basket and a flour sack, both heavy with, "…a few things for that nice Mrs. Graham." John tipped his hat, said his "thank yous' and started back up the lane.

"Katie, that's a fine young man."

"Yes. Too bad he has to go back to the war."

"Yes. Isn't it!"

As John rode into the door-yard and dismounted, Glenn hobbled through the kitchen door, "This must be the famous Captain Jonas P. Markum we've heard so much about this day?"

"I take it you've had company while I was gone?"

"We had an angry Lieutenant and a Private with a busted face. You do that?"

"We had a discussion up the road on Military Protocol, and the proper way to draw a weapon. I did find out something about myself. You know, it's a good thing I was never made an officer….I'd probably of been a real bastard."

"You're not being an officer has had no sway on that result, you still made it there and back just fine! It's fortunate I got so mad about that compass when you first showed it to me. Otherwise I would not have remembered the name."

"It was the only thing I could think of when they stopped me. Did they accept your story?"

"What story? I told them the truth, just like my ma always taught me. That you're a combat crazy Yankee, out of uniform, behind the lines and they should hang your carcass as a spy, and be heroes."

"Well, they truly ought not to try. We've still got room for some more plantin' up behind the barn."

"I remembered the Captain's name, and after they looked at my papers, they seemed satisfied and rode off. I frankly don't think they wanted any more of you anyway. The Lieutenant wasn't all that certain you were a Captain, but I explained to him you were always in a foul mood and would probably ship the Lieutenant's ass off to the war in Virginia just for spite."

John handed down the basket and flour sack. "Tell Sarah these are from Mrs. Purcell. I'll be in after I tend to the mare and clean myself up. I'll also tell her about going into the cattle business. Is there any coffee? I've got a bad awful ache in my head for some reason."

Author's Note: On March 3, 1863, President Lincoln did sign the first Union Conscription Act. Enrollment was demanded of males between the ages of twenty and forty-five, although hired substitutes, or the payment of $300 could be used for an exemption. Draft riots followed in the major eastern cities of the north.

Chapter Nine

"THE DUKE"

John saw to the needs of the gray mare first, then to his own. Afterwards he hurried to the house anxious to share the news of this day with the only friends he now had in the world. As he opened the door to the summer kitchen, the wonderful aroma of the coming evening feast filled the house. Sarah was excited about having such a variety of foods to work up a supper with. The flour sack and the basket from Mrs. Purcell held items Sarah had not seen since before John Henry left for the war. When she turned to greet John the excitement was mirrored on her face and in her smile. John couldn't remember anyone ever smiling at him in just such a way... her entire face smiled. "Oh John, this is going to be a real celebration meal, come sit and have some fresh ground coffee! Tell us all about this cattle business."

"Well, Mr. Purcell and I struck a bargain for two calves, ready to be weaned and enough ground meal to carry them over to the grass. I'll take the wagon up there in a couple of days and carry them back. Mathew could be lots of company for me, if you'll let him go along."

"Sure he can go, be a good experience for him and he loves being with you. John Henry had always thought Mr. Purcell a tough trader, what did you have to bargain with?"

Glenn could no longer stand being excluded and jumped in, "certainly not your charm or winning ways, and how is it you're going to get those calves home?"

"I had a five dollar gold piece from before and I traded Mr. Purcell with that."

But Glenn wouldn't let it go, "From before what?"

"From before you, now get off of it", John snapped. Then as he turned to Sarah, John's smile returned and his voice again softened, "I figure to fix up the spring wagon, and match-up a team out of a couple of the horses the renegades aren't going to be needing anymore. They won't be strong enough to bust sod with, but they can drag a wagon around. One of these days you'll need a way to get to town to pay the taxes, now that you are a lady of means."

Then realizing he had not only stolen away the attention from Glenn, but had cut short one of his only two friends, John turned back to Glenn and added, "You saved me by the way you dealt with that conscription patrol this afternoon, I appreciate you gettin' me off the hook. Had you done it less well, their suspicions would have brought more of them back next time. That Lieutenant was more than a little bent out of shape over me."

Glenn smiled and nodded, "actually, it was the Private that you bent out of shape with your rifle barrel."

With that they all had a good laugh together.

Over a supper of fried ham, eggs, potatoes, golden brown skillet biscuits, strawberry jam and coffee, they talked about the new calves and about getting some kind of a cash crop going for Sarah so she could meet the needs of her farm and of her son. Now that the milk cow was on full pasture and was producing much more than the house could use, they just needed a way to store it and keep it fresh. John offered that he could dig the fill dirt out of the spring-house and repair the roof so they could keep the extra milk and cream cool there. Sarah could skim the cream and sell it, or she could churn butter from it. That was a cash crop that would provide well for their needs. In a couple of years when the calves came fresh, they could be the start of a herd. John realized how excited he was at the prospect of more work, and would later wonder about that. He for sure had never been that excited at the work on his pa's place.

They talked and planned the future for Sarah and Mathew just as though John and Glenn would actually be a part of it. As if it all was something that the three of them would be doing together. Finally, as the conversation wound down, John said his 'goodnights' and went through the night air up to the barn. He was much too excited to sleep, so he got a cigar and a little more of the renegades' sour mash, and then eased himself into the cool water of the watering trough. John's thoughts would not leave Sarah. He knew he was developing strong feelings for her and thought she was maybe feeling something for him. He wanted her and Matt to come to Texas with them when he and Glenn would leave in a few days. Yet, everything he was doing on this farm only made Sarah more independent and made it more possible for her to stay here and for him to go on alone. How stupid was that? Yet as a friend, if that was what he was, he could do no less for her. Once they traveled to town and paid the taxes she could be on her own and independent for some time to come. John intended to ask her to come on to Texas with him, or at least join him after he got his start, but he knew before he asked, she was just not going to leave this farm. And he knew just as well, that he could not stay. He had given his word to see Glenn home and would do no less, even knowing Glenn would let him out of his promise, if he asked. Besides, he had a dream too and it had nothing to do with working a poor dirt farm in southern Arkansas…at least before meeting Sarah, it certainly had nothing to do with a poor dirt farm. Now he was having a problem sorting out just what was important to him.

John's sleep was not restful at all…too many thoughts of Sarah with no conclusion, and a little too much sour mash. He was up early and when Glenn hobbled out for his morning ritual he found John leaning on the top rail of the fence, watching the horses.

He sensed Glenn more than turning to see him. "Which of those renegade horses do you think I might match-up for a decent team?"

"Well, those two bays are about the same color and size. They're a little light weight but might work together."

"Unusual as it may be, I agree with you. Here, you hold the gate 'n I'll head the two of them into the barn and leave the rest out here."

Later as the two men got ready to head to the house and wash-up John offered, "They stand well together in the barn…I think they'll work alright."

Glenn stopped and turned toward John, reaching out to take hold of his arm. "John, there's something more we need to talk about than how those damn renegade horses look standing together. In a very few days I will be about as recovered as I'm likely to get and I'm gonna' be anxious to travel on home. It's about as obvious as a horse's ass in an apple tree that you and Sarah are getting some feelings for each other." John started to protest but Glenn held up his hand to silence him, "let me finish, we may not get another chance soon. You have brought me a long way, friend. I'm alive today because you got me off that battlefield, and you've placed your own life at risk for me on more that one occasion since Shiloh Church. Hell, I will always think you would have shot up that Yankee patrol the first day on the road. But, I can make it from here on my own and I want you to know I release you from your promise so you can stay here with Sarah and make that new life you're always talking about. You help me get my gear together and I'll go on and no hard feelings. You've done more for me than any other man ever has."

"You don't miss much lying on that cot in the summer-kitchen, and I thought you were asleep all that time. I do have some strong feelings for Sarah, enough so that I worry about how Sarah and Mathew will get on with this farm after we're gone. I would like them to come on with us to Texas, if only so I don't have to worry about them. I a...well, I a...guess I just feel some responsible for them cause they done so much for us. But I just don't know what my situation might be after we get there. And, not a word has passed between Sarah and me on this subject. So I have no thought as to how she feels about me, nor am I certain how she might feel about leaving the farm...she and I will need to speak of that and soon. But no matter her response, I gave my word to see you home and that I shall be doing. I appreciate your offer to release me from that promise, only a damn good friend would do that, but it's my pledge...I made it, and I'm the only one who could release me from it. Sarah either does feel strong enough that she'll come on with us, or she doesn't...and she won't. Hell, maybe I'll take you home, see Texas, not like the damn ugly place and come back. But no matter, I'll be moving on with you when you think you're fully ready. Now then, you and I don't need to speak on this promise thing any further." As was John's practice, when he had said all he had to say on a subject, he turned, left Glenn standing there looking after him as he walked alone toward the house.

Two days later John was in the barn fitting his pieced-together harness to the renegades' horses, when he heard what sounded like a strange man's voice up by the summer- kitchen. Remembering the last men who had called there, John moved quickly to his bedroll, retrieved the Spencer, and chambered a shell as he stepped to the open half door that looked toward the house. Standing in the shadows, rifle at the ready, John saw a fancy, two-seat, black carriage with a cover on top and a fine looking matched sorrel team standing at the gate to the door yard. The man who stepped-down was about average in most respects, except he wore a black bowler hat...not something you see everyday out here, which he swept off to reveal his thin, slick plastered hair to Sarah as she came through the kitchen door. He looked every bit the gentlemen with his slight bow to the lady of the house, so John eased the hammer down on the Spencer, but did not leave his post at the half-door. Besides, Sarah did not seem the least alarmed at his being there. Soon, a pitcher of cold tea and glasses came out the door and they moved to the bench John had started to build in the shade of the cottonwood. Maybe the gentleman would get a splinter in his butt...serve him right. Finally, John lied to himself that he was no longer interested in Sarah's caller; he had more important work to be doing, and moved back to fitting the harness. But the work seemed to go slow, and not very well as John continued to take long glances at the yard. For a man not interested, he frequently lost his concentration on fitting the harness. But then, it was his duty to provide her protection, should it be needed.

He could not hear what they had to say to each other, wasn't even interested, but the conversation seemed agreeable and pleasant for both parties as they smiled and sipped their tea. Some later, as John continued to take glances, Sarah suddenly stood up tall and straight as a ram-rod, with her clinched hands on her hips, it certainly looked like she was giving her guest 'what for'. She snatched up her tray and glasses, spun on her heel, and went into the house. The guest moved slowly to untie his team and glancing back toward the door through which Sarah has disappeared, tipped his hat to the closed door, snapped the reins and headed the beautiful matched team down the lane. John didn't know what had just happened, but whatever it was...he wasn't disappointed at the obvious outcome. John finished his project, hoping Sarah would reappear and come to the barn, but she did not.

That evening at supper, John waited for Sarah to open up about her visitor, but she remained silent on that subject. Finally, he could stand it no longer. "Noticed you had a caller this afternoon. Wouldn't have noted, but he was drivin' such a beautiful matched team." No response from Sarah, and Glenn just continued looking down at his plate and concentrate on his food. "Looked some like maybe a drummer." The silence was deafening! "Seemed to leave suddenly, like maybe you weren't needin' whatever he was selling."

Sarah turned and quickly stepped in front of John, "you're not going to leave this alone, are you?" Those dark green eyes were flashing, just like the first day she had confronted John in the door-yard with the scattergun. "That distinguished scoundrel with the beautiful team you seem to admire so much is Mr. Bruce Simcox, the Tax

Collector for Ouachita County. He made a special trip out here from Camden, me being the poor widow of a Confederate officer and all, just to remind me that the taxes on this farm were now two years past due. And he wanted to express his concern that Mathew and I might have to give up the place. But just like you told me John, I gave him no indication that I had any ability to pay. With that, he suggested that I could be extra sweet to him and he would just make all of my problems go away and Mathew and I could continue to live here with no worry about any taxes. He would drive out and visit me on occasion and if I was sweet to him, then he could adjust the past-due balance on the tax rolls to keep the farm from a forced sale. I told Mr. Simcox what he could do with his offer of help, and sent him down the road with instructions never to darken my door-yard again. There now, is your curiosity satisfied? May we please eat this supper before I just throw it out?"

John was not worldly wise in the ways of women; his Pa always warned that no man ever became such regardless of how long he lived. But a male instinct told John he should follow Glenn's wise example, and he began to concentrate on his plate of food. Both men finished their meal in record time and beat a hasty retreat to the wash bench in the door-yard. As they were enjoying a renegade cigar and talking about anything else except Sarah's visitor, she hipped open the kitchen door with three cups of coffee in her hands. She handed them around and then sat staring off into the sunset. Finally she offered, "I'm sorry. I'm so very upset, but I didn't aim to take it out on the only two friends I have. I just can't help but wonder, as a young widow with a child, if this is now what I have to look forward to."

"Sarah, Matt and I will be going to get the calves tomorrow, then the day after you and I'll go to the county seat in Camden and pay those taxes. I'll have a little polite conversation with Mr. Simcox. You can introduce me as your brother, or some other relative just come to help out. I think I can discourage his attention. As to the others...well, in a few days Glenn and I are going to again start for his folks' place in Texas and we'd like you and Mathew to come with us...I mean with me. Glenn says you'd both be mighty welcome and well a...I'd...we'd like you to come along."

In the silence that followed, when John turned toward Sarah, her face was flush, her eyes bright and immediately her hands went to smooth her hair, though as always, every strand was nicely in place. Finally she mumbled something about having to think on it, and retreated through the summer-kitchen door.

Glenn looked at John, "Well Yankee that was certainly smooth! Nothing quite like slowly building up to the big question."

"I said it like I thought it…I don't know how to put the words any different." Then having said all he had to say, John picked up his hat, bid "goodnight", and again walked away into the dark toward the barn.

The first rays of the new day were just breaking over the eastern tree line when John tied his newly matched team and wagon to the hitching rail at the door-yard gate. The milking was done, the cow turned out and John was anxious to get on with this day…especially considering the last one had not ended just as he'd planned. He knew Glenn's remark was correct. This would be a big decision for Sarah and he could have eased into it better, besides he realized while trying to get to sleep, the word 'marriage' had never quite come out. What must Sarah be thinking he meant…just what the hell did he mean? Sarah had ham frying in the old black iron skillet, plump biscuits browning and coffee perking in the ancient blue coffee pot. She looked up from her work, but did not make eye contact with John, "good morning, the coffee's ready and Mathew will be out shortly." John poured a cup of coffee, then mumbled something about seeing to the team and went out to sit on the wash bench just as Glenn came into the yard. "Well, if it's not my smooth talking, Yankee friend. You spend the night there on the wash bench waiting for an answer?"

"I truly feel bad about the way this is turning out and I don't have much tolerance for you riding me about it this mornin'."

"John, if you care about Sarah, and I believe you do, then you need to find a way to have a conversation with her on that subject. That's all I'm sayin'. Let her know how you feel about her". Mathew came through the summer-kitchen door with a big smile and a bag of ham and biscuits. "Mamma said we could eat these on the way, cause she knew you wanted to get started. Also, we're to take this basket back to Mrs. Purcell…can we go now, John?"

"Soon as I get me some more coffee."

They went along with out much talking, just eating the biscuits and ham that Sarah had packed for them. John wished for another big mug of hot, black coffee, but they both settled for the cool water in John's canteen. John was pleased with the way his new team moved out smartly together. Only an experienced eye would have noted how new they were at this. John glanced at Mathew sitting up stiff and straight in the spring seat, "you want to drive the horses?"

"Sure. Could I? You know ma wouldn't like it for me to do that."

"Well, it could be our secret, but you're almost seven. Its time you learned how to handle a team. Besides, when Glenn and me leave, you're back to being the man of the place again, and you've got to be able to handle a team of horses."

"You really gonna' go? I thought you liked ma and me and would maybe stay on till pa comes back. You're my bestest friend, if you're gonna' go, I want to go to Texas with you."

"We'll talk on it some more. Now, you want to learn to drive this team?"

"Sure I do. I just don't want you to go away,"

"Wipe the tears so you can see what you're doing. Put the lines over the top of your first finger, through the palm of your hand, and then close each hand around them. That's it. You're going to be a natural horseman. Now, put a little tension on the lines. You don't want to saw on their mouths, but you want them to know you're in charge. If your team gets startled and jumps or tries to run, you've still got a tight grip on your lines."

And thusly did man and boy go down the road together, each filled with unspoken different thoughts, on the same subject.

"You best let me make the sharp turn into the Purcell's' lane. When I was about your age, I turned my team too short and put the wagon in the ditch."

"Did your pa beat you?"

"Na. When he found out neither the horses nor I were hurt, he just sat down on the bank and laughed!"

Mrs. Purcell had seen the wagon turn into the lane and met her visitors at the yard gate. Something was said about milk and fresh baked cookies as she headed for the back-door with Mathew in tow. "Papa is down behind the barn with the calves. He figured you'd be here one of these days. Go on with ya' now, I'll tend to this boy."

Later, their deal done, the two men were back in their favorite spot of shade in the side yard. Two Black Angus calves were halter-tied to the wagon, the bags of ground meal loaded, the team standing easy, and the cigars and the first drink of whiskey of the day in their hands...it being just after the noon-hour, the drink was considered hospitable.

"You made a good choice Boy, with a bull and a heifer calf, Mrs. Graham's got the start of a good herd. You decided what you're gonna' do now?"

"I'm goin' on to Texas, just like I planned."

"Damn. I was hoping you'd either stay and marry that nice lady and raise-up that boy to be a man, or maybe go back to your army."

"Well the first is very tempting, 'cept I'd like them to go to Texas with me."

"What about going back to the war?"

"Can't do that. I've seen all I can handle. That's why I left."

"Thought as much. They say if you look deep into a man's eyes you can tell how much war he's seen. I'd say you've seen one hell of a lot of this war. But I like you, you're a good man and I'd hate it if you got cross-ways with your army."

"I'm done with them, 'sides my time's long up."

At that moment, Mathew came running around the house with his arms overflowing with puppy. There wasn't any spot on Mathew's face that wasn't smiling.

"Look John, look, a puppy! Mrs. Purcell said I could have one if it's alright with mamma. You think it would be alright with mamma... you think so, John?"

"She'd want to know if you would take care of it...feed and water it, clean-up after it and see it has a warm, safe place to sleep. It's just a baby and needs someone who will care for it."

"Oh I promise to do all of that, and it can sleep with me so it won't be lonesome or scared at night."

"Well, since your mamma's not here it's up to me...then I'd say it's alright 'cause you promised all those things. Which one do you want?"

"This one, I want this one cause he likes me best of all of them."

John turned to Mr. Purcell, "I told you the boy would be able to pick just the right one."

As the sun headed toward the western horizon, John and Mathew said their 'goodbyes' and pointed the team up the road. The Purcells stood side-by-side in the yard until they were out of sight. "Jackson, you think John 'll marry with Sarah and give that boy a father?"

"Don't believe so Mother, he's got his mind plum set on goin' to Texas."

"Too bad. That boy sure loves him. That's all he talks about is John. Did you know John and that Mr. McCord killed four Confederate renegade soldiers at the Graham place protecting Sarah?"

"I know Mother, but best we just never heard any of that."

It was near dark when John headed the team up the lane. Mathew and his new pup had long since gone to sleep nestled up tight to John, with the pup lying over both their laps. They had decided that 'Duke' would be a good name for his puppy. From the spread of his paws, John thought he was going to be of regal size, besides John's dog had been named Duke and Mathew like that. As John stopped beside the door-yard gate, Mathew came alert and while John held Duke, Mathew climbed down and taking the pup in his arms, headed for the house on a dead run.

"Please tell your mother I'm going to tend to the stock before I come to the house." As John urged his team forward, he could hear Mathew's excited voice from inside the house.

Later, after caring for his team, turning the calves into the pen he had build, and feeding all of the animals, John came to the wash bench to clean off the day's accumulation of dust. Sarah heard him and came stomping through the door. "Just what made you think another dog would be welcome in this house, after what happened to the last one?" But seeing the astonished look come over John's face, Sarah could not hold her pretend anger and a beautiful smile spread over her face. She quickly wrapped both arms tightly around John's neck, reached up on her tip-toes, her body tight against his, and kissed him full on the mouth. A shock ran through John's body like a close-by lightening strike. The sensation was so exciting he hoped it to never end. That had only happened once before in his entire life, but he had sure thought about it since! "John Michael Kelley you are the most thoughtful man God ever created. In seven years, I've never seen Mathew so full of pure joy. That's why you wanted him to go with you; you knew the Purcell's had pups at their place."

"Yes ma'am that's true, I just hoped you wouldn't be mad when we showed up with one. Mr. Purcell wanted me to bring one the last time I was up there, but I wished Mathew to pick out the one he wanted."

"John, he is so full of love for you. He thinks you are the most wonderful man in this world, and…so do I. Now get washed up, I've kept you supper waiting on the back of the stove."

My, thought John…that surely did feel good.

Mathew was plum worn out and didn't make any argument about bed…especially when he was told, 'yes, Duke could sleep on a mat beside his bed'. Before retiring, he came over and put his arms around John's neck and whispered, "I love you."

"I love you too, Mathew."

John told Sarah and Glenn a little about the calves and what Mr. Purcell had told him about the Angus breed. Then just before going to his own bedroll in the barn, he said, "Sarah, I believe tomorrow would be a good day for you and me to go to the county seat in Camden and get your taxes paid. That should help keep Mr. Simcox at home in the future…especially after he and I talk some about his manners. Also, you could speak with the store keep there about bringing in cream and butter for groceries and cash."

"John, I don't want any trouble to develop between you and Mr. Simcox over what he said to me."

"You forget, I've seen him! I don't 'spect there'll be much trouble at all. Now, goodnight to you both."

John went out into the cool, dark night. As usual, he stopped to look at the sky for weather signs and stretched the stiffness out. Later, while not being able to go to sleep, he thought again, for at least the tenth time, of Sarah's unexpected kiss and the feel of her body tight against his. He wished he had been more ready so he could have done a better job of returning the kiss, but even unprepared, it was a great kiss. She surely did that well! Next time he would be ready...if she would allow a next time. Smiling, he drifted-off to sleep...thinking about the next time.

Chapter Ten

"THE TAX COLLECTOR"

Camden, Arkansas, is the location of the seat of county government of Ouachita County. It is situated between the bluff of the river valley and the Ouachita River, named by the Choctaw Indians for "sparkling waters". The town is set at the head of the navigational waterway; so much of its commerce is related to the river.

Early trappers and French fur traders came and went from the area for many years before 1825 when John Nunn came from Missouri to become the first permanent resident. It was believed he brought the name, 'Camden' from the place of his birth in Alabama. The town was laid out about 1839, but not incorporated until 1884. However, by 1840 a cluster of stores and saloons had grown up around the steamboat landing. In 1841 over 40,000 bales of cotton were sent down river, and the following year the first cotton gin began operation. The biggest shipper became the Lotawanna Steamboat, captained by Captain Jessie T. McMahan who had been severely wounded in the jaw in the early days of this Great War.

As John and Sarah, and their wagon rode the Bradley ferry across the river, the sights he gathered from the river side of the town were not impressive, and, in fact, somewhat concerning. There was almost a frantic level of activity on the docks, much confusion and noise around the steamboat landing, all of which tended to make his green team some spooky. From what he could see as they drove ashore, there were more saloons than homes and at mid-morning the drunks were already whooping it up in the street and the painted women were beckoning from the second floor windows... John saw the dome of what thought might be the Court House and pointed his team away from the rowdies and toward town. He was concerned was that one of them might see the beautiful Sarah and make a remark that he would take offense at. He'd then have a killing on his hands before they ever got all of Sarah's business done. As they were moving along what appeared to be the main street toward the town, Sarah inquired, "John, you are aware that there is a garrison of Confederate soldiers quartered here, aren't you?"

"No, I was not! How'd you know about that?"

"John Henry brought me here only one time, but I recall him pointing out the soldiers at Fort Southerland over on the Bradley-Ferry Road. They're here to guard the ferry crossing. The Officer in charge, General Sterling Price, lives in the McCollum house just up ahead here on Washington Street. John Henry being a Confederate Captain and all, we were invited to tea with the General and his wife."

"Wonderful! I come all this distance and still wind up a prisoner of war. How does it come you only were here the once?"

"A drunken riverboat man made a dirty remark about me and John Henry shot him, even though the man didn't carry a gun. I did find it strange, John Henry would kill an unarmed man to preserve my 'honor', and then he'd get drunk, come home and beat me."

"Sarah, look at all that celebratin', is this some kind of a holiday or somethin'?"

"Pull up there by the telegraph office and I'll go find out."

"John, I'm sorry to be the one to tell you what the celebration's all about; the telegrapher has been getting details about what their calling the Second Battle of Manassas Junction, in Virginia. Seems the Union was soundly defeated with over 16 thousand causalities and General Lee has now crossed the Potomac River and invaded the North." She could see the pain grow in John's eyes as he directed his attention to his skittish team, and turned silent. "John, that would have not been your fight even if you'd stayed. The Union didn't lose that battle because you weren't there."

John's face remained drawn and he became quiet as the old debate raged again within him; should I have left...'yes, your time was up'...'no, you should have stayed until the army said it was right'. 'Then Glenn would be dead...that has to stand for something!' Sarah interrupted the mental tug-of-war, "We best go about getting our business done and get out of here. Go to the Emporium first and I'll give the shopkeeper my supply list and ask about bringing in the cream and butter. It'll be handy cause the Tax Office is just over Washington street. What can I get for you in the Emporium, John...what would make you smile?"

"Don't need much of anything...maybe a few cigars." Then... almost as an after thought, "I would sure enjoy a tin of those yeller peaches in that heavy, sweet syrup. Haven't had a canned peach since mamma's."

John pulled his knife, wiped it on the leg of his pants and sawed his way nearly around the lid, then bent it back. He tilted the tin and slowly, deliciously drank off the sweet nectar. He speared the peach half on top, popped it all in his mouth and began to chew as the juice found its way around his smile and down his chin. Before again looking to the can, his attention was pulled away from the next peach by Sarah's act of closing the door of the tax office behind her. John jammed the knife blade into the soft wood of the wagon seat and wedged the precious tin of peaches between the seat back and the blade. This team could run away, but when they finally stopped, his peaches would still be sittin' there.

He moved up the boardwalk to get the glare of the sun off of the front window of the tax office. There….he could now see inside, see Sarah talking to Mr. Simcox. John squatted on his hunches, back leaning against the board store front, to watch. As Sarah tried to explain what her business was, Simcox made no move to retrieve the tax ledger. He was smiling but shaking his head, 'no'. John knew Sarah was getting angry; the fists balled-up and went to her hips, as her stance became a little taller. All 120 pounds of her was ready for a fight. As Simcox came around the high counter toward Sarah, John stood and readjusted the Colt on his hip. As Simcox reached out and took hold of Sarah's upper arms, John snapped the rawhide loop off the Colt's hammer and stepped off the boardwalk into the dust and traffic of Washington Street. He walked as a man with a single purpose toward the office, his eyes never leaving the two inside.

John's jaw was set firm and his eyes narrow as he came striding through the tax office door. By the time Simcox could shift his attention from his intended victim to the unwelcome intruder, John was in his face. John slapped him hard on the left side of the face with his open hand, and then with the back of his hand on the right side, with equal velocity. With his left hand, John grabbed up a hand full of boiled, white-shirt front and pulled the startled man back up close to his face as he drew the Colt. John's first impulse was to jam the muzzle under his quivering chin, then in mid-motion stopped and pushed the muzzle hard into Simcox's groin. Simcox exhaled sharply, his eyes went so wide, white shown all the way around them. Seeing the expression, John had to sneer to keep from smiling. "Sir. There seems to be some misunderstanding here. All my sister desires of you this day is a receipt for the two years of back taxes on her farm, and a receipt for the next two years forward, all of which she wishes to pay at this time. That should be about $80.00 and you'll find that Mrs. Graham has sufficient of President Davis' new paper money to cover that."

"I…, I…, that is the county, would prefer gold coin for tax payment, Sir."

"I'm certain you would Mr. Tax Collector, but our President, Mr. Davis and his Treasurer, Mr. Memminger requires that each of us do our government business with his new money. Besides the promise to redeem the money for gold within two years after the ratification of peace is printed right on it for all to see." John holstered the big .44, smoothed out the now badly wrinkled shirt front and said, "I'll just wait over there with Mrs. Graham's team while you good folks finish your business. Remember Sir, she'll require receipts signed by you. I do not want to have to come back over here! Good day to you, Mr. Tax Collector…Sir."

God, but that felt good, the best part of this day…at least, thus far!

As the team stepped off of the Bradley ferry on the eastern bank of the Ouachita River, John felt himself exhale for what seemed the first time in hours. As much satisfaction as he had derived from jamming his Colt into Simcox's groin, he had to admit it was a stupid stunt…effective, but stupid. If Simcox had run after them as they crossed Washington Street from the tax office hollering for help, John would have been picked up immediately, and about 20 minutes later he would have arrived, a Union spy under armed guard, at Fort Southerland. Far as John knew they still shot 'em publicly in front of a firing squad. But here they were on the opposite bank from Camden, they had a wagon loaded with supplies, Sarah had a promised buyer for her butter and cream, and in her dress pocket paid receipts for four years of taxes on the farm. And to make John even more satisfied, his green team had behaved well in the noise and activity of a Camden in celebration. They stepped smartly on and off of the ferry…hell, the gray mare wouldn't do that without a blindfold. Now, if he could teach Sarah to handle them so she could get to town when she needed.

She had been very quiet since they left the Emporium. Earlier, John looked at her profile as she stared ahead and while he was thinking how beautiful she was, she broke out laughing. It was a most pleasant sound, but did dampen his mood of the moment. Now she looked at John and a devilish smile danced around her mouth and the darkest green eyes John had ever seen. "You weren't seriously considering shooting Mr. Simcox…in the…there…ah…where you had your gun pointed, were you?"

"Not really. I don't remember making a conscious choice to point it there. I guess the devil made me do it. Did turn out to be an effective way to focus his mind on our business though."

"It was that! I can't imagine Mr. Simcox will be stopping at the Graham place again anytime soon. I do understand a little of how he must have felt at that moment. After this many weeks and months, I keep thinking I know you, but, you certainly scared me. What I saw in your face when you came through that door was pure rage! I almost felt sorry for Mr. Sincox. I would definitely not have wanted to be the focus of that!"

As John was about to move on to another subject and talk about teaching Sarah how to drive the team, She reached over and took the lines from his hand. "Here, I'll drive; you can finish your peaches."

"I didn't know you could handle horses."

"Just like a man…you never ask, you just assume. I grew up on a farm till pa sent me off to Little Rock. I've farmed horses since I was twelve years old."

John speared the last remaining peach half, and with it on the way to his mouth, he saw Sarah watching him, he stopped, cut in half and made two bites. He drank the last of the sweet juice, wiped the knife on the same leg of his pants and took back the lines. "Thank you for driving and thank you for the peaches. The last ones I had were ma's home canned."

"You did look like you were enjoying them, and you are welcome. The least I could do for someone so bent on protecting my honor."

At the crest of the hill John pulled up in the generous shade of a big oak tree. "Going to let 'em cool down a bit." He wrapped the lines around the break handle, then turned toward Sarah to see her watching him intently. 'Lord God, her eyes are beautiful…I can't do this looking into those deep eyes.' With that realization, John turned again to look forward.

"What's wrong John? You're as nervous as a mother hen with a new hatch."

"I've got something important to say to you, but the thought of speaking of it makes me nervous and I can't seem to get the words started."

"John, in the recent few months you've fought in the biggest battle of this war…and lived to tell about it, you've saved an enemy soldier's life, beat up a Confederate patrol, threatened to shoot up a Union patrol, killed four men in my door-yard while saving my life, and made Mathew the happiest I've ever seen…and that's all before your little talk with Bruce Simcox today. Any of that make you nervous?"

"No. Most of the time I just didn't think about it, I just did it."

"Well, quit thinking on this so much and just say it!"

John took off his hat, ran his fingers through his long, straw colored hair and took a deep breath. He knew he could not look into those eyes and concentrate, so he focused on the tree line up ahead. "Sarah, I find I care a great deal for you…and Mathew. I'd admire to stay on here, help you with the farm, build up the cattle herd and help raise up Mathew to be a good man." Sarah started to speak her excited, affirmative response, but John held up his hand to stop her flow of words.

"But, I can't do any of that, at least not now. I gave my word to see Glenn home alive and safe, and that's what I must do. But I can't just blame it on Glenn, it's more than that. I've had the west and Texas in my head for such a long time…thinking about it and planning how to go there has been the focus that has probably kept me sane through much of the war I've seen. If I don't go see it now, I'll be forever looking at the western horizon wondering what's over there and what I've missed. For these reasons I've just got to go, but I wanted you to know what a hard decision it is for me to leave you…and Mathew."

"I guess I understand what you must do, but I want you to know Mathew and I would like you to stay…you'd be most welcome to. You've become very important to us…both of us. You are part of our lives; we owe so much to you. I know you wonder about what you might miss by not going on, but have you ever thought about what might be missing…by not staying?" She could tell by the color rising in John's cheeks, he had indeed thought about it!

When John turned he found Sarah very close. He knew the kiss was coming as they each moved but ever so slightly to close the distance. 'The nose…where do you put the nose?' He was determined to be ready, not surprised like last time. As the distance closed and their lips touched, John knew that lightening had again struck close by…every nerve fiber was charged and alive…Surely each hair on his arms was standing at attention. He moved his hands to her waist, how slim and firm she was…as Sarah's arms went around his neck and her fingers became entangled in his hair. Her lips parted slightly…they were soft, yet firm against his. Her tongue lightly brushed his bottom lip, darted just into his mouth, then withdrew…he could see bright lights exploding behind his closed eyelids. He had no intention of moving away, but no worry, the pressure of Sarah's hands on the back of his head held their lips in place…tightly together. When they finally parted John's head felt light, he had forgotten to breathe. He gulped air as a man in the last stage of suffocation. "Remember that kiss John, and also remember that's only a part of what you gonna' be thinking about and missing on the trail to Texas. But then, I don't want to influence your decision. Now, we best get on home so I can get supper ready while you do the chores. Just like old married folks!"

Their supper that night was an unusually grand spread. With all of her new supplies, and now the assurance of more to be available, Sarah had prepared enough food for group many times their number. There was skillet fried beefsteak dipped in real milled flour, mashed potatoes and gravy, corn and beans, cabbage slaw and if you still had room, apple pie with plenty of real, fresh ground coffee perking in the old blue pot. Sarah told Glenn and Mathew of their experiences in town and of John's convincing 'conversation' with Mr. Simcox. But all grew quiet when she told Glenn of the war news. When Glenn glanced at John, his eyes were downcast on his plate as he picked at his remaining food. But silently, John was thankful that Sarah's stories did not include any details of the drive home.

John waited until Mathew had left the kitchen to take Duke outside, and then said to Glenn, "Unless you knowing any reason why not, we should get our gear and supplies together tomorrow, then be riding on come the day after. I invited Sarah for she and Mathew to come along to Texas with us, but she decided not to leave the farm." Glenn nodded his agreement as all three fell silent. 'Now that's unusual…you'd think Glenn would be excited about starting again for his home.'

John rose from the table, moved his dishes to the counter as he announced, "I'm gonna go scrub this road dust off in the watering trough. Sarah, thank you for that mighty-fine meal. That's the best I've eaten in all the years since I left my ma's table. You truly did yourself proud!"

Sarah turned, and as she did, John again saw that devilish look come around those deep green eyes and her slight smile. "You're most welcome John, and I thank you for what you did for me this day. I'm glad you enjoyed the meal. Besides, I felt the need for you to have one more thing that you could think about and miss, after you rode down my lane and went back to cold beans and hardtack." With that, she stood on her tip-toes and planted another wet, open-mouth kiss on John's mouth. 'This is gettin' to be a mighty fine habit!'

The cool water felt soothing to John's sore body. He could tell that he had not been riding wagon or horse in some time. The rays of the now long-gone sun had been just enough to warm the water to a comfort point, after coming up from almost 20 feet below. The cigars that Sarah had bought him were better tasting than the ones he had removed from the renegades…Mr. Purcell would like these, but then he did seem to enjoy the others as well. The sour mash seemed to mellow the closer he came to the end of this last bottle. He'd save a bit for tomorrow night before they left. This would be all until they hit a town John could chance entering. Apparently many of these towns maintained garrisons of either regulars, or home guard, although John couldn't quite figure why. Other than himself, there wasn't a Yankee soldier closer than Fort Smith.

John laid his head back, cigar glowing in the corner of his mouth, corked sour mash bottle floating near-by. The night sky had always fascinated him, especially after all the stories Eye of The Hawk had told him about their gods and spirits. John stared at the blackness as though searching for the correct answer to his debate; Sarah or Texas?

Sleep would not come for John. His bath had been quite relaxing, the cigar…enjoyable, and the near last of the sour-mash whiskey… tasty. But, none of it made his thoughts of Sarah retreat to the back of his mind so sleep could come, and such warm thoughts they were! As he turned to look out through the open hay-mow door at the night sky beyond, he detected movement just a few feet away. "John, please don't shoot me, I just wanted to talk to you one more time before we run out of the opportunity."

"Woman, you might of said something rather than scaring me to death. Why aren't you in the house sleeping where you belong?"

"Probably for the same reason you're not sleeping; that wonderful kiss in the wagon."

"Yes, I have thought on it some. There's a bench there if you've a mind to continue to disturb my rest."

"John, I came out here in the middle of the night with the full intent to lay with you in that pallet of yours. To give my body to you, so you would realize how very much I care for you and how grateful I am for all that you've done here…and to make you want to stay with me for the promise of more to come. But I decided on the way to the barn; as much as I would like that, I care for you too much to do that to you. You're so damned noble! Afterward, you'd stay on here with me just because you felt some obligation to my honor. Oh, I'd get what I wanted…you, but as you've said, you would forever be wondering what was over that western horizon. Sure, you'd be good to me and loyal to me, I don't doubt that…but you'd forever be thinking on what you'd missed in Texas."

"Sarah, I'd…"

"Oh just shut-up John! I love you and I just want you to go…go over that next hill and see what's there. If we're intended to be together, you'll find your way back…and if we're not, well we can both just move on with our new lives….you in Texas and me here."

In stunned silence, John looked again to the night sky. When he looked back, Sarah was walking away. "Sarah, I'd…"

Through her crying voice, "Goodnight, John."

"Sarah…thank you. I…I care for you too."

The next day, sleepy-eyed, John stayed busy with the gear and the horses, and avoided the house except for meals. He and Sarah worked to keep conversation to a minimum and to seldom find themselves alone. Sarah even sent Mathew to the barn with a mug of coffee, rather than come herself. Now the men were ready, horses packed and standing impatiently at the door-yard gate; both men and animals were anxious to get started for the west again. How different they all were from the bedraggled specimens that had arrived so many weeks before…how much had changed in each life since! And how much this farm had changed.

The men were mounted and just waiting for Sarah to come out into the door-yard so they could say 'goodbyes', again. Mathew had cried when he found out about the leaving, but was once again distracted by Duke, so he was okay. Sarah had called through the closed screen-wire door to wait as she had a bag of fried ham 'n biscuits for them to eat on the road. John felt like they were again burnin' daylight, hell the sun would be up shortly…but he waited. 'Women…always made a body wait.' Sarah came through the door, a vision of beauty that took John's breath. She wore a new dress that John had not seen in all the weeks they'd been here…fit her extremely well, he noted. Her hair was loose, brushed out and hanging to her shoulders, pulled back by a matching ribbon…it shown as gold in the day's first light. She had color in her cheeks, a bright light shown around her deep green eyes and a beautiful smile on that mouth John already missed. She moved to Glenn's side and handed up a bag of food to tie around the pommel horn. They smiled at each other and Glenn reached down and shook her hand as he said his 'thanks'. As she moved to John's side he took off the wide brim hat and hung it over the pommel. As she handed up the bag to him, he leaned down from the saddle, snaked his left arm under her right arm, around her back and again under her left arm, then straightened in the saddle, lifting her off the ground and up to his level. He looked deep into her beautiful eyes then clamped his mouth firmly over hers. She quickly got over being startled and put both arms around his neck and leaned into him. Only then did John become aware of the soft mound cupped to over-flowing in his left hand. He couldn't move for fear of dropping her, and she made no move to reposition herself against him. So they exchanged a long, deep kiss while John's hand continued to hold her firmly. When he finally returned her to the ground he noted that his breathing problem had returned…'wonder if you ever get used to that…God, but I hope not!' That warm smile had returned to Sarah's face and especially around the eyes. All John could think to name it was, 'a smoky look'.

Then with the devil in her eyes she said, "Take good care of that left hand, John, and at night on the cold Texas trail remember where it's been. Maybe that's one more thing you could miss."

At the end of the lane the two men turned their horses, stopped and looked back at Sarah, standing just where John had set her down. John again took off his wide brimmed hat, and just as a Confederate officer had done on the top of White Mountain, swept it down across the front of his gray mare, as he bowed to her. When he straightened, Glenn said, "you don't have to do this, you know you can stay."

"We've been all through that. Now, if you still remember which direction is west, lead out. If not, I lend you a compass...you're burnin' daylight!"

Author's Note: With his latest success against the Army of the Potomac at Manassas Junction, Lee makes a strategic decision to invade Maryland. After writing of his plans to President Davis on September 3, 1862, Lee placed his army on the move the following day, before Davis could take exception. Lee's tactical purpose was not to find and destroy the Army of the Potomac; in fact he wished to avoid contact. Instead being desperately short of food, shoes and supplies, he wished for his army to live off the land of Maryland and Pennsylvania, while taking the pressure off of the farmers in northern Virginia and allow them to complete their harvest. Lee also planned that he could recruit replacements for his depleted forces in Maryland. Lastly, he planned that such a bold move would convince England and France to come into the war on the Confederate side. None of these objectives would result.

What did come about was the Battle of Antietam (called The Battle of Sharpsburg by the Confederates) which resulted, on September 17, 1862 as the bloodiest day in all American history. The Federals lost 12,000 casualties in the three day battle while Lee would lose almost one-third of his invading force. The retreat of Lee's army also gave Lincoln sufficient confidence to issue The Emancipation Proclamation on September 22. While its effect did not free even one slave, it did keep England (who had outlawed slavery) and France (who did not have slavery) from entering the war on the Southern side.

Chapter Eleven

"THE WAY WEST, AGAIN"

John brought the gray mare's head around to the west and was happy, perhaps even relieved, that he was again on his way to his future... at least his future as he imagined it to be. Once again Glenn had moved into the lead, as though he was the only one who knew where the west actually was. And, once again John was left to look at, this time, the east end of a now west-bound horse. He was extremely conflicted about leaving Sarah, and Matt...and the farm he had worked on so hard, while Glenn healed. But even with that tugging behind him, he was glad to be moving on into whatever was over that western horizon.

Given the recent "unpleasantness" which had occurred during John's last visit to Camden, it was decided the men would not chance a return visit! But getting men and horses over the Ouachita River did present a problem. Rather than heading south of Camden as Glenn had first planned and having to risk exposure at a ferry crossing, they decided to move north into the foothills of the Ouachita Mountains where they could ford the river near its headwaters.

The first two days on the road were thankfully, uneventful and quiet. A definite rarity of late when one traveled any distance with John. The few travelers they met paid them little attention, and neither John nor Glenn did anything to attract it. Two of the travelers had been in Confederate uniforms, which did give Glenn concern that his traveling companion might do something which would provoke an incident...but thankfully he did not. 'Could it be that John was maturing?'

The fall weather continued bright and beautiful with pleasantly warm days, less humidity and fewer flying pests. As they moved further into the foothills, the nights became noticeably cooler. Sarah had filled their saddlebags to overflowing with the food she had purchased in Camden, including another tin of yellow cling peaches in heavy syrup for John. So, they traveled easy, ate well and stayed dry. They spoke often of how much this trip contrasted with their trip from the Mississippi River. Glenn's health was much improved, although he tired easily; they had real coffee to drink, the rotten uniforms had long since been buried, the gray mare and the bay were fat and frisky, and best of all...no rain. And, no one seemed to be chasing them!

Where the men and horses crossed the Ouachita River the stream was cold and fast, but not deep. The gray mare showed her displeasure by snorting and dancing sideways as the swift, cold stream moved up her forelegs, but having expressed her opinion, she then moved on to the western bank. They made an early noon camp under the thick white oak and cottonwood trees. They refreshed in the cold waters, filed canteens, and then Glenn squatted to draw another of his 'dust maps'.

"We're about 20 miles north of Camden now. We'll move on to the north of Poison Springs, then strike southwest around Hope and toward Texarkana. If all goes well, we'll camp on the banks of the Red River later tonight."

"That's a far piece. What's this Poison Springs place?

"The story is that when the Confederates were defeated at Elkhorn Tavern, ya'll called it Pea Ridge, they retreated down this way. Knowing the Federal forces were close on their heels and would be looking for water, the Confederates poisoned the springs to slow 'em down. It worked then, but the water is still too bad to use or drink."

"Sounds like a damn trick an Indian would use."

"Well, we're not going to change that. There's a good road heading toward Texarkana and since we're not drawing much attention now, so we'll use it. I think we should avoid going into Texarkana though. It's a frontier town gone wild with out any law and filled with gamblers, deserters, whores and whiskey."

"Just which one of those are we trying to avoid?"

"Every wanted man from three states heads there to avoid the law."

"Three states?"

"It's on the state line of Arkansas and Texas, and only 25 miles north from Bossier Parish, Louisiana, and also close by The Nations. Come along. Let's move out, I just hate it when you're burning daylight!"

Author's Note:

Poison Springs, Arkansas. Is also noted for the Confederate victory that for the moment changed the course of the war in the west. On April 18, 1864, a Union forage train of 200 wagons, escorted by 1170 men was attacked and captured by Confederate troops, commanded by Generals John Marmanduke and Samuel Maxey. The wagons were loaded with corn for the Union Army of General Frederick Steele at Camden. The loss of these supplies forced Steele to abandon his base at Camden and retreat to Little Rock. This was the beginning of the end of the Union's Red River campaign. Union causalities; 301, Confederate; 114.

It was after night-fall when they finally came upon the Red. Glenn directed they would move down the eastern bank a ways to camp, and then find a spot to ford at first light. Giving the horses their head, they had carefully followed a rutted wagon road about two miles when Glenn spotted a small campfire in a clearing just off the road, next to the river.

"There's a fire and a covered wagon. Perhaps we could furnish some coffee and bacon and join their fire."

"Sounds agreeable enough to me." Then John added, "I'm getting a mite hungry; I must be getting soft from all that easy livin' on Sarah's farm. Go ahead call out and use that southern charm of yours to get us an invite Say, look how strangely that wagon is sittin'; must be in a rut or maybe has a broken wheel. And, where's the horses, I don't see 'em or hear 'em?"

"Hello the campfire! May we come in and share your fire? We're two tired, but friendly soldiers heading home."

A decidedly female, decidedly southern voice shouted back from the darkness beyond the circle of fire light, "You don't sound like any friends I know! There's a rifle on you, make a move toward my fire or my wagon and this will be as close to home as you're going to get!"

John grinned at the exchange, "Seems like I'm not the only one who thinks your southern charm is wearing a bit thin. Think I'll just relax behind this tree while you two southern folks just have a neighborly chat. Please ask her not to shoot my mare though, she's southern. Got the brand to prove it."

"Ma'am, we mean you no harm. We're just two road weary, former soldiers traveling to Texas. We have some coffee and bacon in our pack we'd be pleased to share at your fire."

"Soldiers in which army and where you headed in Texas?"

"One of us is from each side."

"Traveling together? That don't seem very likely in this day. Is one of you the prisoner of the other? Did the other one shoot you?"

"No Ma'am. We're going together, and neither of us shot the other."

"At least not yet!" John added.

"We're heading for the Hill Country, just to the west of Austin."

"That plan take you close to Tyler?"

"Yes Ma'am. Now may we step into the firelight so you can see we mean no harm?"

"You deserters?"

"No Ma'am; I'm wounded and going to my home to recover from my wounds and my friend here served out his time in the Union army before he left."

"You be certain he's not the one who shot you?"

"No Ma'am, I did not, at least I've not done it yet. But there's still time!" John contributed.

"If you're wearing side-arms unbuckle 'em and hang them over the saddle-horn then lead your horses with your right hand on the bridle. Come in very slowly; remember there's a rifle on you all the way. I'm not feeling very social after the last two who stopped here."

As they unbuckled, John observed for Glenn, "This is so reassuring Lieutenant, after 1,500 miles of avoiding patrols from both armies and bounty hunters from neither side, we've just been disarmed by a sweet sounding Southern Belle."

But carefully following instructions, the men led their horses into the circle of firelight and suddenly their eyes, used to the black of night, became blinded. John reacted by moving his left hand to shadow his eyes, "Hands at your side, and stand by the fire. You must be the Yankee given the way you can't seem to follow even simple instructions!" With their limited vision they could make out the shape of the covered wagon where the voice was coming from, but not the person behind the voice.

"Sit on the ground by the fire and keep your hands in sight." They sat and waited for their vision to clear. As it did, their 'hostess' came into view. This decidedly female, decidedly southern person with the rifle was also decidedly with child. As she came into the firelight the latter was most obvious. John thought, 'I have only met two women in the entire state of Arkansas, and both of them pointed a gun at me on the first meeting. That likely means something'; but before he could get deeply into pondering what, their hostess moved a box to the other side of the fire, sat heavily, but with her rifle pointed just to the left of them and ask, "Okay, what's your story?"

Glenn, exercising further his smooth southern ways, began their story at Shiloh Church. As John listened, it occurred to him that Glenn's charm did needed some exercise. John closed out the drone of Glenn's story and instead, studied the woman on the opposite side of the fire. She would be about 25 years old John judged, and from her size and the difficulty of her movements, looked to be very late in her pregnancy, but John wasn't very knowledgeable about such things. She was somewhat shorter and with a darker coloring than Sarah, but quite attractive, pregnancy and all. She looked very tired.

John finally heard the part where they were intending to cross the Red River in the morning when Glenn asked her, "What are you doing out here alone and in your condition Mrs.....?"

"Lieutenant McCoy, my name is Mrs. Lewis Wagner; Savannah Wagner. My husband is a Lieutenant is the Federal Navy and is being held a prisoner-of-war in Camp Ford in Texas, which I am told is close by Tyler. My family has been informed he is quite ill from the wounds inflicted during his capture and is perhaps near death. I am heading there intending to arrange his release and pardon. At least I was intending to do so until the wheel broke on my wagon and two scoundrels stopped to help, but stole my horses instead. And as for being alone, I'm not. My daddy's servant is traveling with me, but just now he's gone to the next town to try to recover the team of horses."

"Servant?" John questioned. More likely your slave you mean."

"No Yankee, Joshua's a freeman with papers. My daddy manumitted him his freedom and gave him papers as a reward for seeing me to obtain my husband's release."

"Likely with those papers in his hand, he's not to be seen again. He'll just take off, maybe with your horses if he can find 'em."

"He'd not do that! Joshua's been with our family all of his life, and he's had plenty of chances to leave me on this trip if that was his mind."

Suddenly, John dominated the conversation with his questions; "You've likely never been to the North, how is it you're married to a Yankee Naval Lieutenant? What makes you believe you can arrange a pardon for your Yankee husband from a Confederate prison? And where did the two bastards, excuse me ma'am, head with your team, and how long ago?"

"Mr. Kelley I'll answer your questions, but can I also get some of your bacon and coffee started on the fire, I've not eaten all day? I met the Lieutenant in my hometown of Vicksburg, Mississippi, when he was stationed there on riverboat duty before the war. We fell in love and were married. Then when your Mr. Lincoln started this damn war, Lewis was given command of the "USS Queen Of The West". She was a fast, lightly armed, Federal ramming ship on the river, named to honor the City of Chicago, up in Illinois I believe. When his boat was captured in Louisiana, the officers were initially held on the second floor of the Federal Courthouse in Tyler, Texas, until the camp was readied for prisoners. Lewis was severely wounded in the battle that lost his boat and, from the reports my family received, he has not been able to receive the needed medical treatment."

"But what makes you think you can get him pardoned and released?"

"I was a Clayton before my marriage to Lewis. My father is Alexander Clayton, a lawyer in Vicksburg who is a leader in the Democratic politics of Mississippi. He was appointed one of seven delegates to the Secession Convention in Montgomery in February, 1861, and is a close personal friend of Mr. Jefferson Davis. The Convention, with my daddy's help wrote the constitution for our new nation and appointed Mr. Jefferson Davis as its first president. I am carrying a letter from President Davis, signed by his personal secretary, Mr. Burton Harrison. I am prayerful that will prove sufficient to my husband's release. My immediate problem however Mr. Kelley, since I have a wagon with a broken wheel and no horses to pull it, is finding a means to arrive at Camp Ford in time that I might yet save my husband's life."

"How is it your pa let you go on this fool trip in the first place, and in your condition?"

"Well first, my daddy did know of my condition, as you call it, and he believes the war must to come to Vicksburg, and very soon. He saw this as a chance to get me, and his soon to be grandchild out Vicksburg ahead of the fight, while there was still time. Your General Grant now has 100,000 men waiting in Corinth while he is chasing General Beauregard all over Mississippi looking for a fight. As soon as our capital Jackson falls, and daddy says it will quite soon, the Union will turn its attention on Vicksburg. Pinned against the river like it is, when that battle starts, no one will be able to get out. The Union just has to have Vicksburg in order to open up the Mississippi River to Yankee commerce and split the South. At least that's so my daddy says."

"How long ago did the thieves leave with your horses and did they say anything about where they were headed?"

"They left me about three hours ago, just about dusk. They mentioned Texarkana, but I didn't hear exactly where. Then Joshua left about an hour later on foot."

Glenn was listening intently then added, "They likely headed off to sell your team, get drunk and raise some fun; Texarkana is the closest place to do that. Most likely they'll cross over to the Texas side to avoid the Arkansas law, just in case someone should show up looking for 'em. They can't be very worried about that however, or they wouldn't have left you alive."

"Gentlemen, the bacon and coffee are done and I've some biscuits left from morning. I don't know about you, but I'm starved. Having your wagon break down, your horses stolen and then being left abandon in strange country at night will certainly give a body an appetite."

They ate quickly and began to formulate a plan. It was decided, after some heavy and heated discussion, that John and Glenn would first put the spare wheel on the wagon and get it ready to travel, and then John would head in to Texarkana and try to recover the horses, while Glenn stayed to provide protection for Mrs. Lewis. Glenn wasn't happy to be left out of the recovery attempt, but had to admit, that plan made more sense than any he could suggest. They removed the double-tree and then the wagon tongue and used it as a pry-lever over a boulder to lift the wagon. After they hoisted the wagon off the ground, Glenn held the pry down while John put the new wheel in place. "How'd you know to do that?"

"Something I've helped my pa and brothers do many times." While Glenn re-saddled the gray mare, John checked his weapons, then mounted, smiling reassuringly to Mrs. Wagner. Glenn handed up the reins and shook John's hand, "Go get it done Yankee."

"That I'll do, Reb. That I'll do!"

With a touch of his hand to the wide brim hat, John moved the mare through the willows and down the bank to cross the now dark Red River.

John and the big gray came out of the river bottom, found the Texarkana Road without a problem, and headed southwest. This was the first time in all their adventures together that the mare had stepped into a dark river without any hesitation. She must have a sense that this was not the time to fool around. The night was mostly dark, with but a quarter of the moon showing, and the road was clear of other travelers. "No one with a lick of good sense would be out in the dark of such a night," John said to the mare. He pulled the Spencer, chambered a cartridge and laid the rifle across his lap in front of him. Then feeling a little more secure put the mare into a mile-eating lope and gave her her head. He decided not to spend much time or energy thinking about what he might be riding in to, or he might just decide to head northeast, back to Sarah and Matt. They…she…had been much on his mind these last two days. He had frequently recalled the many things she had noted to him…with her instructions to remember them, and her on the cold trail. Remember them he had!

The night sky was littered with stars as though God had just thrown them out there by the handful. John knew many of the stories about the figures that were supposed to live in the night sky; warriors, animals, fish and such…but he could never make those pictures out. Took more imagination than he had, but he thought, 'Grandma could probably do that.' He could usually find the Big Dipper and from that, the North Star, but they were well behind him now…as were many of the other things from his life. A short time later, he topped a rise and there it was below him; the place Glenn had said just a half-day earlier, they would take all possible steps to try to avoid.

Author's Note:

Texarkana. The Great Southwest Trail was the main-line of travel from the Indian villages of the Mississippi River country to those of the South and West and had passed close by a Caddo Indian village originally on the site. Later in the 1850's, the builders of the Cairo & Fulton Railroad crossed Arkansas, then crossed the Red River and continued to the Texas boarder at the present site of Texarkana to join the Texas & Pacific Railroad (originally in 1852 called the El Paso and Pacific Railroad). The settlement was not formally established until 1873, but had actually came into existence as a lawless frontier town as soon as the railroaders arrived.

There is no absolute certainty as to the original source of the settlement's name, but three popular stories abound:

1. The name was derived from a steamboat known as the "Texarkana" which sailed the Red River in 1860.

2. Col. Gus Knobel who made the original survey for the St. Louis, Iron Mountain & Southern Railroad before 1850, coined the name and erected a large sign on the present site.

3. A tavern keeper named Swindle from Bossier Parish, LA, created rot-gut liquor he called "Texarkana bitters", and the settlement's name was derived from it as the drink's fame spread.

Chapter Twelve

"THE ROBERTS BROTHERS"

It was long after dark, but still the main street of this poor excuse for a town was busy. The saloons were many and going full tilt. Their drunken patrons spilling out onto the dirt road. Even the emporium had a lamp in its windows but few customers inside. Many of the saloons consisted only of large tents, bleached white from the sun, with wooden store-like fronts facing the street. There probably were banks, apothecaries and millineries and other stores for the "good" citizens, but on this main street it was mostly saloons and rowdies. The roadway was deeply rutted even though there had been no significant rain in weeks. John remembered what Sergeant Mullins had said about the town of Cairo in Illinois, "It was the only place in the world where you could stand in mud up to your knees, with the dust blowing in your eyes." John planned to follow Glenn's thought that the horse thieves had likely crossed over into Texas, so he slumped in the saddle, kept his head down, but with his eyes alert, and rode on through the Arkansas side of town. The lantern light spilled through the open doors, often bringing laughter and drunks with it. A taste of whiskey would certainly be good right now. But that would have to wait, as over the state line he rode into Texas. At long last, John had reached his objective…Texas, but so far it looked a great deal like the Arkansas he had just left!

The roadway was still bad; the saloons still lively and plentiful, only the flag had changed from a field of stars and two bars to one of a single star and two bars. John search the hitching rails along the main street, but doubted the thieves were dumb enough, or drunk enough, to leave a matched team of Appaloosas in harness standing at a hitching rail. Unfortunately, they were not. At the end of the street was a livery stable and John thought that's where I'd leave 'em, so he reined up and dismounted. Leaving the mare at the hitching rail, he moved through the open double doors. The interior was dark and John stepped out of the back light of the open door to let his eyes adjust. The sounds and the smells announced there were horses in the near-by stalls.

"Hello by the door. Who you be and what's your business here?"

John's sight was improving and he could make out a shadowy figure in the rear of the stable. "My name's John Kelley and I'm here looking for a team that belongs to a friend of mine. I'll just be checking your stock and then be on my way."

"Ain't no team here. You get out of my place or I'll be a calling the Town Marshal. Now get!"

"Mister, I mean you no harm, but I do intend to see your stock. The horses I seek were stolen this evening by a couple of renegades who then left a very pregnant, Mississippi lady alone and stranded up on the Red with a broke wagon. If I find those horses here, then you could be in as much trouble as the other two, so just call for the Marshal and we'll let him help with my searching!"

With noticeably less anger in his voice, "What's this team look like and how'd I know your stories not made up?"

"Their matched Appaloosas in harness, if you've seen 'em, it's not likely you'd mistake 'em for anything else. And, as for my story, ol' timer, I'll gladly tell it to the Marshal if you'll but call him over here."

"There's no need, besides he's a cousin on my ma's side and we don't much care for each other anyway. You say the team was stolen? You know we don't take too kindly to such in Texas."

"You'd know if you've seen 'em…how damn many matched pairs of Appaloosas you get in here anyway?   I've not seen the team but they've been well described to me, as have been the two men who took 'em. Now ya' got 'em or ain't ya''?"

"How'd I know they belong to your friend? There was a big buck nigger in here a couple of hours ago looking for the same team."

"Mister, I don't much like that word! Where'd this Negro go from here?"

"Don't know…don't care, but I think ya'll are looking for the same horses. And, I do have 'em. There standing back here."

"You got any money resting on this arrangement?"

"No. I told the two to come back later and I'd make 'em an offer. I figured they be a sight easier to deal with drunk and they is a beautiful team so's I could make a few dollars in gold."

"So when I take this team back to the rightful owner, you've got no complaint coming! Where'd the renegades go to do their drinkin'?"

"Up to The German's. It's truly Bill Friel's saloon, but everyone here abouts calls it 'The German's'. But Boy, you best not go up there alone. Every bad ass in this part of the country winds up at The German's some time or other…and these two are bad asses for true. They smelt so bad they even spoiled the air in my stable."

"You give that team a little feed and secure their harness for travel. I'll be back shortly. If I don't happen to make it back, you give the team to the Negro...he'll take 'em home. Here's a gold coin for your trouble and feed."

John picked up the loose reins and walked the gray mare up the dirt street in the direction the old man had pointed. Friel's place was just beyond the last town structure, sittin' off by itself. Out of the corner of his eye, John thought a couple of times he'd seen a shadow following him, but when he looked quickly, nothing was there. Damned spooky place...he wished Glenn was along to watch his back. He looped the reins over the hitching rail, released the rawhide loop on the Colt, pulled the Spencer instead of the scattergun, and pushed through the open half doors. If the renegades did smell as bad as the old man had said, no one would know it in here. The heavy cigar smoke mixed with the stale beer, mixed with the smell of a half dozen men who hadn't seen soap 'n water for weeks would almost bring tears to your eyes. The old man was correct; this group could give a decent stable a bad name.

It was a slow night; there were four men playing cards at a felt covered table in the corner to his right and while they looked up, no one took much note of John's entry. Ahead at the rough-cut bar were the two he was looking for, standing drinking with their backs to him...but closely watching in the mirror back of the bar. The bar-keep was standing talking to the two, but his eyes were following John also. John stood in the middle of the room, waiting for what, he did not know, but from that spot he could see everyone's movements. Finally he called out, "You two stinking horse thieves at the bar turn around very slowly...hands clear where I can see them. Mr. Friel, if that's your name, you move down the bar and when your hands come up they best not hold anything but a bottle of the good whiskey you keep out of sight."

"Who in the hell you calling horse thieves kid? What's your business here?" The one talking sounded like a big man, but as they turned, their hands were empty and Friel moved out of the way and as his hands came above the bar, there was a fancy bottle and a glass in them.

"You two stole a team of horses from a true lady up on the Red River tonight and left her stranded and alone with a broke wagon. You left the team in the livery…I've seen 'em. Now we're going to walk down and tell our stories to the Marshal. You unbuckle your belt and let the guns drop."

From off to the right, "Kid if shooting starts, I'm not believing you can get all of us, you see, we're all friends and relatives here."

"I don't have to get all of you, but I'll start with those three at the bar, and definitely get two of 'em."

"Give it up Kid and back out of here while you still can, you're just plain out-gunned and we're not going to let you take our friends just for stealing horses." The four card players slowly stood and moved away from their game.

"I always heard Texans didn't care for horse thieves, besides this was a fine southern lady and heavy with child."

"Cut the crap Boy, we're not from Texas so that don't work. Make your play or drop your guns and back out. Maybe we'll be generous and let you live to grow-up. And then, maybe not!"

John shifted the Spencer to his left hand and gripped it like a revolver, and moved his right hand closer to the right hip. No way he was going to get all of 'em, but his first two shots would be the pair at the bar. That's why he was here.

"Who's the nigger in the door with the scattergun? He got some part of this?"

John took a quick glance in the bar mirror as a big Negro man, over six foot tall, stepped into the room with a scattergun level at his hip. "You Joshua?"

"Yes sir. That's what I'm called."

"That the scattergun off my saddle?"

"Yes sir, trust you don't mind I borrowed it."

"You know how to use that?"

"Yes sir. I used to keep my family fed by bird hunting."

"That's real good, Joshua. Suppose you just plan on taking those four mouthy card players when the shootin' begins."

"Now wait a minute, he's got no part of this. Ain't his fight."

"That's true, but if its goin' to be your fight, then anyone can get in and welcome. Besides, he and I don't like that word you folks here abouts keep using. Suppose you four just sit back down at your game, but keeping your hands out on the table so Joshua can see 'em."

"Joshua, if they move, don't blink; just shoot 'em, both barrels. That's not a twist steel barrel so it'll take the force just fine"

"Now horse thieves, seems we're all through chosen up sides, what are you two at the bar going to do, pull 'em or drop 'em? And, Mr. Friel while you're holding that fine bottle so tightly set two glasses on the bar and pour a drink of your good whiskey for me and my new friend here. We'll be having 'em when we finish."

The two at the bar sneered in John's direction, then turned again to the bar. They continued to show John their backs as they returned to their drinks, but their eyes were glued on John's reflection in the back-bar mirror. John moved slightly to his left so he could see Joshua's reflection and he wanted the horse-thieves to see him also. With all eyes on him, John made a show of shifting the Spencer in his left hand, holding it beside his leg by the pistol grip. With his right hand he slowly reached over and cocked the exposed hammer. The 'click' was alarming in this quiet room where no one spoke, but just waited…. waited for John to move, or more likely to cut and run.

John took two deep breaths to put some calm in his hands and in his voice. "Alright you vermin ridden bastards, you turn around and face me or look in the mirror and watch it coming, because coming it is!" Slowly, deliberately they turned together like dancers. John thought those are two of the dirtiest, meanest looking, most unkempt pieces of human garbage I've ever seen. Just by riding into her camp they must have scared the livin' hell right out of Mrs. Wagner.

"Boy, you've got a smart mouth on you, its time someone teached you some manners since your ma didn't get it done. I just believe this ol' boy will be your teach this night." They wore their guns low with the holster tied down. As they turned, each pulled their duster open to clear his holster. They were ready for John's play. "Boy, I don't think you're fast enough to take us both, besides our brother, Garth is at that poker table yonder, if you get lucky with us…he kills you. With that invitation to join, brother Garth pushed his chair back and started to rise. That was the moment Joshua cocked both barrels of the scattergun and locked the butt to his hip. The leader at the table ordered, "Sit easy Garth, besides, I want a see how this comes out; see if that kid's all mouth and no belt buckle." The leader had just saved Garth from being cut in half by a shotgun blast.

"We don't need you Garth, Clint an' me can take 'em. Boy, even if you get a shot off, the other ones gonna' kill you, then the rest of us, we'll skin your nigger."

"Its possible you might get me, that's why I'm gonna' take you with my first shot. In case ol' Clint there gets lucky, I still get you!" With that announcement, the one called Clint took two sliding steps sideways to gain some space. John again checked the image in the mirror; Joshua was in place and ready. John would have felt much better if that image backing him up had of been Glenn's. John's eyes darted back to the pair at the bar. They now stood about four feet apart with "The Mouth" directly in front of him and Clint off to John's left; he was going to get the Spencer. From this range it might put him right over the bar. The moment had arrived! "Alright you bastards, your times up; either pull'em, or unbuckle and let 'em drop!" Clint, well into the night's whiskey, made a not-too-swift move with his right hand as the Spencer swept up and exploded. The report was followed immediately by the report of a handgun. Those in the room were nearly made deaf by the two captive explosions. The Spencer's round slammed into Clint in the right side of his chest crashing his back into the bar. His cocked handgun had cleared the holster when he was hit and it discharged into the floor at John' feet, then spun away. With the impact of the Spencer's round Clint's head snapped back, as he hit the bar his hat disappeared behind it.

The German's right hand was moving under the bar when the round from John's Colt splintered the bar top no more that six inches from Friel's left hand. He stood, eyes wide in surprise, and quickly backed away from the undisturbed scattergun he had hidden there.

'The Mouth' looked in horror at his brother slumping forward into the filth of the unswept floor. Then to his left as the bar top splintered… then as he looked back to John he started a fumbling, drunken move to his hip. John's calm voice broke the sudden stillness in the room, "Your decision time is now, Mouth! Either pull that thing and join your brother, or unbuckle the belt and let it fall."

"I have a name, damn you…call me by my name…it Eugene, Eugene Roberts. You shot my brother, you bastard!"

"Alright U-gene, it's still your move."

As Eugene's whiskey slowed mind pondered his limited choices, brother Garth jumped up from his chair at the table, slamming his chair into the wall and tipping over the poker table in front of him. His gun had cleared the holster and begun its upward arc when the round from the scattergun hit him full in the chest. He took a staggering step backward and slammed into the wall, a look of disbelief on his face, then died slowly slumping down the wall into a sitting position, leaving a blood trail behind.

"That's my other brother. You kilt' Garth!"

"Times up U-gene." John walked toward the last standing brother, John's eyes never leaving that ugly face, Colt pointed at his belly. At a three foot distance, John sprang as he swung the Colt in a downward arc, the barrel smashing Eugene's nose. As the horse thief withered, screamed and bled next to the spittoon, John reached down, unbuckled the gun belt and tossed it to Joshua. "Here, strap this on. It should be in good condition; its never been used that I can tell."

John moved toward the bar eyeing the two shots of Friel's 'good' whiskey that had set undisturbed through it all. The German moved quickly to stand behind the two glasses and with a new gusto announced, "We don't serve those boys in here!"

"If he was a "Boy" yesterday, he's sure as hell a Man today. Besides, you're not serving him, I am. Now stand away!" John picked up the two glasses and nearly spilled the beautiful amber liquid, his hand was shaking so. First time he'd noticed that. He handed Joshua a glass, then over it mouthed the words, "thank you". To which the big black man nodded his head ever so slightly. They tilted their glasses, drank together and then smashed the glasses against the brass rail at the base of the bar.

They left the mess they had created where it had fallen. John, leading the gray mare and prodding U-gene with his Colt went to talk to the Town Marshal, while Joshua headed to the livery to claim Mrs. Wagner's team. Joshua was waiting in front of the barn holding the matched Appaloosas when John rode up. "Alright Joshua, let's head for the Red River." With that Joshua began walking off leading the team. "Wait now, you're not going to walk back. Get up behind me...you can ride and lead."

"You gonna' let me ride double witch you, what'll these white folks think?"

"Sure. I really don't give a damn what these folks think. If I'm gonna' share my fights with you, might as well share my ride too."

Later, as the pair passed out of the town and into the dark countryside John reined up and turned toward Joshua. "One thing though, if we're gonna' be riding on to Texas together, when we get back to camp you've gotta' get those clothes and your big black ass into that river for a damn good scrub-down…with soap. Man you'd kill flies!"

Some later after a long silence, "Mr. John Sir, since you've bought it up, you've got's to get in there witch me…I just didn't know how to tell you before."

Chapter 13

"THE EASTERN CAMP OF INSTRUCTION"

Author's Note:

Camp Ford, Texas. With General Earl Van Dorn's army transferred from Arkansas to Tennessee, the entire northern frontier of the Trans-Mississippi was left unprotected against intrusion by either Union forces or Indian raiding parties coming down from The Nations. Massive efforts were undertaken to recruit and train new units in Texas to fill the manpower quotes under the South's new Conscription Law. The camp, established for that purpose just outside of Tyler, was officially called, "The Camp of Eastern Instruction". It became known however as "Camp Ford", after Col. John S. "R.I.P." (rest-in-peace) Ford, a Confederate officer, Texas Ranger, fierce Indian fighter and the State's first Conscription Officer. The Camp would later become the largest prisoner of war compound west of the Mississippi River with over 5,300 prisoners at its peak population. Initially the camp contained about 3 ½ acres confined by a "dead-line", but without a stockade. The civilians of Tyler began to complain that the prisoners were coming to their houses and begging, or stealing food and supplies. In response, the locals provided their slaves to enclose the compound with a 16 foot high log stockade. Later after the Confederate successes in the Red River Campaign, Poison Springs and Mark's Mills in Arkansas, the prisoner population soared. The camp was quickly expanded to 11 acres by lopping off the top 10 feet of the stockade logs and enclosing the entire 11 acres with walls only six feet high. In spite of the large population, Camp Ford experienced a relatively low prisoner death rate. This was due largely to the organizational control inside the walls and the ample supply of fresh water. By contrast, Salisbury (NC) prison was the south's most deadly with over one-third of those confined there dying.

There were many naval prisoners at Camp Ford, with most of them having been in captivity since the early days of the war, and they were still the last to leave. The first prisoners to arrive at Tyler, were from the captured "USS Queen Of The West" and the "USS Diana". Most Union naval officers were not paroled by the Confederates until May 19, 1865; six weeks after Lee surrendered at Appomattox.

This strange traveling company consisting of a very pregnant Southern Lady, her soon to be free slave, and two former soldiers; one from each army, made an early camp on the south bank of the Sabine River, three days travel out of Texarkana. For all of that period, various members of this band had proposed various plans of action for when they arrived at Camp Ford. Now tomorrow they would arrive, and were still without an agreed plan. Joshua just might be a problem! All did agree that the only role he could play was that of a slave; but he refused to take off his holster and side-arm. And, slaves just do not walk around packing a side-arm. At least, not in east Texas, they do not…makes white folks some nervous. Joshua had buckled on the holster in Friel's when John had tossed it to him, and had slept with it on since. Mrs. Wagner and Glenn both believed John could talk him into storing it in the bottom of the wagon, but John refused to try. He figured Joshua's bravery in the saloon, in the face of dire personal consequences, probably saved their lives.

So, if Joshua wanted to wear the gun, he had earned the right. The two men had become good friends and as they traveled, John taught Joshua how to draw and cock the hammer in the same motion, aim and fire. John was a good teacher...Joshua a willing student.

As the two men talked to each other about every small detail of their shared experience, some details not remembered until the most recent telling, Glenn realized he was sorry not to have been a part of it. He had never seen two more satisfied men that those two as they came riding double over the ford on the Red River leading the Appaloosa team. When they stopped at the Town Marshal's office the following day for Mrs. Wagner to tell her story, Glenn heard for the first time the entire story as it was told to the Marshal. He just sat there quietly, with nothing to contribute. Seems the Robert's brothers were wanted for horse thievery in two states and there was a $50 bounty on the head of each. John was excited about the prospect until he remembered where they were, and what money would be used to pay the reward. John just gave the $150 Confederate to Joshua so, "he could be not only a free man, but a man of means." Besides, John still had the small silk bag of gold coins from Shiloh hanging around his neck. Joshua told John, "I never did have a white man for a friend before."

"Makes us even. I never had a Black friend before either...an Indian, but never a Black. Hell, I never even knew a Black person before." John wanted to pay a morning 'social call' at the German's and, as he said, "pass the pleasantries of the day with Mr. Friel and have a drink of the good whiskey he kept under the bar." But, Mrs. Wagner's wisdom and strong will prevailed and the small band headed out to the southwest.

The three men sat by the campfire having their first meaningful discussion about tomorrow and Camp Ford. Mrs. Wagner had retired to the wagon, following which John produced cigars and the bottle of sour mash he had 'borrowed' from the German.. "Joshua, I'm concerned that I am contributing to the corruption of your soul; you've taken to packing a gun, you've got money in your pocket, you had your first drink of whiskey at Friel's the other night, now three days later you've taken to smoking cigars and you never miss a pull on that bottle as it goes around. Only one more thing I have to teach you; when we arrive someplace with a general store, you need to learn how to buy. Don't look right for a free man of your means to be mooching drinks and smokes off of your friends all the time."

"Oh Mr. John, I think you're ribbing me."

"No Joshua I'm serious. You need to start buying!"

Their conversation gradually became serious as it moved to a plan for tomorrow and with that, Mrs. Wagner appeared at the fire carrying four tin cups for coffee. "Enough of the sour mash, we've serious business tomorrow!"

Glenn pulled the soot encrusted pot from the edge of the wood coals, and filled cups for each of them. Mrs. Wagner had definitely given this some considerable thought. "There are two things that are certain; John can not speak, not even when spoken to. And, there is no other play-acting role for Joshua except that of a slave and Joshua that means you take that damn gun off and stow it!" Joshua started to protest, but stopped when he saw the slight shake of John's head.

"What's the matter with my voice that I'm not allowed to talk?"

"John, you may have saved my life and by that become my best friend, but you're an Iowa farm boy who sounds just like an Iowa farm boy. Even Mr. Purcell told you that you couldn't fool anyone south of the Iowa-Missouri line. As soon as you open your mouth, no one will ever believe you're a soldier in the Confederate army. You'll speak to answer a question or to control your horse and we're all caught."

Mrs. Wagner listened to John and Joshua protest, then held up her hand and announced to the three men, "this is my mission to gain my husband's release, so if you're going with me, this is the way it's going to be done!"

"Joshua, your freedom may have to be short-lived, but like it or not, tomorrow you will be a slave. That means you will take off that gun and holster and you will store them under the pallet in the wagon. You will walk beside my team keeping your eyes on the ground and your mouth shut! Do not speak unless I speak to you first. If the guards require help bringing Lewis out, you will go into the garrison to identify him and help fetch him."

Then turning toward the other two who were watching silently, "Now for you two. You are both wounded Confederate soldiers who my father hired to escort me. You each have a 'CSA' brand on your horse so that will help. Mr. McCoy you shouldn't have any problem in that role. Most of the guards are likely to be local Texas boys and old men so your speech pattern will be helpful. If anyone gives us any problem, you should speak right up. But you, Mr. Kelley, you are a problem! The only role I can think of is that you were shot in the neck at Shiloh Church, destroying your voice box. I have some white muslin I will cut into a long strip like a bandage and wrap around your neck That should provide the excuse, but I know that for you the most difficult part will be at all times to just keep your mouth shut. Remember, you can not utter a word! Mr. McCoy will talk for both of you."

"Now that's what we're going to do, and do it just that way. Pour a little of that sour mash into my coffee, and let's all retire. Tomorrow just might be a very long day."

There was no burnin' daylight this day. None of the four slept soundly or long, and all were up well before the sun. John had the fire built up and a pot of coffee boiling. Glenn had the bay and the gray mare saddled and the gear stowed, while Joshua had the harness on the team and gave them their morning ration of oats. As Mrs. Wagner returned from her 'morning duties' at the river bank, she noted the preparedness of her escorts. "Slow down men, it's much too early to start. We don't dare ride up on that camp until the sun is well into the sky for fear of getting shot. I will fry up some bacon and make us some skillet biscuits to eat on as we travel today. Have yourself some coffee and relax a little, this will be a long enough day."

As they ate in silence, each deep in their own thoughts, Mrs. Wagner came to John with the strip of muslin rolled up in her hand. It was about three inches wide and long enough for three complete turns around John's neck. Then she unwound the last turn, tore the wrap in the middle and tied the ends together to hold the bandage snuggly in place. John started to protest, but she extended her index finger and placed it firmly over John's lips. "From this moment on you have no voice box and thus, you can not utter a word or a sound. If you forget, we may all die." The expression in John's eyes told her he understood.

The morning sun was well up, but little of it filtered through the tall pine trees that surrounded the small party. They had left the Tyler Road about three miles back following the one faded, hand lettered sign that promised 'Camp Ford' was to the right. This lane had been hacked through the dense pine forest and was just wide enough to accommodate the wagon and hopefully did point the correct way to Camp Ford. John had never seen trees standing so thick and was about to comment, but the tight muslin wrap reminded him; he was unable to do so. Rather than a winding lane just wide enough for the wagon, it was more like a 'pine tunnel'. Then with out any thinning of the trees, the tunnel abruptly ended as they came to the edge of a vast cleared area; more than 50 acres of just pine stumps and dead trimmings. They blinked and shaded their eyes from the sudden brightness of the unfiltered sun light. This had to be the area where they had harvested the logs for the prison camp stockade As they topped the rise, there it was below and to the south of them; the largest prisoner-of-war camp west of the Mississippi River; Camp Ford.

The enclosed area looked to be about four to five acres, surrounded by a 16 foot high, rough log stockade. The only visible gate was around on the west side and this wagon road, such as it was, led to it. Adjacent to the gate, on the outside of the stockade, were a number of secure looking log structures; likely the Confederate headquarters, barracks and hospital. Inside the stockade, was a vast array of log huts, lean-to's, tents made from blankets and roofed-over burrows hollowed out of the ground. There appeared to have been a few spring gardens, both with-in and with-out the stockade. About a hundred yards down slope from the south wall there was a free-running spring feeding a small stream with many log catch-basins. Surprisingly, the inside of the camp area looked orderly and well policed. The prisoners' living quarters were, for the most part, laid out in rows with walkways in between. It gave the appearance of some strong leadership on both sides of that pine wall. John wasn't certain what he had expected a prisoner of war camp to look like, but this wasn't it. He had been in many training camps in his 14 months of service that were much worse than this, although the still, warm air was full of that unmistakable smell of too many men permanently confined in too small a space.

When they arrived at the gate area, they were met by a Confederate Lieutenant and three armed guards who had been carefully watching their slow progress across the bare field. John thought they were a sorry looking lot; the officer was 45 years old if he was a day, and the three young guards' total age would hardly equal that. This home guard was made up of young boys, most now yet 13 years old, old men and wounded veterans. Glenn moved forward, snapped the Lieutenant a smart salute, identified the members of the party and stated their purpose. Upon learning who Mrs. Wagner's father was, and especially who had authored the letter she carried, the Lieutenant said it was a matter for the camp commander and fell all over himself to report. The commander was identified as Colonel R.T.P. Allen, who the Lieutenant had further identified to Glenn as 'a West Pointer'. Shortly the Colonel appeared, escorted by the Lieutenant, and was also smartly saluted by Glenn. Glenn was certainly on his good military behavior, John thought. They visited briefly, but John was out of ear shot. When the Colonel looked him over, John knew he had been identified, but quickly turned his eyes away rather than offer a salute. The Colonel was a small man with a thin dark mustache and darting nervous eyes; his small stature and delicate features were almost female. His empty left coat sleeve, however, suggested he had seen other duty and some of this war's action.

As if on a cue, Mrs. Wagner emerged from the back of the wagon dressed in her finest flowing gown with hat to match, and wearing her biggest southern smile. The Colonel stopped in mid-sentence, John thought he saw the thin mustache twitch, then recovering, he hurried to her side, his good arm extended. Mrs. Wagner accepted the arm, spoke a few words from behind a white handkerchief, and glancing from Glenn to John, was escorted by the Colonel to the headquarters building. John turned his attention to Joshua and when they had made eye contact, nodded his head from the team to the water. Joshua unhitched, and led the team toward the catch basin. A gathering of wounded 'home guard' was in heated discussion a few yards away, and now were paying particular attention to Joshua; John eased the gray mare close enough to pick up on their discussion. The subject was the Emancipation Proclamation that Mr. Lincoln was going to formally issue in the near future. One guard was telling the rest, "The Sergeant says Lincoln's paper ain't gonna' be worth a cup of warm spit. Lincoln said he's gonna' free the niggers in the Confederacy but he can't do that from up north. Mr. Greeley up in New York City said much the same thing; he's freeing the niggers he can't reach and left as slaves the ones he could have reached, meaning the niggers up there in the Union."

"There's one of 'em watering those horses, let's ask him if'n he thinks he's free! Hey Nigger, get your black ass over here." Joshua continued at his task without looking at the group. John, on the other hand, began to pay close attention. Again, "Darky, gets yourself over here, last time I'm gonna' be telling you for we comes to bring you over!" When Glenn's attention was pulled in that directed by the hollering, what he saw made his blood run cold. John was pulling the rawhide loop off the hammer of his Colt, as he began to side- step the gray mare between the noisy group of wounded Confederate veterans doubling as guards, and Joshua returning from watering the team. 'My God, John's going to take 'em on and if he opens his mouth, we're all dead.' Glenn ran toward the group, with John easing the mare up on them also. "All ya'll leave that black alone. He's the slave of Mrs. Wagner who is with your commander carrying a letter from President Davis. Ya'll don't want to be messing with that! Joshua, get that team back hitched so's we can be leaving when Mrs. Wagner says." The group turned away, John retied the Colt, Joshua passed on back to the wagon and Glenn just exhaled.

"John, you damn fool, get on back up there by the wagon. If you're gonna' survive to be old enough to vote, you're gonna' have to learn to do a better job picking your fights. Try remembering just where you are, who you are and what brought you here!"

About an hour later Mrs. Wagner and the Colonel emerged from the headquarters building. He called the Lieutenant over and the three of them spoke briefly, then Mrs. Wagner returned with quickened steps to the wagon. "We've done it! The Colonel has agreed to release Lewis as it's very unlikely he will even survive, let alone to fight again against the Confederacy. Joshua, you will go into the Union hospital with their party, identify Lewis and help fetch him. Now be off with you before something happens to change the Colonel's mind. You two get us ready to travel just as soon as they return. I don't wish to remain here a moment longer than is necessary."

It was at least an hour of pacing back and forth before the big, double gates opened enough to emit four men, one on each corner, carrying the litter and following the Lieutenant. Two were young 'home guardsmen' and not at all happy with their assigned duty of carrying a Yankee, one was Joshua and the fourth a Union prisoner, probably a hospital orderly or helper, but the remains of his uniform were not sufficient to offer a clue. Mrs. Wagner rushed to meet the party. The happiness radiating from her face quickly disappeared as she looked down into the litter. Her hand flew to her mouth to suppress a cry, then recovering; she reached down and took the hand of the passenger, holding it as she walked along side the patient. As the four lifted the litter into the wagon John caught his first glimpse of the man they had risked so much to rescue. His first thought, 'we've come way too late to do this man any good. We've put much at risk to rescue a dead man'. The uniform was so tattered as to nearly disguise the branch of the service, or even the side the wearer had fought on. Two remaining brass buttons were about all that could identify the coat as navy. The man wrapped in the dirty coat was very pale, almost ashen in color, with eyes sunken and in dark contrasted to the skin of his face. His left arm had at sometime been amputated just above the elbow and the stump continued to leak through the dirty bandage. He had been a big man, but all that remained to suggest that were his height and the slack in his coat.

As the litter was positioned in the wagon, the two home-guard stepped away, as if to put distance between themselves and Joshua. At that moment the Union prisoner turned to John and with sad eyes said softly, "My name is Martin Kutcher from Company C of the Iowa 19th Volunteer Regiment. My family's home is in Henry County, Iowa. Could you kindly somehow let my people know I'm alive, just like you'd want yours to know if you were up there in Camp Douglas?" John was so shaken, he nearly spoke out. But Glenn had heard the plea and moved quickly to cover for John, "Sir, you're speaking to a mute Confederate soldier who has no way to do as you ask, even if he was inclined. Now get on back so's we can be on our way!" As the Union soldier again looked into John's face for help, John looked into his eyes and nodded his head ever so slightly, then looked away as the prisoner was pulled to the ground.

The two men quickly mounted, Joshua settled into the wagon seat, and Mrs. Wagner held her husband's head in her lap as the small band moved out in the direction of Tyler. "Lewis is badly in need of a Doctor if he's to live. Perhaps we could find help in Tyler."

Glenn was quick to put that into reality, "In February of 1861, when the secession election was held in Smith County the vote was 1,150 for, and only 50 against leaving the Union. And, three of those 50, the Whitmore brothers and George Rosenbaum are now guests of the place we just left, so don't expect much in the way of help hereabout."

Tyler's only Doctor, a man of 68 years, who had been pressed back into practice due to the shortage made by war, was out in the countryside attending at a difficult birth. Thus, this small band moved on through town; proceeding to the southwest to camp in the willows along the banks of the Trinity River. A quiet, peaceful spot with little disturbance save the singing of the birds and the running of the river. There, two days later, Lieutenant Lewis Wagner, recently of the Union Navy, died of his long untreated wounds. He would be but one such death of over 650,000 of the four-year war, but the young river boat Captain would die peacefully, without much pain, and as a free man held tightly in the arms of his beautiful wife as she sang softly to him. He was surrounded by three men he did not know who had risk their lives to bring him to this moment.

Lieutenant Lewis Wagner was buried in a small cemetery on what Glenn explained were formerly the grounds of Fort Houston, named in honor of the Texas hero, Sam Houston.

Author's Note:

Fort Houston. At its best, Fort Houston had been little more than a blockhouse and stockade built in May, 1836, by the Republic of Texas to defend against Indian raids, but then abandoned in 1842. The surrounding small town took as its name the name of the Fort, but the town too was abandoned in 1857 when nearby Palestine, Texas, became the seat of Anderson County. In that year, 600 acres were purchased by John H. Reagan, the then US Congressman who would became the Post Master General of the Confederacy, as a site for his home. Thus it was that a young Yankee Naval Officer and river gun-boat Captain was buried on the home site of a Cabinet Officer of the new Confederate Nation.

Chapter 14

"THE END OF THE TRAIL?"

Author's Note:

The Hill Country of Texas: The Indian tribes of the Hill Country had their initial encounter with Europeans in about 1690 when Father Darnian Massenet came to the area to establish his mission. There he met the tribe that would eventually be known as the Llanos. The Spanish and French travelers who explored central Texas in the 1600 and 1700 had used numerous variations for the spelling of the tribe's name. By 1789 they were called Yanes, then Llanes; not until the early 1800's did the name become Llanos. In 1756 a Spanish expedition led by don Bernardo de Miranda, who was the Lieutenant-General of the province of Texas, arrived seeking the legendary silver mines in the La Lameria, as the Spanish called the Hill Country. In 1816 the Rio de los Chanas became known as the Llano River after the Indians who then inhabited its banks. However, they were soon pushed out of the region by the much larger Lipan-Apache and Penateka-Comanche tribes.

The white man gained control of the area with the Meusebach Treaty of 1847 and the forcible relocation of the remaining tribes began, along with the Tonkawa to Fort Cobb in the Indian Territory (Oklahoma). But the tribes again reappeared in force in 1861 when the army and the local young men began leaving for the war. The tribes conducted frequent raids into Blanco and neighboring Llano counties for supplies, horses and white slaves.

John Pitts laid out the town of Pittsburg in early 1850. The name was later changed to Blanco, meaning white, which came from the name given by the Spanish Aquayo expedition of 1720 to the nearby river cliffs.

When Angus and Lucinda McCoy arrived as a new husband and wife in the spring of 1840, she had never seen a country so beautiful. The air was much clearer and drier than her home in New Orleans, and the hills were carpeted with native wild flowers; bluebonnets, Indian head, and paint brush. The vast areas of range land were abundant with game; bear, panther, deer and wild turkey. With the plentiful game, the area also became the home range to many Indian tribes. The young woman from the city, loved the beauty, but hated the isolation. Beyond Pittsburg to the southwest it was 50 miles to the nearest settlement. Taming and holding this land would take great energy and greater courage.

Glenn was completely in charge of the small traveling band now. Since leaving Camp Ford they had traveled over range that was very familiar to him. They passed just north of Bryan, where Glenn had gone to college for two years before the war and were headed straight southwest toward the junction of the Pedernales and Llano Rivers, where Glenn's family made their home. Here on the banks of Lake Granger, fed by the Little River and the Brazos River, would be their last night camp on the trail before arriving tomorrow. They were down to their last 30 miles!

As the four sat around the last camp fire, Glenn was like a school boy. "You know, I never really expected to see this country or my folks again. John, if you hadn't helped me and stayed with me, at risk to your own freedom, I would never have made it."

"I had to stay with you; you told me you were the only one who knew where Texas was. Glenn, I believe in the early morning you should go on alone to lessen the shock for your people when we all come in on them."

"I will not! We started this together and by God we'll finish together. I'm not going in without you, John. That's just the way it is."

"We'll be right along behind you, but think of this from your folk's standpoint. Just look at what you're bringing in on them. You're traveling with a Yankee soldier who you yourself described as a deserter, riding a CSA branded horse he stole; a very pregnant southern widow who's husband, a Yankee naval officer, we just broke out of a Confederate prison; and a black man who until very recent was a slave and now wears a gun he knows how to use and won't take off and has $150 Confederate in his pocket. Don't you think we might require some explaining before we ride up to your folk's front door?"

"That does make some sense, providing I can trust to come on. You're not going to take off are you?"

"Where am I going to go, and what am I gonna' do with these people? You just tell me how to get there and we'll all be along."

"My folk's house is at the junction of the Perdernales and Llano Rivers in Travis County, though their grazing range sweeps well into Blanco County too. Were camping in Williamson County leaving about 30 miles yet to travel. You're gonna' follow this road to the Marshall Ford and cross the Llano River, and then just follow the river on up stream. The gate post will have their brand on it; the *A bar L*. About five miles up that lane is the house. Even you can't miss it! I do think you should put that throat bandage back on and if you meet anyone, let Mrs. Lewis do the talking. In spite of all my best efforts with you, you still sound like a damn Yankee."

The sky was mostly still dark with just a faint glow in the east when Glenn felt the tapping on his boot and heard those words that had haunted him and disturbed his sleep since Shiloh Church; "Come on. Get up. You're burnin' daylight!"

At the top of the rise Glenn reigned in the bay and looked back at their camp. He could see John in the dawn's light, still standing where he had left him minutes before, watching as he rode away. As Glenn turned in the saddle to wave, John came to attention and raised his right hand in a salute. 'What the hell' thought Glenn, 'A few months ago John had refused to call me Sir or Lieutenant, in fact had made a hell of a fuss about it, now as I ride away he salutes?' Glenn squared the bay around, brought himself to attention and snapped a return of the honors. Each of these two former enemies who had depended on the other for his survival for the last eight months was saddened and touched by their parting. Glenn dropped his arm, put his heels into the bay's flank and disappeared over the rise. John turned to the task of breaking camp and getting his party on the trail.

John had them moving at a good pace. Joshua, as always gun strapped to his hip, moved the Appaloosas along at a quick step as Mrs. Wagner rested in the back of the wagon. The roadway was flat and smooth and at this pace the road dust billowed up behind the wagon instead of coming up through the bottom. John, muslin wrapped on his throat, had scouted ahead to the Ford and returned without seeing any other riders. Glenn had made such a point about Indian raiding parties since the war; so John rode with the Spencer in front of him and kept his eyes moving around the horizon as he scouted. He could see where the bay had crossed the stream about three or four hours ahead of them, but no other fresh tracks showed in the soft mud. The bay's track looked like a loose shoe on the right front hoof; he'd need to remember to tell Glenn about that.

With the river so low this time of year, John figured they could have crossed anyplace, but Glenn had directed, 'cross at Marshall Ford', and this was his country. Mrs. Wagner refreshed herself beside the running stream while Joshua filled their canteens and watered the team. As John prepared to scout ahead he noticed the pained look of Savannah Wagner's features. Her time was near at hand, John only prayed to get her to the ranch first. He had found since leaving his pa's farm. there were many things that he could do that he never realized he could, but he didn't number delivering a baby among them. But when he thought about it, how different could it be from birthing a calf, and the cows did all that pretty much by themselves.

While John was scouting the trail ahead on the west side of the Ford, Glenn was nearing the point where the lane turned on to his family's ranch. There were no fences to mark the beginning, or the end of the ranch. It didn't make any sense to try to fence 3000 acres. Besides everyone around these parts knew where the "McCoy place" started and ended. Those in the past who forgot, Angus had a not too gentle way of reminding. Glenn did note during the last couple days of travel where people had started to string "Elwood 2-point" barbed wire, likely before the war had started. There was no one around to string it now and no money to buy the wire if there was. If that caught-on, it would change the way of life as they knew it in the open range country.

Glenn stopped before the sun faded "*A-L*" sign; a wide smile came to his face. He never thought to see this again. He rode under the arch and put the bay into an easy lope. Up on a rise well ahead of him a rider suddenly appeared outlined against the bright mid-day sky and studied this interloper. Glenn continued his pace, he belonged here, but his eyes never left the watcher. There was something unnerving about being watched, even from a far piece. Suddenly his observer jerked his mount so sharply the horse reared, then at a full gallop headed for the ranch house. In the still air Glenn heard the words, heavy with a Mexican accent he recognized as Pedro Alvarez, "Mr. Andrew coming...Mr. Andrew coming!" Well thought Glenn, so much for the surprise, and he put the bay into a hard run also.

Glenn, while still a half mile away, now clearly saw the familiar, sprawling Spanish house with its distinguishing red tile roof, and the barns and out-buildings. The stately cottonwoods were giving mid-day shade to the house and to his family gathered to greet him

169

under the veranda, waiting…for him. Glenn remembered how beautiful the Wisteria vine was there when in full spring bloom and was immediately sorry he had missed it. Pedro held open the yard gate and swept off his big Mexican Sombrero as Glenn walked the bay through the opening. "Thank you my Lady of Guadalupe, Mr. Andrew comes home." Glenn reigned-up at the hitching rail, but did not dismount. He just wanted to drink in this moment, this moment he thought would never come…this moment of his homecoming.

His Pa and Ma looked much the same, maybe a few more streaks of gray, but having your only son off in a war would likely do that. Suzanne was even more striking than he had remembered; he'd have to keep an eye on John when he arrived. Maybe on both of them!

"Howdy folks, I'm home. I told you I'd be back."

For the next hour there was much huggin' and kissin', and many tears of joy shed all around. As Mrs. McCoy went to direct the preparation of the noon meal, Glenn, now suddenly once again Andrew, finally got a break to announce that some friends were following by wagon and would be here before dark.

"That's fine", said Angus. "Any friend of yours is most welcome here."

"Perhaps before you get too filled with welcome Pa, I should tell ya'll a bit about them. There's a recently freed slave from Mississippi named Joshua who carries a gun and has become right handy with it."

"Now where in the hell did a slave get a gun and what damn fool taught him to use it?"

"My friend John gave it to him after Joshua backed John in a saloon gun-fight in Texarkana when the two of them shot three horse thieves."

"What were ya'll doing mixing with horse thieves anyway, and who's this John?"

"Well Sir, I'm working up to telling ya' about John. The two thieves had stolen a matched team of Appaloosas from this pregnant woman from Vicksburg who was on her way to break her Yankee husband out of the Camp Ford prison over by Tyler; and then they just left her on the trail." While Angus was trying to comprehend what his son was telling him, Andrew quickly moved on.

"John and Joshua killed two of the three brothers, recovered the team and collected a reward, which John gave to Joshua because it was paid in Confederate dollars; and then John took a Colt off a dead one, gave it to Joshua; then as we traveled on from Tyler, taught him how to use it."

"Doesn't this John friend of yours know it's against the law and against all common sense to arm a slave?"

"John said when Joshua stood in the middle of that bar-room and held four men at bay with a scattergun, he didn't look like no slave, he didn't even look colored. Besides John said it wasn't his law."

"Well it damn well is his law! It's the law of every southerner. And I'd like to know, why'd he give his country's money away, and to a Darky?"

"Were coming to that part, but John says the money's only good for when you're walking off into the woods first thing in the morning."

"I hate to hear it said quite like that, but it's close to the truth. It troubles me to ask, but how'd you plan to break a Yankee out of the largest Confederate prison west of the Mississippi River?"

"He was a Union Naval Captain and, well Sir; we had this letter from President Davis."

"President Jefferson Davis, the head of our Confederate nation? Just how'd you manage that one?"

"Yes Sir. Mrs. Wagner's father, she's the pregnant lady, was a delegate to the Confederate Secession Convention in Montgomery where they appointed Mr. Davis President. So he got the letter for his daughter, and that's what we expected to use. We did get the Captain out, but unfortunately he died two days later, so we buried him on the Postmaster General's ranch."

"You buried a Union Navy Officer on the ranch of Mr. John Reagan, a member of the Confederate President's personal cabinet?"

"Yes Sir. It was the only place handy and the weather was too hot to transport him far."

"Are we up to you telling about John yet? You seem to have some reluctance to enter into that part of your story."

"Just one other matter first. It's very close to Mrs. Wagner's time to deliver. John's much concerned that he gets her here first, so you might want to tell Momma and Mrs. Alvarez what to expect. I'll just wait here."

"Yes, you do that. I somehow feel we're just coming to the good part."

"Alright, everyone's alerted and I've sent Pedro out to lead them in. Now, let's hear about John, shall we?"

"Just one more thing first; ever since I left you and Momma I've been called Glenn, not Andrew. That happened cause the Army got my records wrong at enlistment. John and I have been trailing together for eight months, so he's always called me Glenn and so does all of the people coming here with that wagon. I suppose I could have corrected it, but I liked the name, especially since it was Momma's father's name, so I stayed with it. If you don't mind, I'd like to be known that way here also."

"I recon it'll take some getting used to for me, since I picked the name Andrew, but you're all grown up now and you should be able to decide how you want to be called."

"Thank you, Pa. John and I met the night following that second day of the battle of Shiloh Church, in Tennessee. I had been wounded hard toward the end of that day's battle; shot in the chest with two broken ribs and also shot in the thigh with the ball still in there. And when John came on me he was trying to decide if he should kill me, or leave me there to die on my own. You see Pa, John's a Corporal in the Union Army."

"He's a what! You're bringing a damn Yankee into my house?"

"He's turned out to be a good man Pa. Instead of killing me, he put himself at great risk to save me. He took the ball out of my leg with a pocket knife and some whiskey, he bound up my ribs so's I could ride, found two horses for us, gathered supplies and gave me a gun."

"I think you mean either he stole what he needed or looted the bodies of the dead, or likely both."

"John's explanation was that the former owners weren't needing them anymore, and had no further use for them. It took me a while to realize it too; those items were put to a much better use helping the two of us to survive than being left to the plunder of renegades from both sides. Anyway, John bound me up, equipped us and we headed west before any of the next daylight could be wasted."

"Who did you and this Union looter report to that you were leaving?"

"No one."

"So you both deserted! So now this friend of yours is not only a Yankee looter of the dead and a horse thief, he's also a deserter?"

"Maybe you just had to be there Pa. I would likely have been dead before anyone came on the following day, and if not then, severely wounded Confederate Officers do not survive for long in Union prison camps. As for John, he volunteered for one year, went through five major battles and then left after 14-months; two months longer than he and the army agreed. I know this because John showed me his papers before he burnt them. But putting all of that aside for the moment, this family, and me most of all, owe John Kelley a great debt of gratitude, On the first day together on the trail, he faced down a Union patrol when their Captain tried to take me as his prisoner, he kept me fed and my wounds tended when I couldn't care for myself, and when I became too sick to travel on instead of leaving me, he put himself at great risk by taking me to the home of a Confederate Captain in Arkansas for care. It's because of all his care and putting himself at considerable risk that I even get to be here so you and I can have this conversation. And I tell you this Pa, if you cause him to feel so unwelcome that he leaves, I'll go with him!" With that said, Glenn stood, looked his Pa, who he had never-ever spoken back to, in the eye, and walked away.

"Our son left us but a boy, but he came back home as a man. Damn I'm proud of him!"

Glenn felt the sudden need to escape from the house and from his Pa, so he saddled the bay and started out the lane to find John and Savannah Lewis. Strange, he had just thought of her as Savannah, not as Mrs. Lewis.

As John turned his small party under the gate arch of the *A-L* sign, his former Iowa company, along with 31,000 other Union soldiers, under the command of Ulysses Grant and William Sherman, launched the initial battle, of what would be become the Vicksburg campaign, when Grant attacked John Pemberton and 14,000 entrenched Confederates at Chickasaw Bluff. At that moment, neither John nor Savannah knew of this battle, but it would prevent either of them from ever returning to their homes, or to their old way of life again. In truth, the old way of life they left would never exist again, for either of them.

Glenn and the bay fell into step with John's big gray mare. "I'm glad to see you John, how's Savannah holding up under the travel?"

"I gave her my watch a piece back and she's reported that her pains were very sharp and about twenty minutes apart."

"Well we're about a half hour from the house and they are all ready and excited about the event."

"I assume you have explained all of us to your Pa?"

"Yes, he's likely gonna' want to talk to you some. He may sound gruff, but there's no need for you to feel uncomfortable."

"Glenn, when I spent eight days of fighting and walking in the mud between Fort Henry and Fort Donalson in a cold February snow storm; that was uncomfortable. When I watched you Confederates roll 60-some cannon on to a ridge, all looking down on my position; that was uncomfortable. This will be like sittin' down at my Momma's table; all full of love and good feelings. I do hope you explained to your Pa that he has nothing to fear from me!" Glenn's laughter warmed them both as it broke the stillness of the twilight.

Their first meal together had been polite but rather quiet. Mrs. Lewis had been moved immediately into a bedroom readied for her. The McCoy women were mostly absent from the table in their attendance to her. When the men finally pushed back, Angus suggested, but in a tone that sounded more like a command, that he and John would take whiskey and cigars on the Veranda while Andrew, or Glenn as he now wants to be called, checked on their horses and then got himself settled back into his own room. Besides he stated, "Andrew doesn't use whiskey."

"Oh yes Sir, I do."

"And just where did you pick up such a foul thing?"

"From John. John always said whiskey may not cure you, but it won't kill you either."

Well, thought John, this first conversation is starting off well.

A fire had been set in the round, open fire pit and was burning brightly driving back the December chill. John noted how the fire light danced on the glass of amber liquid in his hand; a double warmth against the cold and the threat of Mr. McCoy on this early night air. "Mr. Kelley, I do not wish to embarrass you, but that having been said, Mrs. McCoy and I wish to express our great appreciation to you for bringing our boy home safe. He's told us much of the story, though most likely not all of it. You would have been within your right and your duty if you had killed him on that field of battle, or turned him over as a prisoner, or since you had your own mission, just left him to die, which he believes he surely would have, had it not been for you."

"I had to take him Sir, he said he's the only one who knew where Texas was. He convinced me that I couldn't make it on my own, and that's likely true." John started to respond further, but Angus held up his hand for silence, then continued. "This family is greatly in your debt Mr. Kelley, and we both would like you to stay on here with us until you decide about your future plans. There is one condition that we require from you however; that's you write to your folks so's they can know your fate. As parents, Mrs. McCoy and I have been in great agony for many months not knowing about Andrew and would not want that for any other parent, on either side. If you can't write, Suzanne said she would write your words for you."

"I can write just fine; my Momma was a school teacher and she taught me and my brothers. I'll tell 'em about me and where I am but don't believe I could tell 'em about what I seen and done since I left home."

"Don't be concerned about that, what they need to know is that you are alive and for now, at least, out of the war. Since the beginning of time, most men in war have done things and seen things that they can never speak again of, not even to others who have done and seen the same things. Those few who can, and do talk of it, are usually politicians and have neither seen nor done much."

"I've always been filled with the wanderlust, recon' in a way, still am. This whole experience of goin' off to war started out to be the grand adventure for me. The chance to get away from home, see what's over the horizon, to enjoy the thrill of life. That all lasted until our first battle; from then on its been trying to learn quick enough to stay alive and keep my men alive, while Americans go on just slaughtering other Americans."

"Wars are started by old men, to be fought by the young. I seen this war a comin', the politicians on both sides have, through their incompetence, so mismanaged events that now other men have to kill and maim each other just to settle the matter. There are farmers just like you on both sides, there are educated men like Andrew on both sides, but American men all and they are killed and maimed alike. We are one men of one blood, speaking one tongue and believing in one Almighty God, yet we must kill each other. It will end someday, but this country will never be the same again. Our innocence will have been taken from us. It was some that way for me as well, and I've not seen or experienced even a small part of what you and Andrew have been through, however." Both men paused for a drink and to relight their cigars, then Angus continued. "When we joined General Sam Houston all we wanted to do is fight, to avenge what had happened to our friends at the Alamo. I felt quite strong about it as I had just missed by a few days being there with Colonel Crockett and his 37 men. But General Sam was so badly outnumbered by Santa Anna, all we could do was hit 'em and retreat...hit 'em and retreat. The Mexicans finally got tired and got careless; stopped advancing on us and set up a big camp; then on April 21, 1836, at San Jacinto, General Sam turned and attacked, just all but wiping them out. With that battle the "War For Texas Independence" was over and we won. From those Mexicans' still alive, we took the boots and guns and horses and made them walk back home, and Santa Anna was sent off to Cuba...should have killed him too. Andrew said your Pa was one of those who had to come back in '45 to finish that job."

With their glasses refilled and cigars relit, "Mr. Kelley, what do you have in mind to do with yourself now that you are here and away from the war?"

"We've been riding through this country for some days now, it's absolutely spectacular, some of the most beautiful country I've ever seen. I think I'd like to learn about the cattle business and start a place of my own here."

"Well the first thing you need to know about the cattle business is that there ain't no cattle business, least ways not in the south since this war started. The war took away the people who used to work the cattle, the blockade shut-off the world markets and the markets in the north, and the only money we got around here won't buy nothin' and ain't worth even working for."

"Come to think about it, I don't even recall seein' many cattle on the way. Where'd they all go?"

"With no one to keep 'em corralled, they mostly just turned wild. Why south of here in the canyons between the Guadalupe River and the start of the Medina River are as many as a hundred thousand wild, unbranded cattle that nobody claims or wants."

"Why not just go get some of 'em. How far is that anyway?"

"Oh I 'spect its about 200 miles, but what do you figure to do with 'em after you get 'em?"

"Oh I don't know. But how can you say you be in the cattle business if you don't have no cattle?"

"I'll tell ya', I've had this, what Mrs. McCoy calls Angus' crazy idea for awhile. In fact whenever I mention it, Lucinda bids me come out of the noon day sun, but now with you and Andrew here, we just could mite do it."

"Do what?"

"I'd like for us to go down to the Guadalupe, find a big box-canyon with good water, and round up about 3,000 head of them wild cattle, then drive 'em north to sell for Union gold."

"Could that be done?"

"Well getting' the horses we'd need ain't no problem. Then we could have Pedro get some of his people together with the three of us and there might be a few other crazies around home from the war. We'd all have to agree to do it on shares, cause there's no money for paying help. But the more I have thought on it, the more I believe it could be done with the right people."

"Where'd you take 'em?"

"Perhaps to the mines in Colorado. Perhaps through the Indian Territory and into Kansas. There's markets out there in the north and there's gold to pay for beef. The problem would be to get the beef and the gold together. Now that would be the way to learn the cattle business; takin' about 3,000 head up-trail at about 10 miles a day. Yes sir…you'd learn cattle in a hurry! But if we made it, it would mean some serious money…gold money."

"Could you do that, put your beef in Yankee bellies?"

"This war ain't gonna' last forever and when its over there's some major rebuilding to be done by the survivors. I intend me, mine and the A bar L to be among those survivors. No question!"

As they paused their conversation to visualize a suddenly shared dream, Mrs. McCoy came onto the veranda. "From the look on your faces, I expect Angus has been talking about his fool plan to drive cattle up north.

"What's the progress with Mrs. Lewis, woman?"

"She's delivered a fine baby boy and both mother and baby are doing fine."

"How big is it?"

"I figure about nine pounds."

"Well, that's keepin' size."

"Mr. Kelley, Mrs. Lewis would like to see you and the son we now are calling Glenn. Kindly fetch him and you both come to her room. And Mr. Kelley, kindly leave your whiskey and your cigar here."

"Yes Ma'am. I'll find him, right away."

Minutes later the two young men stood side-by-side admiring the mother and her baby. John thought the baby was too red and wrinkled to be beautiful, and the mother drawn and tired. Glenn, by contrast, thought he would never see a more beautiful sight than this beautiful woman and her new baby. As long as this was still happening, the world was going to be alright.

"The reason I ask you both to come see me is that I have a big favor to ask of each of you."

"Yes Ma'am."

"This new boy comes into a very harsh world and without a father he's going to need fine strong men in his life that he can look to for the example of what kind of man he should strive to be. He's going to need a man's love and understanding, a man's training, and, when necessary, a man's correction. For all of these reasons I would like the two of you to be his god-fathers. Had it not been for each of you, his chances of making it into this world at all would have been close to none. Would you two accept that responsibility for me? It would surely make me rest easier."

"Yes Ma'am…yes Ma'am."

"Good. Now if you are going to be his god-fathers, then he rightfully should carry your names. With your permission I would like to use each of your middle names and call this baby, Michael Glenn Lewis. Do I have your permission for this baby to be your name-sake?"

"Yes Ma'am, I would be most honored."

"Yes Ma'am, I'd be just fine with that, thank you!"

"Alright, now out of here," Lucinda McCoy ordered. "Mrs. Lewis needs her rest. Maybe if you'll both clean yourselves up tomorrow, we'll let you hold your new god-child."

When the two turned toward the door, the light from the oil lamp danced on the extra moisture overflowing their eyes. As they stepped into the court-yard, the moon shown in all it's full glory, much like the first night on the Shiloh Church battlefield. John ask, "I've just lost complete track of time. What time of year is it that our god-child was born?"

"I know it's December, and I think it must be almost Christmas-time."

"That's appropriate. You know Glenn, suddenly, and perhaps for the first time, I'm damn glad I didn't kill you back there at Shiloh Church when I was so seriously considering it. Yep, maybe glad for the first time."

"Ya, I know. I'm damn glad too. John, together we've finally reached the end of our long trail."

"So?"

"It's gonna' be okay if you want to burn a little daylight tomorrow."

THE END

The Epilogue

The Hill Country of Texas

January 2, 1863

Dear Pa,

This letter leaves me being in very good health and I pray it will find you and my brothers Mathew and Luke also enjoying the best of health. I hope too that things on the farm have gone well for you in the year since I last saw you; that you have just completed another bountiful harvest and your horse herd is continuing to expand, just as we had always planned. I do so miss all of you and being a part of that dream we were working for. I, of course, have no way of knowing if anyone from the Army has been to visit with you and Momma about me. If they have, they likely informed you I was killed at the battle of Shiloh Church in Tennessee, or perhaps captured there by the Rebels. Thankfully, neither of those conditions would be correct.

Pa, recall almost two years ago next March when you went with me into Fort Madison for me to volunteer for Mr. Lincoln's new army. The Captain there said I was volunteering only for one

183

year then would be back home, and then you and I each signed our agreement on his paper. Well, the Army lost track of me somehow and forgot to tell me to leave when my year was up. Just had too many people to keep track of, I recon'. So, after I waited for over thirteen months and then not hearing from 'em, I got tired of waiting and just left. It was after the two day battle at Shiloh Church. By then I had fought in five major battles in that thirteen months and had lived up to everything on that paper we signed.

I've seen and done some terrible things Pa since last I left you at that train station. Things I won't ever get out of my head. Things much worse than any you ever told me about from Mexico in '48. At White Mountain in the Boston Mountains of Arkansas, 9,000 Confederates made repeated charges all afternoon over an open field into our fortified and protected positions, till by night fall they could no longer get over their own dead and did not have enough men left standing to carry their dead and wounded off the field. After they retreated down the mountain, we dug 20 foot long slit trenches and dumped in their dead six and seven bodies deep. When I looked down in that trench before the dirt was shoveled in I realized that every blank, dead face there looking back up at me was an American. It could just a well have been me laying down there. They were likely boys just like me and their Pa and Ma loved them but would never ever see 'em again, and likely never know where they was buried. The Captain who had hid behind the redoubt ordered our company to follow the retreating Confederates down the mountain and kill all the rest of them; but thankfully Colonel Thomas Moore, a fierce fighter but a good Christian man in his heart, changed that order and we let 'em gather their wounded and withdraw.

Three major battles later, I was with over 100,000 men who fought for two days in the April rain at Shiloh Church; that's the one Mr. Horace Greeley now calls Pittsburg Landing. In those two days, the two sides suffered over 20,000 killed, wounded and missing. That's just short of twice what was suffered in all the years in the Mexican war. I was not hurt bad; was kicked in the head by a horse and knocked out when a Confederate cavalry unit over ran our position. Of the twelve men in my squad at the start of that battle, five were

184

wounded and five killed, one of those had his head cut off with a broad sword right in front of me. The Confederates put 62 cannon on a high ridge and every gapping, black eye seemed to be looking right down at me. We were told that there were not 62 cannon in the entire south, but there they were. They fired down at us for over three hours without let up, each time blowing perfect, white smoke rings down toward the valley. The Union would have lost that battle and maybe the entire war in the West except the Confederate General-In-Charge got killed at the end of the first day. It was the night after the battle was over and I came to alone on the battle field, but still alive, that I knew I would take advantage of my time being up and leave. I found me a good horse, some supplies and in the dark of night just rode away.

Mr. McCoy, that's where I'm stayin', was in the fight for Texas Independence. He says one of the hardest lessons for a warrior is one not learned until long after the combat has ended. It is that you'd never live any moment in your life quite so intensely again. He says, that don't mean you won't enjoy life. Having looked death square in the face will make you enjoy all the things of life just a little more than the one who has not . But you'll learn the moment of your life when you were the most frightened will become the moment when you were the most focused, and that will become the moment you'll have been the most alive; and that moment will have passed, never again to be equaled. Is that the way is was with you Pa?

I know I have shamed you and our good family name by riding away from the Army and war like that. You were with Captain Lee in Texas and Mexico for two years and came home a hero, but only after the Army said you could. I did not last near that long and did not wait to be told. That is why I did not come back to the farm, 'cause I would not be able to stand the look in your eyes after you heard my story. Besides, I figured the Army would come there first looking for me, and that would put you in a spot to have to lie to save me. If you want, you can just tell people I was killed in the war and I will stay away. At least Grandpa is not alive; I could just not stand to have to tell him. Did you know your friend from Mexico, Captain

Lee's a General now, but out east and for the other side? Some say he's rather a good one.

I am in the Hill Country of Texas now. I brought a badly wounded Confederate Lieutenant home alive after I took a bullet out of him when the Shiloh Church battle was over. I know I was expected to kill him and move on, but after what I'd seen in those two days I just couldn't bring myself do it. We are at his Pa and Ma's ranch where his Pa said I could stay, but only if I wrote you this letter, so you would know I wasn't dead. Don't know yet just what I'm going to do. They say this country is beautiful in the spring after the rains, so perhaps I'll stay and see that. Mr. McCoy says the country south of here is full of wild, unbranded Mexican cattle nobody owns. He thinks maybe we should round-up a few thousand head, drive 'em north to Kansas, and sell 'em for gold. Ya' see there's no money around here. About the biggest problem would be finding enough able-bodied men for a drive like that, and gettin' the cattle and us through the territory of the Indian Nations. But if Mr. McCoy still wants that in the spring, I'll likely have a go at it.

I'm told this letter should reach you in but a couple of months. This is a strange war where we kill each other and dump the dead in unmarked slit trenches, but pass letter mail back 'n forth through the lines with out interruption.

I love you all very much and miss you greatly, but I know that for all our sakes I must stay away from home and on the move. I hope in time you can see you way clear to forgive me for what I've done, or at least give some understanding as to why I did it, and with that, maybe out-live the shame I've caused you, for which I am truly sorry.

Your son, John

My Dear Momma,

I know you're bound to be worried about me, shucks you worried about the three of us anytime we were out of your sight. I know Pa will share with you some of the things I wrote in his letter, but I thought you should have your own letter, especially seeing it was you who taught me to write. 'Sides, there are some things in Pa's letter you don't need to hear and there are some things in this one to you that he probably wouldn't understand. But right up front, know that I am in quite good health, but you would say, "John you are so thin". I have just been away from your table for too long, and have not had a mouthful of mince-meat pie since I left with Pa for the train. Army food will keep you alive, when you get a meal at all, but will not add any meat to your frame. Much of what we get to eat we must find and cook for ourselves, and you know I was never much to cook.

I am now well away from the war and here in central Texas, and with no wish or intention to see any more of the war. I left just in time as I could not have absorbed much more. But for all the ugly things I have seen there has been much of beauty and wonder too. I have seen pine trees that seem to reach to the sky and standing so thick you could not ride a horse through them. Where we crossed the Mississippi River is the widest I have ever known. Much wider than we have just above the seven-mile rapids. And majestic Bald Eagles. In one short distance along the big river I counted 20 and missed many more. They build very large nests of sticks and mud near the top of the dead trees along the river where they get fish for food.

For all the ugliness of people to each other in war, there are many more that are good. The one's who helped me the most were all on the side of our so-called enemy. Mr. Miller, who was killed while taking over the big river on a raft at night, and his wife who fed us the best meal I have had since leaving your table. She was later, as was Mr. Miller, killed for helping us. Seems like God would be inclined to give protection to such good people. Then there is the beautiful woman in Arkansas with her six year old son, who took

187

us in and saved our lives by her care. That in spite of her husband having been killed in a battle I was also in. Had I not promised to see Glenn safely home, I just might have stayed and ask her to be my wife. Might go back there yet as she stays much on my mind. You know how it is? You said when I meet the right woman I'll know, 'cause I won't be able to forget her. If you are right, Sarah's then likely the right woman for me. Something about her eyes that won't leave my mind to rest.

I am at the McCoy ranch in what is called the Hill Country in Texas. It is a beautiful ranch that stretches past the horizon in all directions. Pa passed close by here in about '46, so he could tell you about the beauty of this place, ask him especially about all the blue flowers in the spring, they're called bluebonnets. I have not seen them yet, but expect to stay they winter, so likely will. The dry grass this time of year is belly high on a steer and I'm told when in the spring it turns green it becomes so thick as to wear out a horse run through it and in the wind, looks like the waves of a sea.

I'll likely stay here for awhile and hope to learn about cattle. We might look to start a drive north in the spring. I like what I see so far and just might settle here, or I also might return to see the beautiful lady with the straw hair and the dark green eyes in Arkansas. As I said, she's much on my mind. I love you Momma.

Your loving son, John

The Hill Country of Texas

January 7, 1863

Dear Mr. and Mrs. Kutcher

Whose son Private Martin serves with Company C, the Iowa 19th

Living in Henry County, Iowa

It is my prayer that this letter will reach you so I may tell you of your son Martin. He is concerned that you have had no other word of him in some time. He is a prisoner in the Confederate compound called, Camp Ford, just outside Tyler, Texas. I am recently of the Iowa 14th Regiment, and had the occasion, within the last two months, to be at Camp Ford on other business. Martin spoke with me briefly and indicated he was well and as I saw, he's lost no limbs. He looks thin, but everyone in this war is thin. I know prisoners are being exchanged between the sides frequently, so it's quite possible he may soon be released.

I hope this letter brings some encouragement to you regarding Martin. Hold fast to your faith in the goodness of God and we can all pray for your son's release.

With Regards, your servant, John M. Kelley, III

189

January 7, 1863

My Dear Sarah Graham and Mathew,

I am pleased to report to you and Matt that Glenn and I have arrived at his father's ranch in central Texas. We are safe and have come in good health, thanks to the generous care you gave us. As Glenn and I have spoken many times this arrival, and our now healthy condition would not have been possible without the two of you. You took a great risk to salvage us, and we are forever most grateful. My biggest fear was that we would somehow bring harm down on you after we left to travel on.

The most difficult thing for me now is learning that Glenn is not Glenn at all, but here he's called Andrew. Most of the time when I mention the name Glenn, no one except his mother knows who I am talking about and she just smiles at a thought from long ago. Glenn has a slight limp and a shortness of breath remaining and such will likely always be so, but he tries not to let it slow him down. As for me, I'm in quite good health and pray that this letter finds both of you the same.

I remain sorry that you chose not to take this journey with me. As you bade me to do, I have remembered many things about our short time together. Those memories were most keen at night, in my bedroll around a dying camp fire. Especially warm is the memory of the feel of you as I lifted you up to the saddle to kiss you goodbye. Having now completed my promise to return Glenn safely home, I find my mind free to now think on the promises that you and I might consider for each other. Sarah, I continue to want you and Mathew to join me here. I want you to become my wife and I wish to help you raise up Matt as our son. We could make this happen, if you agree. My thinking on the subject is that I could come back for you, we could then move your stock down to Mr. Purcell's farm for now and let them graze with his herd. I could fix up your wagon and team and drive them back here, or better yet, I could fetch you and Matt to come along with us on the spring cattle drive we are planning.

Think of the experience for Matt and what I could teach him. If you would rather come here now though, I will come immediately to you and we will return here before the spring round up. I know that the things I am suggesting bring with them problems for you in your life and for the separate plans you have made for the farm. But I believe we were picked to be together and we should work our problems to make that happen. Mamma believes there is a Divine Intervention which brings intended people together. Since meeting you, now I believe that also. In the meantime, I trust the taxman is no longer calling on you?

Central Texas is a wonderful land, full of opportunities. When this war finally ends, this will be the place to be and to grow. Mr. McCoy has suggested we round up some of the wild, unclaimed cattle and drive them north for the Union gold. He has offered me shares in the drive and enough land to begin a spread upon our return. While both of these are exciting to me and I think just what I have wanted for a long time, neither would be as valuable in my life as you and Mathew would be. If I should have both, I would be a truly blessed man. I do love you both and pledge to work to make a good life for the three of us, and any more to follow. You know how serious I am about my pledges. I hope you will give serious thought to this proposal and send your response back quickly.

Your loving and devoted servant,   John

Printed in the United States
128692LV00010B/250-258/A

9 781420 876611